DUKE IN ALL BUT NAME

The Entitled Gentlemen, Book One

by

Caroline Warfield

ARE YOU SIGNED UP FOR DRAGONBLADE'S BLOG?

You'll get the latest news and information on exclusive giveaways, exclusive excerpts, coming releases, sales, free books, cover reveals and more.

Check out our complete list of authors, too!

No spam, no junk. That's a promise!

Sign Up Here

www.dragonbladepublishing.com

Dearest Reader;

Thank you for your support of a small press. At Dragonblade Publishing, we strive to bring you the highest quality Historical Romance from some of the best authors in the business. Without your support, there is no 'us', so we sincerely hope you adore these stories and find some new favorite authors along the way.

Happy Reading!

CEO, Dragonblade Publishing

Additional Dragonblade books by Author Caroline Warfield

The Entitled Gentlemen Series
Duke in All But Name (Book 1)

The Ashmead Heirs Series
The Wayward Son (Book 1)
The Defiant Daughter (Book 2)
The Forgotten Daughter (Book 3)
The Upright Son (Book 4)

Dedication

It takes a village to make a book. This one is dedicated to those whose contributions made it and many of my earlier books so much better: Sherry Ewing, Jude Knight, Corrine Lehman, Judy Johnson, Lyss Em—my editor—and all the folks at Dragonblade who work so hard on behalf of their authors.

The weak can never forgive.
Forgiveness is the attribute of the strong.
—Mahatma Gandhi

CHAPTER ONE

Selwyn Court, Dorset, August 1818

THE DUKE OF Glenmoor was dead. Or so Mia's cousin claimed. Of course, Eustace was deep in his cups when he said it, and subject to drama at the best of times, even when seated at his father's dinner table as he was that evening.

He might not have mentioned it at all if his sister Selina hadn't expressed a moony-eyed hope that the young and very eligible duke, their nearest neighbor of note, would return home now that fall approached, declaring she needed a new wardrobe since they had only recently left off mourning for her mother, Mia's Aunt Harriet.

"Well, he ain't coming back soon. I can tell you that. Word in London is he has disappeared," Eustace declared, waving his empty wine glass. A footman rushed to refill it.

Selina's spoon clattered to her plate, and Viscount Clavering—Mia's uncle and Eustace and Selina's father, Ludlow Selwyn—bristled. "Nonsense. Dukes don't just disappear," he said.

Selina's distress no doubt owed more to fear of the loss of a chance to fix Glenmoor's attention than any real concern for the poor man.

Eustace shrugged. "He may be dead. Betting in the clubs is

that he did himself in."

Mia shuddered, and Uncle Ludlow glared at him in horror. If true, the duke's death would be a tragedy however it occurred. Mia loathed Eustace's insensitive attitude.

"But he has to come home," Selina wailed. "Now mourning is over, there could be assemblies, and, and…"

"You'll never get the pair of them married off," Eustace sneered, slurping his wine. "Fee is a Friday-faced Methodist, and Selina's whining would drive a man to drink."

As if you need an excuse to overimbibe. Mia glared at him. She hated her proper name, Euphemia Forbearance Selwyn, gift of a scholarly father and pious mother, almost as much as she hated Eustace's mocking nickname, Fee.

"Mind your tongue, boy. Your sister and cousin are just now out of mourning for your mother. Show some respect." Uncle Ludlow's frown deepened, but as always, it had little effect.

"What am I supposed to do here in Dorset with naught but sheep and the pokey little hamlet of Nether Abbas for entertainment?" Selina said, her tone confirming her brother's judgment about her whining.

Eustace drank deeply. "I'll grant you that, little sister. Dull as dirt is Dorset. If Clavering would—"

"There won't be a farthing for you until quarter day, if that is what you mean to ask. Do you good to rusticate for a while. Time you took some responsibility," the viscount sputtered.

At one-and-twenty, Eustace was a year older than Mia in time but younger in every way that mattered. *When does a man acquire enough age to exhibit some character?*

Eustace certainly showed no sign of settling down so far. He had declared himself finished with university two years before and decamped for London. He only came home when his purse emptied out and he needed to outrun creditors. God only knew what sorts of vice and debauchery he got up to. At least this time, he'd arrived without his rakehell friends to raid the viscount's brandy, ogle both Selina and Mia, and send her uncle into a rage over their profanity.

Uncle Ludlow turned his frown on Selina. "As for you, young lady, you'll get your London season in the spring. We'll see if we can get some fools to take you and your cousin off my hands."

Mia's heart sank. He had grudgingly offered her one season. "No overdoing the fripperies, mind, Euphemia, and just the one. You best make the most of it," he'd said. "Unless we get lucky and some farmer takes you off my hands." She wasn't sure which option sounded more dismal, being dragged through London as Selina's poor relation or being forced on some local swain. Now that her aunt had passed, she had no real role at Selwyn Court, however. Uncle Ludlow viewed her as a burden. Her only other relative was her Great-Aunt Hortensia, widow of a chapel preacher who lived in penury in Northumberland. With no money of her own and no other place to go, Mia could only pray that she might find a decent husband.

"Where did you find that ugly frock, Fee? Did some local trull make it up out of her grandmother's attic?" Eustace asked. "No one will have you looking like that."

Mia ignored the jibe.

Selina seized on it to wheedle for new dresses. "We'll both need new wardrobes for the season." Selina glanced at her father hopefully. "And I don't see why it must wait, now that mourning is over. The Duke of Glenmoor might yet come home this fall, and we will entertain."

"Ha! You'll grow cold waiting for that to happen, you ninny," Eustace said, laughing.

Mia watched the play of emotion on her uncle's face. She could almost hear him weighing the cost of dressing his daughter against the possibility of attracting an unattached duke. "Might be best to puff off Euphemia at a local assembly. If I dress you now, though, I'll have to do it again in the spring. Best wait until we see if he returns to Woodglen."

"Eustace may be right. The duke has been away more than home for the past two years," Mia murmured. Mia found the

Duke of Glenmoor to be a pleasant enough young man, if a bit dandified, and well mannered at least—not that he had ever paid much attention to plain Mia Selwyn, his neighbor's unwanted niece.

"But dukes don't just disappear," the viscount said, nodding to the butler to clear the table and bring the pudding.

"This one's been acting peculiar all year. First, he trundled off to Wales with his stepmother. Came to London just as the season started and left town a week later."

"He didn't come here, I can tell you that," Uncle Ludlow said, shaking his head. "He's come nowhere near Woodglen in over a year."

Eustace shook his head. "Betts and Rowley stumbled on him in some little inn in a nothing of a village near Nottingham during summer, nursing his ale in the corner, sunk in misery. Treated them to the cut direct. Betts thinks he lost his mind when old Hopewell's granddaughter refused him."

Selina's eyes flew open wide, shock—and a bit of satisfaction—in her expression. "Some henwit refused the Duke of Glenmoor? Who would refuse an offer from a duke? Why on earth would she do that?"

"Dunno. The chit was betrothed to an earl's second son by season's end. Her grandfather stayed mum on the subject. No one got a word out of him." Eustace shrugged. "Maybe Glenmoor was mad before she refused him, and Hopewell found out."

Curious… Mia paused with a spoonful of trifle in her hand and tried to puzzle it through. "So you mean he's just spending his life at this inn up in the midlands?"

"No. Disappeared like I said. He came back to town for a week or two. Sold off his phaeton and team at Tattersall's. Betts witnessed Danbury's oldest snap it up. Sold a few other things, and rumors spread that he's bankrupt. But then I saw him at Brook's myself acting normal as you please."

Uncle Ludlow snorted. "Bankrupt? I think not. His father left him buckets. Marshall over at Woodglen says rents are up."

"But what do you mean, 'disappeared'?" Selina demanded.

"I mean one day he was in London, the next day gone. No word to anyone. Ignored Parliament, too, and Glenmoor always votes. Didn't take the knocker off the door. Nothing. Just went missing. Like I said, betting in the clubs is that he…" Eustace lowered his voice. "…did himself in." He straightened. "I bet against him killing himself. Didn't seem the type. Still, if he's mad, who knows."

"Nonsense. Dukes don't kill themselves," the viscount said.

"They don't disappear, either. Some folks think he was done in. Whatever happened in Wales last year may be the problem. Betting is running two to one that he's dead, though." Eustace held his glass for another refill.

Mia dropped her hands to her lap. "How awful! Betting on the poor man's misery."

Eustace sneered at her. "What do you know? It's what men do. There's a whole book on where the body will be found. Betts has that village—Ashmead, I think he said. Rowley says Wales. They'll never find him if the body is in the wilds of Wales. They're both wrong. I put my money on the Thames. He'll wash up, mark my words."

Selina paled.

"Enough!" Uncle Ludlow glared at him. "This is not proper dinner conversation."

Eustace continued as if his father hadn't spoken. "More interesting is the question of an heir. If they declare him dead, who inherits? I thought there was a brother when I was a nipper."

"Crippled half-wit from old Glenmoor's time in America. Bastard in any case," the viscount muttered.

"I remember. Hunched one shoulder down. Walked with a limp. Didn't talk much," Eustace mused. "He died, didn't he? Couldn't inherit if he was a bastard anyway."

The viscount nodded solemnly. "The unfortunate wretch attacked the duchess and had to be sent away. Glenmoor reported him dead."

"So some cousin gets the lot or it all reverts to Prinny?" Eustace asked.

"And the duke is not coming back?" Selina moaned, fixated on the end of her hopes.

"No more distasteful speculation," the viscount pronounced.

Mia studied her uncle's thoughtful expression. She suspected he'd be off the next morning to question Marshall, the Woodglen steward.

When Selina rose as Eustace demanded port, Mia followed, grateful to get away.

Poor Glenmoor! There will be cousins, she thought, walking away. *There always are, and they will leap at the title. No one leaves a duchy to its own devices.*

Kendrick Colliery, Wales, that same month

GIDEON KENDRICK SPREAD the letter on his desk, sank his head into his hands, and read it again. His damned brother had done it. He had run from the responsibilities attached to his title.

At least, he'd tried.

The rich wood paneling of the mine owner's office glowed in flickering lamplight. Though it was barely noon, gray clouds hung heavily over the valley and little light filtered through the window.

Gideon reread the letter in his hands, swore vehemently, and crumpled it up, slamming the desk with his fist, toppling his Sèvres cup, and spilling the dregs of his coffee onto his walnut desk. He grabbed the offending missive, wiped the spill with his handkerchief, and groaned.

...however long I'm gone, I left papers with my solicitors giving you full authority over the Glenmoor estate and all my hold-

ings…

The damned fool was determined to tie the loathsome place around Gideon's neck one way or another. His brother, Phillip Tavernash, Duke of Glenmoor, would have wiggled out of his title if he could, but they both knew that neither the Committee for Privileges nor Prinny himself would rescind a title once it had been confirmed—as it had been nine years before—no matter how much evidence Phillip brought to bear that Gideon should have been the heir and not Phillip.

He could ignore his brother—they'd been strangers for over fourteen years until their recent reconciliation. He could let the duchy sink into ruin. Except Phillip trapped him with more words, arrows to his heart.

My solicitors have a sealed envelope to be opened upon my death. It lays out the truth. Daniel will need you to be familiar with the estate, should something happen to me. Don't fail me.

Gideon unleashed a formidable flood of filthy curses, exhausting every profane word he'd learned in the mines, from his time in the pit to his rise as owner. It changed nothing. His well-meaning but unwise brother sought to burden Gideon's five-year-old son, Daniel, with his title and responsibilities. Except Phillip viewed it as a gift, a privilege, a righting of a grave injustice.

Gideon glared at the letter as long as he could stand, smoothed it out, and folded it. He needed to think. He needed advice. He rose, stuffing the letter in his coat pocket, and lurched to the door, groaning a little. Tension made the curvature in his back hurt worse than usual.

"Alyx! Have my horse brought round," he barked through the door.

He must have been uncharacteristically harsh, because his secretary's eyes flew open. "Yes, Mr. Kendrick."

"And send word to the governess that I will be late tonight. I may not return until morning." Miss Huntington could be trusted with the welfare of his children.

A few hours later, he sat in a cozy parlor and warmed his aching bones before a fire to ward off the evening chill, sunk in gloom, while his host waited patiently for an explanation. Gavin Morgan, a longtime associate who had become a friend during the previous year, was one of the few people in the united kingdoms who knew the truth. Gideon Kendrick, né Tavernash, was the legitimate son of the late duke and rightful Duke of Glenmoor, though the title had been conferred on his younger brother, the product of a later, albeit bigamous, marriage.

Gideon handed him the letter and concentrated on his drink, a hot toddy laced with rum.

After one glance, Gavin whistled soft and slow. "He's handing over the keys to the kingdom, and you act like that horse of yours died. One gathers you don't choose to accept."

"Hell no. I loathe the place. I loathe everything to do with the Glenmoor name," Gideon muttered.

"Except His Grace," Gavin said.

"Except Phillip, yes." *His Pox-Ridden Grace, may he rot in his grave, is the snake who sired me. My brother is something else entirely.* "I didn't think he'd bolt," Gideon mumbled morosely, staring into his mug, inhaling steam for comfort.

"I heard the girl jilted him," Gavin said. "That sort of disappointment drives some men to foolishness."

"There was never a betrothal. We could have buried the whole business, but the benighted fool told her everything, even the probability that his mother's marriage was invalid and the likelihood that their son would never inherit the title. She refused him." Gideon shook his head. "I think he actually loved the chit. Or so he believed. Spent spring hiding in that village in the middle of nowhere."

"Ashmead? Where your stepmother lived?"

"That's the one. Tried to drown himself in the tavern's ale while weeping on sympathetic shoulders. Now this."

"It must have taken him all summer to come up with this

harebrained scheme. Where do you think he went?" Gavin asked.

Gideon had no idea and said so.

"Scotland?" Gavin lifted a brow.

"More likely France. He rather liked Paris, as I recall. Or Rome. Constantinople. Darkest Africa. I have no idea. He's disappeared to God knows where and expects me to step in and take over the whole damned Glenmoor operation—for which I have no desire, questionable right, and precious little authority. No matter what papers he signed, they'd never let me through the door."

"They?"

"My father's warped ideas infested the entire estate, from his steward and butler to the lowest potboy to the neighborhood. I had naught but insult from the lot of them."

Gavin shook his head. "The duke seemed to think your father sent you here to die, but the mines may have been a relief," he said with a twist of his lips.

"Daniel Kendrick was more a father to me than the one who sired me. The colliery is my home."

Morgan didn't have to respond; he shared the feeling. The two men sat in companionable silence, finishing one mug and then another until the warmth seeped all the way to Gideon's soul.

The colliery, the valley, Wales. That was home. Daniel Kendrick had plucked him out of the pit to which his father banished him, taught him the business, and eventually given him his name. Gideon's late wife, Maera, was Daniel's daughter. The only kindness he'd had before coming here had been from Pritchard, the stablemaster, and occasionally from his father's young wife, Madelyn, when she was able.

Gavin brought one more mug, wobbling a bit when he rose. "So what are you going to do?"

Gideon breathed in and let it out on a sigh. The valley was home, but Phillip, in spite of everything, was family. "I'll go, of course." He waved the letter. "To London. Long enough to speak to the solicitors about this nonsense. I may have to rescue my brother from folly."

He would stay far away from the duchy's primary seat at Woodglen, scene of his nightmares. He'd make a quick trip and be back to his motherless children in a month. Decision made, he nodded off.

CHAPTER TWO

Nether Abbas, Dorset, October

DEW COVERED THE grass along the hedgerows and sunlight shone over the stubble in the newly harvested rows as Mia Selwyn made her way past Woodglen's fields to the village, glad for a day away from Selwyn Court, Selina's complaints, and Eustace's sly comments with the horrid friends who had followed him home.

Eustace mocked her reading habits, her gown, her hair, her parentage unless Uncle Ludlow stepped in to stop it. He usually ignored the abuse when Eustace came alone, but with Eustace's friends at Selwyn Court, he probably hoped one of them would take her off his hands. She shuddered at the thought.

Making it worse, her uncle had informed them all that some sort of cousin had turned up at Woodglen claiming to be the duke's heir, sending Selina into a frenzy. She pleaded and begged her father to invite the man to tea, a duke in waiting being even better than a missing one. At least she had left off flirting with Eustace's rakish friends.

When the Norman tower of Saint Peter's came into sight through the yew trees, Mia slowed her steps, letting the country-side work its magic on her mood. She paused to enjoy fall wildflowers in a yard or two as she passed. Her much-loved dog,

Hector, a great furry creature of questionable origins, matched his steps to hers, ever content to be at her side.

She tied Hector to a pole outside Adcock's Stationery and went in to post a letter to her Great-Aunt Hortensia. Uncle disapproved of the relationship, so Mia found it easier to post privately from her pin money. If she asked him to frank a letter, he would read it and impose his opinions on her.

She passed two stores and peered into the window of Hinson's Grocery. Hinson's wife, Martha, managed a small enterprise, a tearoom of sorts, in an alcove off the store. The thought of tea and Martha's pastries drew her. She could refresh herself and delay her return.

"Does your uncle allow that great monster of a dog in the house?"

Mia turned toward the sneering face of the speaker, Evelyn Duger.

"No, we keep him in the stable. My uncle prefers to think of Hector as a stray who will be driven off eventually." The stray part was true enough, but he was Mia's now and the only thing she had in the world that mattered. Hector knew it. He wouldn't leave.

Evelyn gave a sniff and breezed by, into the store. Mia entered and found an empty seat in the far corner. She'd stumbled into a nest of gossips, and most of the tables were full. The buzz of conversation centered as it usually did on the big house, Woodglen, and its happenings.

Mia quickly realized why so many ladies were present. A maid from Woodglen had come down and sat center table with Martha Hinson. One of the ladies peppering her with questions about the famous heir called her Mercy. This lot was as frenzied as Selina about the man.

"Acts like the duke himself, he does. He rode up flashing papers claiming they proved his place a week ago, moved in, and has us running off our feet to do his bidding," Mercy said, tossing her hair and preening.

"Except this cousin isn't the duke. There's no proof Glenmoor died. The courts will wait seven years, won't they?" Martha Hinson asked.

The entire subject of the poor missing duke turned Mia's stomach.

"The cousin definitely exists, though, I can tell you," the maid said, accepting another cup of tea from Martha. She probably thought it her due for entertaining them.

"I'm surprised old Fillmore let him in," Evelyn Duger said. The Woodglen butler was notoriously high in the instep and unlikely to tolerate nonsense.

"Oh, Fillmore objected loud enough, but Marshall let him in."

Curtis Marshall was the Woodglen steward. "Why would he do that?" Mia frowned over her teacup.

"Said he had examined the man's credentials, whatever that is. Next thing we knew, Marshall announced that as next in line, he had a right to 'inspect' the estate until the duke's death is proved or he returns," Mercy said. "None of us have seen the big oaf inspect anything but the wine cellar and the dining room."

"How is the butler taking it?" Milly Adcock asked.

"Fillmore looked fair to swallow his tongue, but that house-keeper, Mrs. Morrit, dotes on him. Neither one can defy Marshall," Mercy responded.

"With the duke gone, the steward has the power?" Mia mused.

Mercy shrugged. "That heir may think otherwise. Though, he's a weak-chinned fop and lazy to boot."

"If there's power to be had, greedy men will try to take it," Evelyn Duger said.

Agnes Pettifer, Evelyn's sister, put her oar in. "If he's as lazy as Mercy says, he's more apt to wait for someone to hand him power than to grab it."

Evelyn snorted. "Some business chap in London may have the reins."

An hour later more than one curtain twitched as Mia made

her way back through the village still wrapped in thought about the mysterious cousin. Clear of the place, a slow smile came over her. Nether Abbas, a nest of spite populated by nosy busybodies, often turned its claws on Viscount Clavering's poor relation, Mia herself. It occurred to her that a much more delicious scandal—speculation about the so-called cousin entrenched at Woodglen—might keep them occupied and push their henpecking over her lack of breeding aside for a while.

Walking, as was her habit, across one of the lower Woodglen fields, she reached the place where she could pick up the lane just before it forked, the left side leading to the massive edifice of Woodglen and the right side to Selwyn Court two miles on.

She stepped through a gap in the hedgerow ahead of Hector. The sound of pounding hooves sent her heart to her throat, and she leaped against the hedges as a massive horse thundered up. Hector wiggled his head between the hedge and Mia's side to bark at the rider who had brought his mount under control just short of where Mia had been standing.

The great black beast danced nervously, and its rider glared down at her. She stared back at eyes dark and lit with anger. His hair, long and as black as the horse he rode and the clothes he wore, flew wildly around his short-brimmed beaver hat. "You damned fool. Don't you check before you dart into the road?" he shouted.

I didn't dart. Mia was so taken with the strange sight in front of her that she couldn't get the words out. The beast was magnificent, its rider… Mia wasn't sure what to make of the rider. She found animals easier to comprehend than their owners even in the best of times and certainly in this case.

The man's face shifted, and for a moment, she thought he would apologize. He didn't. "You could have been killed—you and that great lump of a dog—be careful in future." The stranger stared at her a moment longer, urged his horse on without another word, and disappeared down the lane, taking the turn to the left. To Woodglen.

Mia put a hand to her pounding heart. *Who was that? The cousin, perhaps?* Then she remembered Mercy's description.

…a weak-chinned fop, the sort Agnes had said was more apt to wait for someone to hand power to him than to grab it. The mysterious rider could not be the cousin. The man she just saw would have no trouble whatsoever taking what he wanted. None at all.

"THE VULTURES ARE circling for sure now." Woodglen's butler looked Gideon over from the scuffed tips of his riding boots to his hair, long and wild from the wind, contempt radiating from him.

"I'm equally delighted to see you, Fillmore. Step aside and let me in." Gideon glared at the longtime retainer with as little respect as the old man had always shown him.

"You are supposed to be dead," the butler sneered.

"Sorry to disappoint. I gather my brother didn't share the joyous news when he found me last year. Are you going to move or do I need to push you aside?"

Gideon's hips and back hurt like the devil after hours in the saddle. His meager supply of patience evaporated.

"You aren't the heir," Fillmore muttered.

If only you knew… Gideon took a step forward. For a moment, Fillmore appeared to weigh his chances of tossing Gideon out, but he stepped back. The old reprobate gestured to a footman. "Watch this one closely. I'll inform Mr. Marshall. Keep him right where he stands."

"The steward? Bring him to me." One of the many facts piled on Gideon's shoulders during his unsatisfactory visit to the offices of Sadler and January, Solicitors, in London was the name of Phillip's land steward, Curtis Marshall. His brother had had the good sense to hire someone new after the old duke kicked up his toes.

Fillmore walked away without responding, and Gideon heard

the old man mutter something about "God himself," but whether Fillmore referred to the steward's arrogance or his own, he could not tell.

Gideon pushed his saddlebags into the arms of the bewildered footman. "Take this to my room—any guest room will do. My luggage is following." He swept off his hat, set it on the bags, and limped past the sputtering servant into the nearest parlor, the one his father had used to allow importuning strangers to use to cool their heels until he saw fit to address them, one designed for discomfort. He took a high-backed chair and sank into it, craving willow bark tea and a good brandy but fearing neither was likely to be forthcoming.

The footman stood in the doorway, still clutching Gideon's hat and saddlebags.

Not particularly bright, this one. Gideon watched the boy trying to puzzle out whether failing Fillmore or defying this stranger who seemed to claim some right to be here would be the bigger mistake. Gideon raised one sardonic eyebrow and glared until the footman shuffled back into the entranceway. He heard the thump of heavy bags hitting the polished floor.

My saddlebags will rest by the door until I sort this out. At least they'll be handy if they toss me out.

He thought, not for the first time, that he ought to have stopped at the inn in Nether Abbas, but his memories of the Cockcrow were dismal. He'd forced himself on to get this encounter over with as soon as could be. He had spent two weeks reviewing the investments, reports on miner properties, and the business of the estate at large. He'd almost bolted home to Wales when Sadler insisted there were things at Woodglen that needed his oversight. He still could.

He squeezed his eyes shut. It could be a long wait. He tossed about for a pleasant thought—anything to drive out the sick feeling that had taken up residence in the pit of his stomach as soon as he turned the lane and saw Woodglen looming ahead. Some might take it for the impressive edifice it was meant to be.

To Gideon, the place was a drooling monster ready to open its jaws and devour him. He blinked that image away and thought first of his home and children. They tugged on his heart, and a desire to cut and run back to his place of comfort surged through him.

Not yet.

He turned his mind to the ride down from London. He had reveled in the glories of the English countryside and the beauty of Blackmore Vale, flatter and more open than his home in Wales in spite of the hills rising along the south edge. It had almost kept his demons, unleashed by the need to come to this place, at bay. Even Nether Abbas—seen from a distance—appeared peaceful. He had skirted the village, having no more desire to go there than here.

One memory kept intruding, that of a young woman stepping into the path of his horse's hooves. Not a schoolroom miss, and not anyone he knew. He guessed her age to be twenty or so. She'd have been a small child when he was banished. He let his memory roam over her—slender but nicely curved, she was a woman grown for certain and, judging from her dress, a lady. Her clothing hadn't flattered her, but it was obviously well made. She had spirit, too. He'd thought for a moment she meant to take him to task. He found that oddly attractive. He regretted growling at her. Neither his momentary fear he might have injured her nor his black mood had given him an excuse to be churlish. He would owe her an apology if he ever encountered her again. If he stayed in the area long enough.

"Well, sir, state your business." A man with the square build of a boxer and the face of an ill-tempered vicar stood in the doorway, arms akimbo, feet planted firmly apart, and glowered at him. When Gideon stared back, he went on. "Well, hurry about it before I have you shown the door." Fillmore, standing behind the man's left shoulder, watched with smug satisfaction.

"Marshall, I presume? Horace Sadler told me I would find you here. I'm here to inspect the estate and its operation."

Marshall didn't so much as blink.

"On behalf of the duke."

Gideon had puzzled all the way down how to present himself. The words he used were as good as any. Marshall's lip curled in disdain. He went past skepticism to disbelief without pausing.

"The duke is missing," Marshall said, striding into the room to loom over Gideon.

"Most certainly. He has requested that I have full power to manage his affairs in his absence," Gideon said without rising.

Marshall took a step closer. "Why should I believe you?" he demanded. "Who do you think you are?"

"I suspect Fillmore will have told you who I am," Gideon said, rising with a sigh. He used to wonder how tall he might have been if his spine hadn't been bent but had learned to accept what couldn't be fixed. As it was, he stood taller than Marshall, a cause for some satisfaction. "My brother wrote to request my assistance, and Sadler confirmed that I have been given full proxy power to act on the duke's behalf until such time as my brother chooses to return."

"Fillmore told me the duke's only brother is dead," Marshall growled.

"So he was told. Now he knows otherwise," Gideon said, reaching into his coat and removing a sheaf of paper. He extended it toward the steward but kept a tight grip, saying. "I have additional copies of this. The original and the duke's letters of authority are in a safe with Sadler and January along with his will." He released the solicitor's letter into Marshall's hand.

Marshall's expression didn't improve as he glanced at it.

"What is your name?" he demanded.

Good question. "Gideon Kendrick—as it says on the paper in your hand."

"The brother's name was Tavernash."

"I jettisoned it and took a new one many years ago. I had no use for it in the mines." Gideon noted with satisfaction that Fillmore blinked. "If you'll excuse me, I've had a long journey today. We can talk tomorrow."

Gideon spoke directly to Fillmore. "Send a hot bath up to my room—any guest room will do. Dinner on a tray, a mug of willow bark tea, and brandy."

Fillmore glanced at Marshall, who barked, "Get on it, man."

"What will Tavernash think?" Fillmore asked.

"What I tell him," Marshall answered.

"Another Tavernash?" Gideon demanded.

"Felton Tavernash is the Duke of Glenmore's nearest relative. The heir presumptive," Marshall said, his lips twitching, his eyes glittering.

Mr. Tavernash—some damned cousin, no doubt—is doomed to disappointment. Gideon almost said it out loud, if only to wipe the smug expression off Marshall's visage. The documents Phillip left in Sadler and January's safe would confirm that Gideon should always have been duke and that his son Daniel, God help the little one, would without question be next.

The reasons were complicated. Unless something happened to Phillip, he had no need to tell them. There would be time. Plenty of time. He returned Marshall's avid glare. "Tell him what you wish. It changes nothing. We'll meet in the morning."

"About this?" Marshall hefted the sheaf of papers. "I will check your claims when I have a moment. You may stay tonight." He turned to leave.

"Shall I send for a magistrate, then?" Gideon asked.

It fell on empty ears.

CHAPTER THREE

G IDEON LAY AWAKE in the early morning, studying the drab bedcovers in one of Woodglen's drearier guest rooms, one at the far end of a corridor of empty rooms. Old Fillmore would have pushed him down the servants' stairs at the end of the hall if he could have. Marshall controlled Woodglen, however, even Fillmore. If nothing else had become clear the night before, that had. Faced with an unpromising gray dawn, Gideon considered that he had three options.

His preferred choice—retreating to Wales and family—called out to him. The advantage was peace. The disadvantage, guilt. Sadler had dribbled out enough information to indicate funds were being siphoned off and that unapproved land transactions might be in the works. From London, they could not be certain. Responsibility for the mess lay with Phillip, but Phillip trusted Gideon to pick up his pieces.

He swung his legs over the edge of the bed and leaned on his knees. Gideon had no loyalty to the Glenmoor title or the estate. Sadler's hints, however, touched Gideon's biases. Three things he hated—mismanagement, waste, and dishonesty—were at play or might be. That the estate would one day be Daniel's fed anger over such behavior. The need to find out had driven him here. He would stay, at least for a while. His second option was to take control even if he had to fetch a magistrate, sheriff, and armed constables.

On the other hand, he could allow Marshall to assume he held the power, lull him into complacency while playing the pathetic cripple they took him for, and gather crumbs of information from the background until he uncovered the truth. His stomach curdled at the thought. He should—

A brisk knock interrupted his thoughts.

"Enter."

A footman came in, different from the night before. This one studied Gideon with naked speculation and a canny intellect. "Mr. Marshall assigned me to be your manservant, you coming without one."

Marshall. The assigning of servants should lie with the butler. Gideon knew a spy when he saw one. "What is your name?" Gideon asked.

"Jem." The footman knelt and lit a fire. "A tray is coming. I didn't know if you would want tea or coffee. I ordered both," he said over his shoulder.

"I'll join Mr. Tavernash in the breakfast room," Gideon replied, pushing himself up. He still wore his shirt from the day before; it hung in wrinkles almost to his knees.

Jem snorted. "That one? He won't rise before noon."

Yet the unexpected intruder was to be rousted at dawn. If Marshall planned to make Gideon uncomfortable enough to drive him out, he'd find Gideon to be tougher than that. Planting a spy in his room was equally transparent, but Gideon could work with it. There was a middle ground. He would project his authority while sparring with Marshall and still encourage the man to underestimate him. At least for now.

Jem finished fiddling with the hearth and stood, wiping his hands together.

Gideon spoke with the tones he used to keep miners in line. "Pity Tavernash is a sluggard. I'm generally up at dawn, and I'll take my meal in the family breakfast parlor. When you finish helping me dress, go down and tell cook I want my coffee strong, my eggs coddled, my ham thick, and my toast unburned. I loathe kippers."

Their eyes held for a moment too long, and Gideon braced for open rebellion. Jem broke contact and glanced at the suit Gideon had worn when he arrived, unbrushed but lying in a neat pile on the chair.

"The rest of my luggage will arrive today or tomorrow. You may unpack and press them. There is a clean shirt in my saddlebag," Gideon said. "Help me out of this one." He turned, providing this uninvited would-be valet a view of his back, and raised his arms. Jem tugged the shirt up, and a breath, raggedly sucked in, rewarded Gideon. Gideon knew what Jem saw and deliberately intended to give him something to take to his master. He withheld any comment.

Gideon's spine twisted in a sharp *S*. The doctor Daniel Kendrick had forced him to see in Cardiff had pronounced it the worst curvature he'd ever seen. Gideon knew from hard experience that many folks took physical deformity as a sign of mental deficiency; Marshall could make of it what he wanted. Jem would have also discovered that Gideon's shirts were fine linen, well made, and expensive. Unfortunately, Jem's inspection would also feed the narrative that would flood the neighborhood. *The half-wit cripple has returned.*

Having made his point, Gideon dismissed the servant. He'd grown used to servants since his childhood in his mother's tavern but never to someone helping him dress. He certainly didn't plan to allow the man to shave him; the last thing he needed was a razor to his throat.

The distance between rooms gave him trouble. He had left his walking stick in the baggage coach; he didn't often resort to using it, but Woodglen's stairs and long corridors would challenge his ability to manage without it.

Still, he found the breakfast room easily enough, grateful it hadn't changed since he'd left fifteen years before. By the time he had shaved, finished dressing, and walked the length of the house to get there, his eggs were cold and congealed, the ham thin and striped with grizzle, and toast not only burned but cold. He caught a footman lurking in the hall and sent it back.

So it begins…

An hour later, filled with a tolerable breakfast, he faced an empty house. Neither Fillmore nor Marshall put in an appearance, and he wasn't in the mood to search the maze of rooms for them. He could demand their attendance, but it was early yet. No one except servants appeared to be up. That message about his place in the house wasn't lost on him, either. He decided to check on his mount in the stable. He half feared they'd treat Hannibal as poorly as they treated him.

He found Hannibal well cared for, however, groomed and fed but happy enough to see him and have his neck rubbed. He found the grooms as surly as the house servants. "Does Pritchard still work here?"

"Horse is fine. Whaddya want Pritchard for, then? 'e's not much use with that one arm," the groom grumbled without glancing up from his work.

One arm? "Is he here?"

The man shrugged. "Was studying that peculiar tack of yours a bit ago," he said, gesturing toward the tack room with his head.

The saddle! Gideon's heart sped up. *If they damaged my saddle, I'll—* He cursed himself for letting his emotions about Woodglen distract him from taking time to instruct the groom about his custom gear.

He found his saddle safely stored over a sawhorse, the side braces for his stirrups leaning against it. He leaned one hand on it in relief.

"Y've come back, then. I knew it was you when I saw this gear. Fancier 'n the one we made up for you back in the day." A wizened old man, thin and shrunken, gray of hair with the sleeve of one arm pinned up, spoke from the corner of the room. In the shadows, Gideon never would have recognized Pritchard if he hadn't spoken.

Pritchard was the one who'd believed he could ride if they fashioned a saddle to give him support and keep him from listing to the side. It was Pritchard who had done it. The man approached, his gait slow. "They said you were dead."

Gideon nodded. "The old duke lied."

"Th' young one know? He's not been around much."

"Phillip knows. He found me last year. He turned up at my colliery without warning." Gideon smiled at the memory.

"*Your* colliery? Done well for yerself, have you?" Pritchard shook his head.

"Three of them, actually," Gideon said allowing his pride to show.

Pritchard cackled with glee. "That oughta show 'em. Thought they left you for dead." He sobered at the thought. "Bad doings that night," he murmured.

Gideon's smile fled; he didn't have to be told which night. Pritchard had tried to intervene when his father's servants beat him. A sudden thought horrified him. "What happened to your arm?"

"Broke it the night they dragged you away. Didn't heal right. Gratis had to take it. I almost didn't survive that, what with fever and all." The old man's eyes drifted up and away. "Long time ago."

"Why did you stay?" Gideon asked softly.

"Got no place to go, do I? They give me a place to sleep. I help as I can." From the state of his clothing, he got little more than that.

"Who's the stablemaster these days?" Gideon asked.

Pritchard shrugged. "Isn't one. Just four grooms. Marshall keeps 'em in line hisself. They say the duke has gone missing. Some folks say he is dead."

"Not dead. Just traveling. He sent me here," Gideon replied quietly.

Pritchard nodded his approval. "What are you going to do now?"

"Find out what needs fixing and take care of it." *Starting with a pension for Pritchard.*

"A MORNING CALL is perfectly proper," Selina said for the third time, clutching her reticule to her chest.

Mia loped along the lane beside her and kept her myriad objections to herself. Selina would barge into Woodglen with her or without her. She had come along to try to tone down her young cousin's behavior. "Your father may not think so."

"Of course he would," Selina said. "He said we should call on the man."

"He said *he* would call on the newcomer himself and test the waters. He didn't say we should hoof it over at the first opportunity, unescorted." Mia sighed. Discussion about Felton Tavernash, the heir presumptive to the Glenmoor title and estate, had dominated dinner at Selwyn Court for three days.

Mia wouldn't have initiated this fools' errand, but she admitted to some curiosity about the man. Her opinion of a person who moved into someone's house in his absence—even or perhaps especially when the man a duke—ate his food, drank his wine, and ordered his servants about was already low. She doubted if it would improve on acquaintance, but she was open to the possibility. What preyed on her mind was that Marshall, the steward, had allowed him in. She'd have thought he'd have sent him away with a flea in his ear. Marshall must fear the duke truly was dead and didn't wish to irritate his possible successor.

In complete honesty, she was even more curious about the mysterious rider, the one dressed entirely in black. Who was he and what role did he play in this unfolding drama? He may have been a passing businessman who'd called in at Woodglen and left, but she doubted that.

They circled a small lake surrounded by overhanging trees, with resident ducks artfully placed. At least, they appeared artful to Mia. She suspected one would have to work very hard to create the impression of wilderness this lake was meant to project. She peered up and caught a glimpse of Woodglen's impressive façade, with its central block rising four stories high and wings stretching out in either direction, each end topped with a dome.

"Imagine being mistress of all this," Selina sighed, continuing around.

Mia could not in fact imagine such thing. She didn't answer.

The drive passed through a broad scythed lawn, one with little by the way of garden to soften the cold impact of the place. Even Selina shivered as they approached, but Mia suspected that had more to do with nerves. "It isn't too late to turn around," Mia said, straining to keep amusement from her voice. Selina merely glared at her.

Mia paused at the foot of the curving steps to one side of the portico that dominated the front entrance to gaze up at the columns on top, smooth but topped with ionic capitals. Selina barged on up the steps, forcing Mia to follow. At the top, Mia counted six of the columns forming what she believed would be called a hexastyle, a classical pretense as though this mountain of brick and stone was some sort of temple. *Temple to what?* Her maternal grandparents, Methodist to their backbone, would have been horrified.

She spun to the door when it opened and met the ferocious face of Fillmore, Woodglen's excessively proper butler. He gazed at them rather as he might have looked upon a bug who dared besmirch the portico. Mia had encountered him in the village once and found him intimidating then as well.

"We're here to call on Mr. Tavernash," Selina chirped. "Is he receiving?" She held out her calling card between two fingers.

Fillmore glanced over her shoulder at Mia, quickly dismissing her as the poor relation she was. For a moment, she expected him to close the door in their faces.

After an uncomfortable pause, he took the card. "I will inquire," he intoned. Apparently, Viscount Clavering's daughter deserved at least that much. He stepped back to allow them into the sanctuary. It was the first time Mia had been inside in the five years she'd lived nearby. Uncle Ludlow had dined at Woodglen occasionally, and had taken Selina once, but Mia had never been invited to join him.

They walked through the entrance with its marble floors and, Mia noted, marble columns lining the walls, to a pokey little parlor. Mia suspected Fillmore used it to store unexpected arrivals and unwanted parcels. Selina shot Mia a smug smirk.

"We should leave, Selina. This is a mistake. We were raised to know young ladies do not call on gentlemen in their homes—especially uninvited." Mia regretted succumbing to temptation.

"Nonsense. This isn't some boudoir. And it isn't as if I'm unchaperoned," Selina said, relegating Mia to the faded world of companions and maiden aunts while she gleefully studied every detail of what Mia suspected was one of Woodglen's least impressive rooms.

Fillmore let them cool their heels for half an hour. Either he deliberately wanted them to stew about it, or it took him that long to reach his destination in this cavernous house and come back.

"Mr. Tavernash isn't in," Fillmore said bluntly. He gestured to the door.

"Tell him we regret missing him, and kindly pass this along." Selina handed Fillmore a folded missive. "It is an invitation to tea."

Mia sucked in a breath. She hadn't expected the invitation. Uncle Ludlow would not be happy. He expected to do the inviting.

Fillmore gestured to the door, but Selina dragged her feet, studying what she could see as if cataloging the assets. Mia bit her cheek to keep from hurrying her in front of the overbearing butler. They were almost there when another gentleman, walking across the hall between two rooms, gazed toward them and paused.

Mia's mysterious stranger seemed to recognize her. He approached them as Fillmore impatiently opened the door. Mia held her breath. On foot, he appeared less ferocious. His body tilted to one side, and he walked with a swaying gait that was not quite a limp. He radiated confidence nonetheless.

Who is this man?

"We have guests, Fillmore?" he asked. It sounded more like a demand.

"These ladies called on Mr. Tavernash," Fillmore said with clipped tones.

"As nearest neighbors, we thought to welcome him. You…" Selina's voice faded away under the force of his frown.

The stranger glanced at Mia and then Fillmore. "Neighbors?"

"The Honorable Selina Selwyn is the daughter of Viscount Clavering," Fillmore said, his tight jaw making the words sound as if he forced them out. He glared at Selina.

Mia noticed a flicker of recognition at Uncle Ludlow's name. This man wasn't an utter stranger to this place.

"Kindly introduce us, Fillmore," he said. There was no mistaking the command in his voice this time.

The butler scowled in disapproval but complied. "Miss Selwyn, may I present Mr. Gideon Kendrick." He didn't add anything to explain the man's presence at Woodglen or his air of authority.

Kendrick peered pointedly at Mia.

"And her…companion," Fillmore finished.

"My cousin, Miss Euphemia Selwyn," Selina clarified.

Kendrick studied Mia so intently she had to fight not to squirm. "I'm honored, ladies," he said with a slight inclination of his head.

For a moment, Mia thought he would say more, feared he'd allude to their previous encounter in front of the butler and Selina, but he did not.

Soon enough they were out the door and on their way back

down the long drive. Selina sighed dramatically. "Thank goodness that man is not the heir. Isn't he horrid?"

Mia didn't think so. Not in the slightest. His posture may be odd, but she found his air of authority and his intense dark eyes compelling.

Selina ignored her. "I know who he is. Did you guess?" she asked smugly.

Mia blinked. She had no idea what her cousin babbled about.

"He's the brother, the half-wit cripple. Do you think he's come to cause trouble for poor Mr. Tavernash?"

CHAPTER FOUR

A DAY LATER, Mia held Sally Anders's baby in her arms and let the luxury of the warm little body and trusting eyes soothe her soul. She'd come with a food basket after Selwyn Court's cook alerted her to the family's need. Sally lived in a sad excuse for a cottage at the border between Woodglen and Selwyn Court, one allotted her out of charity after her husband had slipped, fallen on a scythe during harvest, and died.

"You tell Lord Clavering we're that grateful," Erma, Sally's mother-in-law, said, her words a refrain for the sound of her rickety rocker. A tiny boy, perhaps two years old, sat at the old woman's feet, playing with a block of wood, his eyes straying frequently to the basket Mia had brought.

Sally herself sat, as she had during the entire visit, silently staring at her hands folded in her lap. The horror of her husband's death never left her, and the burden of two children and an old woman to feed with no man to work for them crushed her. Uncle Ludlow's only concession had been use of this place free of charge after he asked them to vacate their previous house for a paying—that was, working—tenant. He didn't object to Mia's visits nor to her bringing mending to the two women so she could also pass on a few coins. Neither did he bestir himself to do more.

Mia wondered if Sally's family would have fared better as

Woodglen tenants. She had no idea. The absent duke might have been even less help, and they'd be at the mercy of Curtis Marshall.

The sounds of horses brought Sally alert, fear stark in her eyes as she stared at the door. Hector, who had been left outside, barked at the arrivals, no doubt making it worse. Sally darted glances around the room and sank back into her stupor. Mia suspected whoever had brought her husband home—or news of his accident, at least—had come on horseback. The sound forced her to relive that moment.

Mia handed the baby to Erma. "I'll see to the disturbance."

The old woman nodded; Sally didn't move.

Hector settled down when Mia came out, but he stayed alert. An old man mounted on a bulky black pony, one Mia judged both aged and weary, came to a stop and slid to the ground using his only hand to steady his dismount. She reached up to offer the pony comfort while the man pulled his forelock and nodded, his attention directed to the door. "How is Sally?" he asked, eyeing Hector nervously and untying a rough sack from his saddle.

Mia, distracted by a second rider, didn't answer. Gideon Kendrick was once more clad entirely in black. He stopped several feet away. He did not immediately dismount, nor did he greet her. His inscrutable gaze bore into her, and Mia thought questions lurked behind his coal-black eyes.

What a rude man he is. He was not the half-wit Selina called him, however. Intelligence burned in his countenance. Two could play at rudeness. Mia met him stare for stare.

The old man, who stood forgotten at her side, spoke up. "I'll just pop in on Erma, then," he said, stepping toward the door.

"She isn't well," Mia said belatedly, answering the old man's original question before he could enter the cottage. "Sally, that is. Are you a friend?"

"Aye," the old man said grimly. "I'm that. Needs a few."

"Pritchard, is that you?" Erma called from inside.

Friend, then. Mia nodded at him, wondering fleetingly why

she hadn't seen him here before. She turned back to Kendrick and caught him heaving himself up and off his horse, powerful arms and shoulders bearing his weight. She couldn't help admiring his strength, obvious in spite of whatever caused his odd posture, as he let himself down gently on his left foot.

What she now realized was a custom-made saddle with a tall back, built to cradle the rider and hold him steady, complicated the process. She suspected his clumsy, if impressive, dismount accounted for his earlier hesitation. He did not wish her to watch him do it. Even now he glowered when he caught her gaze.

To break the uncomfortable silence, she said the first thing that occurred to her. "That is a magnificent animal. A Welsh cob, is he? Bit of a big fellow for that breed, though." She walked directly to the horse.

Kendrick raised a hand to warn her away, but she reached her own up for the horse to snuffle.

"Hannibal is not a lady's pet," Kendrick growled.

"I should say not. He's powerful and dependable enough to cross the Alps in winter, I'll warrant. An altogether noble beast," she said.

Hannibal snorted and took a step back. He raised his head and peered over at her as if to acknowledge the praise as his due and to signal the end of his patience with her ministrations.

She smiled up at him. Standoffish he might be, but she liked him. She deferred judgment about his master. "What brings you here?" she asked.

"I could ask you the same, Miss Selwyn," Kendrick retorted, yanking on the cuff of his riding gloves.

"The Anders are Selwyn tenants," she replied, irritated that he expected her to defend herself.

Kendrick glanced up at the ramshackle cottage with its peeling shutters and sagging roof and raised his eyebrows.

Selwyn Court's care for its tenants is pathetically poor. He didn't need to say the words.

The urge to defend her uncle died in her throat. The judgment was fair enough, but who was Gideon Kendrick to make it? The impulse to stalk off in high dudgeon almost overtook her, but her reticule and bonnet were inside the cottage. She turned her back to him and went to retrieve them, ordering Hector to stay.

GIDEON WATCHED THE Selwyn girl walk away, drawn in spite of his good sense by the sway of her hips, the glint of sun on her honey-brown hair, and the grace of her movements. He felt a fool for ogling her, and for the memory that he still owed her an apology for the encounter on the road. He'd been rude again, and now he owed her another apology for that. He couldn't express regret for the surge of attraction that had flooded him when she approached Hannibal, however, not without embarrassing her by revealing it. He hadn't had such a sudden uninvited surge of lust since his wife had died five years before, and it had shocked him.

He followed her into the hovel, hovering near the door while his eyes adjusted to the shadows, regretting his decision to come. Pritchard insisted he see this; he hadn't expected the neighbors to observe his arrival.

Pritchard's voice penetrated his thoughts. "...wouldn't let me borrow a pony even much less bring nutthin. Sorry it has been so long. Master Gideon here made it right. He'll see to it I kin come more." Gideon's old friend knelt on the dirt floor next to a rocking chair, patting the hand of an elderly lady where it held a small baby.

The woman glanced up at Gideon, her expression pained. "Who's this one, then?"

"The old duke's other son, Erma. Remember?" Pritchard said.

"The one what…"

Gideon definitely should not have come. He waited for the words, jaw set. *Half-wit. Cripple. Monster. Brute.* They didn't come.

"Don't go believing nonsense. He's a kind gent, Erma. He gave them grooms what for. Told them I could take all the coal I wanted and use the pony, too. On his *authority*. Authority, he said. I thought they'd balk, but he had such a look on his face. Made him come so he could meet you." Pritchard glanced back with a cheeky grin.

When Pritchard's Erma shifted a bit, Mia Selwyn leaned over her, murmured something, and took the baby from her. Gideon had forgotten her presence for a moment. She cast him a glance that was puzzled at best, as if trying to fit him into her universe. *Let her try.*

Erma stood and dipped a curtsey on unsteady feet, causing Gideon's breath to catch. He took her hand and urged her to sit. "None of that. Mrs. Anders, is it? Pritchard told me you needed fuel and have no one to chop wood. The Woodglen farrier won't miss a bit from his mountain of coal now and then."

The old woman smiled at him and did as he bid. "Thank you kindly, my lord."

"Hardly that. Mr. Kendrick will do," Gideon said, the words coming out as if dragged through gravel.

"Duke's son, ain't you?" she retorted.

"Alas, yes," he replied, setting Erma off in a burst of laughter.

He took the sack of coal and carried it to the hearth. Pritchard held the woman's hand in his tenderly. "Dunno what Marshall will say about this, but I'm here for today, at least. I missed you, old girl."

The younger woman never spoke. She sat staring at her lap. Pritchard described a horrific accident; Gideon had seen women traumatized like that after mine accidents. There was little anyone could do for them except give them time to heal. Time and tasks that needed doing.

Miss Selwyn approached and put the baby in the younger woman's lap, gently wrapping her arms around it and waiting to be sure she took firm hold. "I have to leave now, Sally." She straightened and peered at Erma. "I'll bid you good day, Mrs.

Anders. Thank you for your fine work. I left the coins on the table with this week's mending. There'll be more next week."

"Thank the viscount for it," Erma said.

Miss Selwyn's tight lips when she nodded suggested the viscount, who Gideon remembered as a pinchpenny, had nothing to do with the arrangement. She swept on her bonnet, a plain straw affair, and tied it in a pert bow under her chin before donning her cloak.

She surprised Gideon when she stopped and inclined her head to him, curiosity, held in check by reserve, still lurking in her eyes. "Mr. Kendrick. Thank you for your kindness to the Anders family."

He followed her out, leaving Pritchard with his Erma.

"Miss Selwyn, a word!" he called. The shaggy dog of dubious origins who had been guarding the door stopped when she did and turned to glower at him.

Her eyes, he noted when she turned, were dark blue and bright with intelligence, adding warmth to his attraction. "What is it?" she asked.

"I owe you an apology."

"What on earth for?" she asked.

"The other day. On the road. You startled me, and I feared an accident, but that is no excuse for my rudeness," he replied.

For a moment, he thought she meant to chastise him for a catalog of such sins. She didn't. "Your fine friend Hannibal made sure neither of us came to grief," she said, smiling over at the horse. As if in response, the beast walked right up to her and nudged the side of her head.

What sort of lady attracts so many ferocious animals to behave like lapdogs?

She reached up and soothed Hannibal's nose with a laugh. "No apologies needed from either of you."

"I had been on the road for hours, and I wasn't at my best," he added.

She peered at him speculatively, and he feared she would ask about his deformities. "We all suffer from the trials of travel, Mr. Kendrick. Thank you for your kind words, though."

Their eyes held, but there seemed nothing else to say. She broke contact, dipping her head. "Good day, Mr. Kendrick."

"Good day, Miss Selwyn," he said, returning the gesture.

"Come, Hector," she commanded, and the great lump of a dog followed meekly.

Watching her depart, he was struck by something. "Is it common for young ladies to walk about unaccompanied in Dorset?"

She stopped, her back still to him. "Whyever not, Mr. Kendrick?" He could hear amusement in her voice. "Everyone in Nether Abbas and surrounding knows me. Who would care? Besides, I'm not unaccompanied. I have Hector." She walked on.

Who indeed? A gentleman should. A gentleman should offer to escort her. The urge ate at him, but instinct told him she wouldn't welcome it any more than he would welcome someone rushing to assist him mounting his horse. *Pride is a prickly thing.*

CHAPTER FIVE

"I HEAR YOU make free with Woodglen's coal. You obviously think highly of yourself." Marshall had sauntered in and led with an attack. The steward had let Gideon cool his heels for half an hour in the estate workroom in the lowest level of the great house, the far back wing that held offices and storage of various sorts after Gideon had sent word demanding an interview. Now he scrutinized Gideon across a battered worktable where Fillmore had directed him to wait. The steward's calculating expression hovered between anticipation and triumph.

It's to be chess, then. Good. Gideon played very well.

"Nothing escapes you, Marshall, not even a trivial bag of coal. I'll make note of your diligence about inventory in my report," Gideon responded.

Gideon's talk of a report hit home. "Report? To whom?" Marshall snorted and raised his chin insolently, but his eyes were wary.

The magistrates if you're stealing. But of course, this wasn't about inventory. Marshall's men spied on Gideon, not the coal supplies. "Sadler and January as a first step. The duke ultimately."

"The duke has gone missing." Marshall's response was reflexive. Gideon had actually wondered if Phillip had left clues to his plans here at Woodglen, but obviously he had not. A better chess player would have revealed less.

"Has he? Did he fail to tell you where he went?" Gideon held Marshall's eyes, hoping the weasel took his intended implication that he knew more than the steward did.

"Dukes are not required to explain themselves to their staff," Marshall growled.

"Exactly right," Gideon retorted. *Family is another matter; damn my brother anyway.* "I will need an office. Perhaps I could make use of yours. I will also want clerical supplies and access to the ledgers." He didn't know where they were kept now, if he'd ever known.

For the first time, it occurred to Gideon that family papers would be somewhere in this place. He probably should have considered it before. Phillip would have known. Would their father have kept proof of his bigamy here? Gideon doubted it, and he didn't care to pursue it. Not now. He wanted to keep his time here as short as possible. Besides, Phillip would have told him if he'd found proof about their parentage one way or the other. At least, Gideon believed he would have.

"Who do you think you are?" Marshall sputtered.

"I am the duke's brother and his trusted agent. I have authority to act on his behalf." Gideon gazed implacably back at Marshall, arms folded across his chest. "Did you read the papers I gave you?"

"I don't have time for that," Marshall said, glaring right back at him. "They're somewhere in my office."

Gideon retrieved another copy from his coat pocket. "Shall I read it to you?" He didn't wait for a response. "Horace Sadler, solicitor, etc., etc. Doth confirm and warrant, and so on...," he read. He skimmed down to the meat of it while Marshall's mouth opened and closed and he groped for a retort.

"...all authority to act including but not exclusively, surveying all accounts and contracts, inspecting all premises and holdings, ordering changes, and so on it goes." Gideon glanced up. "My favorites are 'ordering staff' and 'selling property of any kind as he deems fit.' Or not. You can review the whole list once you find that copy in your office."

"No duke gives away that kind of power. Why would he permit it?" Marshall demanded.

"It isn't for us to question him, is it? The last bit here is important," Gideon said, waving the papers. "'Mr. Kendrick has full authority to act, and such authority shall be treated as if coming from the duke himself.'" Gideon smiled then, a cold, dry stretching of the lips. "You may consider me the duke in all but name." *For now.*

"I'll do no such thing. I'll send to Sadler and January for confirmation of this insane document myself. I'll inquire about the duke's sanity while I'm at it," Marshall said, striding to the door.

"An office, Marshall. And supplies," Gideon demanded.

"Fillmore will find you something. I have no time for it." The hostile butler himself stood in the hall. He had been listening no doubt.

"You heard him, Fillmore. Find me a place to work." Gideon raised his voice so Marshall couldn't miss it. "And bring me last year's ledgers. I'll start there." He tamped down resentment. Gideon had lost a pawn but opened up his rook. Compliance would come with resentment and no little pettiness, but it would come.

MIA WROTE TO Great-Aunt Hortensia Hodge, last of her mother's family, monthly, assuring her that she enjoyed good health, remembered her prayers, and remained simple in her habits and rigid in her morals—not that she had much opportunity to do anything else. She didn't tell the old woman she used her pin money to send her letters and hid them from her uncle, avoiding his frank, nor that she retrieved replies from the postal service herself. It was a small rebellion, but it saved her Uncle Ludlow's ugly words about her mother's origins. She had realized quickly that he read everything and was not shy about voicing his stern disapproval of her Hodge relatives.

Aunt Hortensia wrote back reminding her she lacked suitable female guidance now that Aunt Harriet Selwyn, the viscountess, went to her great reward and warning Mia about the pitfalls of idleness, the dangers of society, and the perils of a season—which Mia would be wise to refuse. As if she would.

The missives tended to languish at the stationers' shop that served as the post office in Nether Abbas, awaiting Mia's attention. They were all so similar she didn't rush to read them. They differed only in which bits of random advice regarding everything from dress to eating habits Hortensia Hodge chose to sprinkle in.

A twinge of guilt eventually brought her to town to fetch her aunt's letters as it had this day, a sunny November morning that promised at least an enjoyable walk to the village. Passing a shilling from her pin money to Mr. Adcock, the stationer, for the newest, she felt a similar twinge of guilt when she recalled that they almost always ended with "…and Cuddles sends his love." The old cocker spaniel loved her; there was that. She would read this one. She always did.

"A penny more, Miss Selwyn," Adcock said, "Northumberland being well over three hundred miles."

She paid him, tucked her letter in her reticule, and passed over her reply to the last. That might have been it, but Adcock's sudden frown caused her to turn around to find the cause of his disgust.

Gideon Kendrick stood near the door, frowning back. "Still in business, Adcock?" he asked, peering around the shop with distaste.

She couldn't fault the man his upturned nose. Truthfully, Mia had always found Adcock's premises a bit shabby and in need of a good dusting, if not an actual scrub.

Adcock gazed back at Mia. "Will there be anything else, Miss Selwyn?" he asked impatiently. Was he trying to hurry her along?

Torn between good manners and unbecoming curiosity, she hesitated before stepping back from the counter.

"I need paper and ink." Kendrick stepped forward, gazing directly at Adcock.

For a moment, she thought the proprietor would refuse to serve him. "Not dead, then?" Adcock asked.

"As you see. Kindly fill my order," Kendrick said.

Adcock didn't appear shocked. Gossip up and down the village had informed all of them that the old earl's son had returned alive and well. "Still scribbling incomprehensible drivel, Tavernash?" Adcock spat.

"My name is Kendrick. Fill my order and keep your ignorant opinions to yourself."

"I hear you're at Woodglen. Use theirs." Frozen in inappropriate fascination by the doorway, Mia thought Adcock would give Kendrick cut direct and retreat to his back room.

"Supplies have run out," Kendrick said, every word sharp as a chip of ice.

That stopped Adcock in his tracks, and he laughed outright. "Their monthly shipment went over three days ago. If you ask Fillmore nicely, he might…"

Color rose up Kendrick's neck. "I'll have a ream of paper and two bottles of ink," he said. "Add three empty ledger books, and give me a copy of Woodglen's orders for the past three months."

Mia leaned back against the wall, fearing Kendrick's anger was boiling to an explosion of some sort. She had no idea what she could do about it.

"And how many goose quills, Your Majesty?" Adcock sneered.

"None. I own a supply of Donkin's metal tips. Just fill my order," Kendrick retorted.

"I'll see your money first, Taver—whatever you call yourself," Adcock said. "And I won't show you any damned accounts without Curtis Marshall's say-so."

"Fine. I'll view the copy at the house. Put my order on

Woodglen's account," Kendrick said, his voice growing tight, his effort at control obvious.

Adcock's eyes flew wide. "You do have cheek. Even more than you did as a boy. I'll need Curtis Marshall to—"

"You need nothing. I'm auditing the Woodglen books. Perhaps I should examine the business you've done with the estate more closely. It may be that we need to send our trade to a different proprietor," Kendrick said, holding his ground.

"You're the idiot old Glenmoor always said you were if you think you can get away with that stunt," Adcock said.

"Don't try me," Kendrick replied. He glared at the proprietor, his expression implacable. He seemed to grow before her as he spoke. Mia held her breath in the face of the battle raging.

Adcock sagged; the round went to Kendrick. "I'll do it this time. I'll send a bill to Marshall immediately, however. If it isn't paid, I'll not let you in here again, and I'll see to it you are barred from every store in Nether Abbas."

"You'll do it, or I will personally take Woodglen's trade to Shaftsbury."

Adcock shot Mia a filthy look while he assembled the requested goods. Kendrick caught it, turned, and saw her watching. Red blotches emerged on his face, while his eyes burned with anger. Mia shifted her gaze to her feet.

She fled, breezed past Hannibal where he waited patiently on the road, and was a full block down the market street before a realization brought her to a stop. She thought Kendrick's behavior rude—and it had been, every time she'd encountered him. That didn't give her an excuse to pry into his private interaction with Adcock. She owed him an apology this time.

By the time she reached the stationers' store, Kendrick was leaving, a package in his arms and a world-class scowl on his face.

"I owe you an apology." She blurted the words out before she came to a stop.

Kendrick shook his head. His expression didn't soften. "Did you satisfy your curiosity?"

Her neck and cheeks felt hotter than ever. "That wasn't well done of me." Then she spoiled her apology when she couldn't hold back the question troubling her. "Are you really auditing Woodglen?"

"Yes, and before you ask on whose authority, it is none of your business," he said, tying his package behind his saddle.

"Every shopkeeper in Nether Abbas will want to know the answer to that," Mia murmured.

"Very well. Tell them the duke's authority."

"But…"

"Never mind. I'll do it myself. Good day, Miss Selwyn," he said, leading Hannibal to a mounting block set along the commercial district for ladies' use. He put one foot in his stirrup and heaved himself up with one muscular thrust of his shoulders accompanied by a grimace. He fixed a leather strap around each thigh, studiously avoiding her gaze.

You're staring again, Mia. "I'm sorry," she whispered. He didn't hear her. It didn't matter. She watched him trot off toward Woodglen.

She wasn't alone. Avid faces peered from every window along the market street.

CHAPTER SIX

D INNER AT SELWYN Court hummed with excitement that evening. The duke's bastard brother had been sighted in Nether Abbas, and everyone seemed to have a story.

"Rogers at the Cockcrow told Betts the man is a dwarf hunchback and trouble," Eustace Selwyn said with glee.

Betts, the Honorable Richard Bettinton, one of Eustace's more unsavory friends, confirmed that with equal relish. "Rogers won't have him in the place," he said. "More's the pity—would have liked a good look."

Mia held her tongue with difficulty. Anything she said to the contrary would invite a verbal attack from Eustace. Selina bounced in her seat, fit to burst, but kept silent. Uncle Ludlow had never discovered her visit to Woodglen. If she gave in to the urge to say she'd seen the man, she'd have to explain when.

"The bloke at the stable said he was nearly mute, too." The third speaker, Sir Harvey Rowlinson, the one they called Rowley, spoke quietly.

Eustace leaned forward. "Our grooms talk to those over in Woodglen's stables. George says no one there wants to deal with him. They're all afraid he'll ask them to help him mount, and not one wants to touch him, deformed as he is."

"He doesn't need help mounting his horse," Mia said before she could stop herself.

"How would you know, Fee? Have you taken to consorting with grooms and stable hands?" Eustace sneered.

"I thought you said it was the horses she consorts with," Betts said as if it was a great joke.

She sat up straighter. "I saw him in Nether Abbas." Suddenly the focus of all eyes, she wished she hadn't spoken.

"When?" Eustace demanded.

"Where?" Uncle Ludlow asked at the same time.

"This morning. He came into Adcock's Stationery when I went to…" Mia hesitated, loath to reveal her defiance of Uncle Ludlow's dictate that all correspondence come through him. "That is, I used my pin money to purchase a diary."

Selina leaned across the table. "Was he horrible, as they say? Could you understand him when he spoke?" Her eyes glittered.

Her cousin knew full well he spoke like a gentleman. She had heard him at Woodglen. Mia was tempted to reveal Selina's little secret. Instead, she said, "He had no problem making his demands clear to Mr. Adcock."

"I certainly hope you left quickly, Mia. No lady should have any dealings with that creature," Uncle Ludlow said. Mia opened her mouth to demand why, thought better of it, and dropped her eyes to the fish portion she had shredded on her plate.

"No *respectable* lady," Eustace said with glee. "I heard he was caught in flagrante with his own stepmother."

Betts giggled. "I've heard some women have a taste for the grotesque."

"Enough!" Uncle Ludlow roared. "There are ladies present."

"What news from Woodglen, then, Clavering? Didn't you ride over there a day ago?" Eustace asked.

Selina drew breath and grasped her hands to her chest. "Has the heir accepted our invitation to tea? You left your card, didn't you, Papa?" She leaned toward the viscount anxiously. "Please tell me he hasn't left."

"Mr. Tavernash is still in residence. He's the cousin with expectations, yes, and he has been too preoccupied acquainting himself with Woodglen to socialize so far," Uncle Ludlow replied.

"Forget the bleating cousin. What does Marshall have to say about the bastard?" Eustace demanded.

Selina sank into sullen silence.

The viscount sighed. "The Tavernash by-blow had just arrived. Marshall expected to send him away with a flea in his ear within a day. I'm shocked that didn't happen."

"What did he say? Is the dwarf as mentally deficient as they say?" Betts asked.

Mia kept her face down. Nothing in that description matched the man she had met four times now. Kendrick's obvious intelligence and competence shouldn't need defending, and Eustace and his friends were unlikely to listen. As to his crooked posture—he was hardly some sort of ogre. She thought again of the way he raised himself out of his saddle, his shoulders rippling with strength under a well-fitted jacket, and blushed.

"You put my cousin to blush, Betts. Watch how you talk, but I'm as curious as you. I wonder what he's like." Eustace drained his glass.

"When Felton Tavernash accepts my invitation to dinner, you can ask him. It shouldn't be long," Uncle Ludlow said.

"The heir?" Eustace asked. "I thought... But you say you did ask him?"

"He should be able to tell us why that man is still there. When he calls, that is—and gentleman that he is, I have no doubt he will." A decent pudding arrived, drawing Uncle Ludlow's attention to his meal.

Selina wiggled in her seat impatiently, her most petulant expression on full display. "We need to prod him a bit," she muttered, but the viscount ignored her.

"If we're all so curious about Mr. Kendrick, perhaps we should simply invite him to tea as well," Mia said, drawing gasps all around the table.

Uncle Ludlow snapped to attention at that. "He will not be received in this house." He pronounced each word as if it was a dart. "I remember well what he is like and what happened fourteen years ago, things a young maiden shouldn't hear."

Eustace perked up at that and appeared ready to ask but closed his mouth.

"Still, it might be amusing to actually meet him," Rowley murmured.

Betts broke in before the viscount could chastise that remark. "The one that's coming is the duke's heir. Do you think he knows whether the duke is dead or where the body might be? Maybe we can learn something to give our betting an edge."

"Good idea, Betts, but I still think he did himself in," Eustace said.

"Dukes don't kill themselves," Uncle Ludlow said.

"They don't just disappear, either," Eustace retorted.

"Maybe the half-wit killed him. Came to try to take over the duchy." Betts, grinning over a spoon of raspberry trifle, appeared very pleased with that fantastical theory.

Eustace leaned over. "Wouldn't it just set White's into a frenzy if we bring that little idea to the betting book? Of course, he'd never be able to take over the title. Unless… The unentailed estate, maybe. If I were Felton Tavernash, I'd watch my back, I can tell you that."

"I wonder what old Rogers at the Cockcrow would think of that idea," Betts said. "He knows him."

"Nonsense. Enough unfounded talk, all of you. Ladies…" Uncle Ludlow gazed at Selina pointedly.

Selina rose with a scowl and led Mia to the door. "We always have to leave when it is getting good," she whined.

Mia ignored her. She was too busy watching the glances being exchanged. Eustace and his miscreant friends would be spreading nonsense at the tavern before the night was over. Of that she had no doubt.

FELTON TAVERNASH WAS a fop of the first order who had few ideas not put in his head by his mother, or so Gideon decided when he finally found him on his own fourth day in residence. The Woodglen manor house was massive enough that two men could avoid each other indefinitely, with Gideon housed in the least comfortable guest corridor and Tavernash comfortably entrenched in the family wing. To Gideon's knowledge, the erstwhile heir avoided the estate offices and seemed more interested in the wine cellar.

Still, an encounter was easy enough to arrange once Gideon decided he needed to meet the man. The Tavernash aspirant liked his food. Gideon merely inserted himself into the formal dining room at dinnertime. The dinner hour was predictable enough. Gideon sauntered in just as the staff in full livery began to serve Felton Tavernash, who sat in solitary splendor at the head of the table.

"Set a place for me, Fillmore. I will dine here," he said, taking a chair to the cousin's left.

"I say, what is the meaning of this?" Tavernash sputtered. He narrowed his eyes. "You're that intruder. Fillmore said you used to live here."

"That I did," Gideon said, glaring at Fillmore until the old man laid his place and brought the soup course. "It is my brother's house. I am Gideon Kendrick."

"Wrong side of the blanket, m' mother says," Tavernash muttered. "Can't inherit."

Gideon ignored the jibe and applied himself to his soup before asking, "Who is your father?"

"Was. Passed two years ago. Sir Ronald Tavernash. Left me a neat little pile, Sedgewood Hall, in Buckinghamshire." Tavernash shrugged. "Nothing like this."

"A baronet? Are you not Sir Felton Tavernash, then?" Gideon asked.

"Should be. Still waiting for the worthless College of Arms to certify me."

"How was he related to my father?" Gideon said, gently reinforcing his right to be there.

"Old duke? Second cousin. My pater and the duke shared a great-grandfather."

"I don't recall meeting him here," Gideon murmured.

"Didn't socialize. My mother says Dukes of Glenmoor are too high in the instep for that. She says I'll be the same." Tavernash preened as if that was a badge of honor. He tugged at the lace at his cuffs and raised his chin. Gideon thought he heard the creaking of a corset.

"Are there other male Tavernash descendants?"

The would-be heir grinned smugly. "None. M' mother searched Debrett's and consulted with the biddies she corresponds with in London. Maiden aunts and girls only. There's only me." He glanced around the room with a proprietary smile on his powdered face.

"Did my brother invite you here?" Gideon asked smoothly.

"The duke? Couldn't, could he? He's missing. Probably dead, m'mother says. Betting at White's is he did himself in over some broken heart. More fool he, I say."

Fillmore served the fish course, his face a mask of disapproval.

"My brother, who is very much the Duke of Glenmoor, is not dead," Gideon said.

"How do you know?" Tavernash demanded.

"He wrote to me. And his solicitors confirmed it. He sent me here to manage the operation of the estate in his absence," Gideon said.

"Manage it? You mean like a steward?"

"Something like that," Gideon said.

"Now I know you're mentally deficient like Fillmore told me. Already has a steward. Marshall assures me he has the estate well in hand. I'm to enjoy the fruits, he says."

I'll bet he does. Gideon shot the butler a fulminating glare.

"You are certainly welcome to do that during your visit, but

Marshall has been made aware that I have the authority to oversee Woodglen finances, including household expenses," Gideon said, glancing pointedly at the footman refilling Tavernash's glass. "When my brother returns—"

"If the duke returns, you mean."

"He will. You can ask him his opinion then."

Momentary confusion marred the fop's expression, quickly replaced by smug confidence. Clearly Gideon's claims held no weight beside his mother's belief that Woodglen was his. "He's gone," Tavernash insisted.

Yes, he is, but he damned well better come back, Gideon thought. He was heartily sick of the entire enterprise. Even the glance at the books he'd had so far made it clear Phillip had ignored incompetence and sloppy record keeping no businessman would have overlooked. Gideon certainly didn't intend to. He would stay until he cleaned up the mess.

Tavernash he could ignore. The arrogant fool was no threat. Fillmore and Marshall were another story.

CHAPTER SEVEN

THE SOUND OF three drunken louts stumbling about and guffawing over pointless arguments echoed up from the front entrance an hour or so before dawn. Her sleep thus disturbed, Mia rose and wandered downstairs early enough to see servants righting tumbled furniture and cleaning up substances on the floor that did not bear close inspection. She paused, tempted to order them to leave the chaos for Uncle Ludlow to see, but of course they would ignore her, and the mess would only cause the servants trouble.

She took breakfast in the kitchen so as not to further tax the staff and made her way to the library, seeking quiet and a good book. She hurried in, closed the door to shut out the cleaning effort, and immediately regretted it. The smells of spirits and the expelled contents of someone's stomach struck her first. The sight of a gentleman's waistcoat and a coat with a lady's stocking dangling from the pocket tossed carelessly over a chair came into her line of sight just before she noticed the breeches strewn across the floor.

"Isn't this cozy? Nice of you to join me," a gravelly voice drawled, startling Mia, who had been lost in thought pondering the idea that this mess might get Uncle Ludlow's attention. Her heart pounded when Betts rose on one elbow and ran a hand across his scruffy face, flicking away some unnamed substance caught on his cheek. He lay sprawled across the settee, empty bottles strewn on the floor next to him.

"I was dreaming about your pretty little cousin, but you'll do," he slurred. He beckoned her with one hand.

Mia froze in place.

To her horror, Betts, who was obviously still in the grip of the spirits he'd consumed, muttered something about coming to get her and pushed himself to his feet. Stains covered the shirt he slept in, but it covered him to his knees. *Thank God.*

As soon as he took two lurching steps, the smell of his un-washed body gagged her, and she backed toward the door. He took one more step, swayed to one side, and collapsed on the floor, muttering something incomprehensible.

The fool is senseless with drink! She spun on her heels and fled the room, slamming the door behind her. Three maids stared at the door with rounded eyes.

"Oh, miss, we ran to warn you, but we were too late. We ain't cleaning that room with that man in there. We jist pray the viscount don't sack us."

Mia opened her mouth, but no words of reassurance came out. "I'll be outside," she said, starting for the door, mortified by the way her voice cracked.

"But, miss, it be pouring rain," Maisie, the youngest tweeny, said.

A glance at the entrance sidelights confirmed that unpleasant fact. Mia fled upstairs.

Selina! She might stumble over Betts if she wanders into the library. Eager to warn her cousin, she tapped lightly on Selina's door but got no response. She peeked in to find her bed empty and Selina's maid, Kerr—ostensibly Mia's servant as well, though both Selina and the maid tended to forget it—tidying up. "She's gone," the woman snapped.

"Gone? So early?"

Kerr gave an insolent shrug, one she wouldn't dare try on Selina or the viscount. She had made it clear soon after Mia arrived at Selwyn Court where her primary loyalty lay. There would be no point in questioning her.

Selina must be down at breakfast. She never uses the library anyway, Mia decided. *Besides,* she thought, *Uncle Ludlow probably wouldn't demand that loose screw Betts marry her if she did. On the other hand, he would likely demand marriage to that worm in my case, just to get me off his hands.* She locked herself in her room and dug through her pile of books for one worth rereading.

It was late morning when the viscount awoke and almost noon when he came down. Mia could tell the former from the traffic back and forth to his suite and the latter from the uproar that ensued when he entered the library.

Mia started down and met a footman half dragging Betts up the stairs. She flattened herself against the wall to let them pass, covering her nose with a handkerchief. Betts blinked when he passed, as if trying to remember something.

Above stairs, she heard Eustace. "What the hell, Betts? Sounds like the old man is in a rage."

Rage indeed. Uncle Ludlow bellowed at staff who scurried in all directions. Footmen carried out a stained rug, the housekeeper—scowling deeply—picked up clothing for the laundry, and Maisie came from the kitchen, dragging a bucket of water. Mia took a relieved breath when one of the footmen carrying a second bucket took it from the tiny tweeny, leaving Maisie to carry soap and rags.

"Mia! I hope you stayed well away this morning," the viscount roared.

"I was in my room all morning, Uncle," she said truthfully enough.

"I trust Selina did the same." Very little trust, if his worried expression meant anything.

"I—" Mia paused to choose her words carefully.

"You what, girl? Spit it out," he demanded.

"I checked on her earlier, and she was gone."

"Gone? Where?" he shouted.

"I don't know, and neither did Kerr. Just gone."

When summoned, Kerr curtseyed to the viscount and answered obsequiously, "Miss Selina didn't confide in me, my lord. I warned her the rain would ruin her gown, but she was determined. 'I need to do it now,' she said."

"Do what?" Uncle Ludlow demanded.

"She didn't say, my lord," Kerr said, attempting to project a meekness Mia knew to be false.

"When was this?" he asked.

"Soon after the sun rose. Very unusual for my miss, I must say," Kerr answered.

That was true enough. Something in Kerr's demeanor made Mia think she knew more, but Mia had no way to shake it out of her. "What was my cousin wearing?" she asked sweetly.

Kerr shot her a hateful glower out of Uncle Ludlow's sight. "Her green silk."

Hardly suitable for a simple walk. A niggling suspicion formed. "I hope she wore her sturdy half boots in this weather," Mia said, studying Kerr intently.

Kerr glanced at Uncle Ludlow, who appeared to be watching her, and back at Mia. "She wore her new green slippers," she admitted.

"In this weather? Has she lost what few wits she has?" Uncle turned on Mia. "How could you let her go out like that, Euphemia?"

Let her? Selina did what she pleased, though in fairness, she did not usually go out unaccompanied, unlike now. Unlike Mia.

"Do either of you have any idea where she might have gone?" Uncle Ludlow demanded, running a hand through his hair.

Kerr swore she had no idea and bowed out in craven deference.

Mia, reluctant to give voice to her growing suspicions, suggested the village, drawing a skeptical raised brow and frown from her uncle.

It didn't matter. A messenger arrived at that moment in

Woodglen livery. Wallace, Selwyn Court's butler, relieved to have a normal duty to perform on this chaotic afternoon, took the message, left the man at the door, and bowed to Uncle Ludlow, who grabbed the missive, ripped it open, and crumpled it, grumbling an oath.

"The lackwit is at Woodglen. You need to fetch her." He dropped the message and stalked off in the direction of his study.

Mia picked up the paper and scanned it quickly.

Miss Selwyn was caught in the storm, pursuing a lost pet. Mrs. Morrit has seen to dry clothing and a warm bath. Please advise.

Kendrick

Lost pet? Selina? Mia shook her head. She approached the door. "Has the rain stopped or merely paused before another deluge?" she asked the man in Woodglen livery.

"I believe it is finished, miss," the man said.

"Order the carriage, Wallace," she said.

"I fear Mr. Eustace requires it this afternoon," the butler said.

It would take her almost two hours to walk to Woodglen. The muddy fields would force her to stick to the roads. "Did you walk?" she asked the messenger.

"Yes, miss."

She glanced at Wallace, resigned. "Send someone to check if Hector is still in the stables. I will dress for the weather, gather warm clothing for Miss Selwyn, and accompany this man."

Not long after, she set out. Hector had been let loose as she suspected, providing Selina with her excuse to invade Woodglen dressed for a dinner party in the midst of a deluge. God knew what scandal Mia might find there.

CHAPTER EIGHT

GIDEON PORED OVER notes and columns of numbers in the closet Fillmore called an office. The space had the advantage of its proximity to Marshall's more spacious work space and a window that gave him a view of the kitchen garden. Marshall had grudgingly provided him with the oldest of the Glenmoor estate books, at least the ones that dated from the beginning of Marshall's tenure as steward nine years before, soon after his brother had succeeded to the title. Phillip had been merely twenty-three and green behind the ears.

Poor penmanship and sloppy methods made the work slow going, and his plan to deal with things swiftly faded more each day. The last thing Gideon needed was distraction from a pea-brained miss who had wheedled her way into the house, half-drowned and presuming.

With Marshall out checking on a fencing issue and Tavernash asleep, the servants had called on Gideon to deal with the girl. Apparently, he was now deemed adequate to handle troublesome problems. Ones Fillmore found distasteful, at least. After he walked the quarter mile or so from the estate office to the front entrance, the blasted chit had wrinkled her nose at him and asked for Tavernash.

She'd come in a gown inappropriate for morning calls that had become positively indecent when soaked to her skin. Gideon had been even more grateful than usual that no one knew how close he stood to the inheritance; he might have to endure this hen-witted girl or others of her ilk pursuing him as doggedly as she did Tavernash.

Mrs. Morrit, rigid with disapproval, appeared to have the situation in hand. She'd insisted the chit couldn't be turned back out in the rain and whisked the girl upstairs. Thank goodness. With luck, she'd be dried off and sent on her way again without any further effort on his part. Or Felton Tavernash could deal with her fantasies of acquiring a duchess's coronet on his own. Gideon had work to do.

He was redoing a column of numbers that didn't quite add up a few hours later when Fillmore interrupted him again.

"There's another one," Fillmore said without preamble. No "Mr. Kendrick." No "Sir."

"Another what?"

"Selwyn lady."

"It's raining lost chits today?" Gideon asked, rising. For a moment, Fillmore appeared close to amusement. It didn't last.

A smile winked to life as Gideon walked. The other Miss Selwyn must be the appealing miss who visited tenants and didn't simper or back down. Perhaps she'd come to shake sense into her cousin.

This Miss Selwyn, who had been left standing at the grand front entrance, was dry, warmly clothed, and appropriately dressed. She inclined her head when he approached. "I understand my cousin is in difficulty. I've come to fetch her home," she said.

Thank goodness. Her direct manner and calm common sense drew Gideon as the filmy evening dress clinging wet and indecently to her cousin's form had not. His day improved at the sight of her. As he was distracted by her face and form, his wits went begging. "Viscount Selwyn sent you promptly," he said by way of greeting. It came out more harshly than he intended.

"Are you surprised? Or did you think he sent her here? I assure you he did not," Miss Selwyn said, glowering.

What is it about this woman? He'd been caught wrong-footed again. "I didn't mean to imply any such thing. She said she pursued an animal—your dog, if I remember the animal correctly. Does he run off often? I had the impression you had him well trained."

"Hector never runs off," she said, raising an indignant chin. "And my cousin stays as far from him as she can."

"So the great hairy beast of unusual heritage corralled in our stables is not yours?" he asked.

The lady raised her hand to just above her waist. "This tall? Brown—a chocolaty color? One ear with a notch in it?"

Chocolaty? Gideon would have said muddy. He nodded solemnly.

Miss Selwyn pinched her lips together and sighed. "That's Hector. Someone must have encouraged his misbehavior."

He'd known it was her four-legged shadow but couldn't resist tweaking her. Gideon could guess who misbehaved, and it wasn't the dog.

Miss Selwyn's irritated expression didn't surprise him, but her words did. "Uncle Ludlow wishes to chase him off. He usually ignores him, however, believing he'll wander off on his own. He won't. He's mine. I'll take him home. If you would alert my cousin, we can be on our way quickly."

Escorting her to the cousin would be the proper action. It sounded simple enough, or it would have if Gideon didn't prefer to avoid unnecessary trips up the stairs. He sent the footman stationed in the entrance scurrying instead.

Waiting for the cousin or for word from Mrs. Morrit took more time than was comfortable. He was about to escort her to a parlor and ring for tea, but she spoke first.

"I should go fetch Hector and wait outside for Selina," Miss Selwyn said as the silent wait grew awkward.

"Didn't I say? I asked that he be brought round to you. He is a massive great beast, your guardian angel."

At that description, Miss Selwyn's habitually solemn face blossomed in a smile that could make angelic choirs sing. "He is that!"

She ran to the window, watching earnestly until a figure came into view with the mountain of canine energy on a lead. Gideon came up beside her. It was Pritchard, of course. He, at least, obeyed Gideon without question. The dog, Hector, must have caught a glimpse of her in the window because he bounded up the steps to the door, barking.

"He follows you everywhere. Does your uncle permit him in the house?"

"No." The smile disappeared.

"I think it best if we don't, either," he murmured.

"Uncle mostly tries to pretend Hector doesn't exist. I try to keep him from uncle's notice."

"From his notice?" He choked over the idea that she could keep a dog the size of a small pony from someone's notice. He began to laugh. Determined not to give offense, he tried to stop but couldn't. "I'm—" he started to apologize, but by then, she was laughing, too.

"Fruitless, I know. I could throw a blanket over him," she suggested, gulping over her laughter.

"You'd need a small shed," he said, sending her off again.

Tears ran down her cheeks by the time laughter subsided. He handed her his neatly folded handkerchief, his bare hand touching her gloved one, and ripples of feeling shot through him. She paused, her hand on the offering, as if she felt it, too. Their eyes caught momentarily before she glanced away quickly, dabbing her eyes with the handkerchief.

Gideon clasped his hands behind him to avoid the temptation to take the linen back and wipe her tears himself. *You're almost old enough to be her father, Kendrick—fifteen years older, or more. Rein yourself in.*

MIA FELT THE heat along her neck and knew her face must be red as a strawberry. She pressed the gentleman's pleasantly soft handkerchief to her cheeks longer than was necessary, letting it soothe her nerves. It smelled of pine and some other very masculine undertones, causing a warm rush of feelings she could hardly identify but that she wanted to cherish.

"Excuse me!" The preemptive command behind them brought her abruptly to attention. She dropped her hands to her side and pivoted around, still clinging to the piece of linen. Mr. Kendrick turned as well. Mia could hear Hector barking on the portico and, unless she was mistaken, throwing himself against the massive door.

A woman in a prim white cap and the dark-gray gown of an upper servant stood in the center of the entranceway, hands clasped tightly, mouth in a thin line, disapproval radiating from every line of her body.

"One improper lady is quite enough. We don't need another hoyden," she said in clipped tones. "You are the vis-count's...niece, I presume." If her tone wasn't exactly sneering, neither was it respectful. Mia noticed she hadn't addressed Mr. Kendrick by name or as "sir."

"I am Miss Euphemia Selwyn. I've come to escort my cousin back to Selwyn Court."

The housekeeper breathed in so sharply her nose pinched shut, causing a whistle. At least, Mia assumed this vision of fury was Mrs. Morrit, Woodglen's famous dragon of a housekeeper, since no mere mortal servant would be so haughty. "Unfortunate-ly, Miss Selwyn cannot traipse back where she belongs. She has taken a chill," the woman announced.

"Are you sure?" Mia asked.

Mrs. Morrit's eyes blazed. "Are you questioning my judg-ment?"

"I'm questioning my cousin's…determination." Mia drew back from accusing Selina of lying outright.

"Her shivering is genuine. She's flushed and warm. I can't vouch for the sore throat she claims. The foolish chit walked here in a deluge when the sun was just rising."

"What is to be done, Mrs. Morrit?" Kendrick asked. "We can't—"

"I'll not have this house accused of harming a guest—even an uninvited one. The rain is gone, but the wind is sharp and cold. We are obliged to send for the physician. Dr. Gratis should decide whether to move her."

"Gratis?" he muttered. Mia had had few dealings with the local physician, but something in Kendrick's tone gave Mia a cold blast of dread.

"Do what you must, then, Mrs. Morrit," Kendrick said. He took a step away. "And kindly see this lady to her cousin." He left the entranceway, his odd, swaying gait carrying him swiftly down the corridor that led to the back of the house. Mrs. Morrit watched him go with a sour frown.

The housekeeper dispatched the lurking footman to the village. "And order that ugly dog driven off or locked in the stables."

"Let me speak to him," Mia said quickly. Someone needed to calm Hector lest he harm himself or someone else. She didn't wait for permission. Hector's enthusiastic greeting left mud on her skirt and slobber on her face, but he calmed, and when she sent him off with Pritchard, he went meekly. Grateful she still had Kendrick's handkerchief, she wiped her face, took another sniff of pine, tucked it in her sleeve, and returned to face the housekeeper, left to wonder why Kendrick wished to avoid Dr. Gratis and nonplussed by the housekeeper's obvious disdain.

Mia clutched the bundle of clothing she'd brought with her and followed the housekeeper up the stairs, eyes on the woman's rigid back, resigned to whatever misery Selina would have brought down on her.

CHAPTER NINE

Mrs. Morrit led Mia up three flights to a narrow, unlit corridor. There was no sound of life behind the long row of closed doors. The housekeeper opened the second door on the right, gestured Mia in, and hovered in the open doorway.

Selina lay, pale and wan, on a narrow bed. "Fee, did Papa send you?"

"I'm to fetch you home," Mia said.

Selina was ready to object, but Mrs. Morrit got there first. "Not until the doctor sees you." Mia thought the woman's mouth and nose pinched so tightly her face might crack. "You will not leave this guest wing," Mrs. Morrit went on. "There will be no reason for you to wander the house." She left without another word.

Mia peered around the room, still holding the bundle. In addition to the bed, the space contained a pine dresser and washstand, a single straight-backed chair, and a writing desk. No flowers broke up the dour impression. The pitcher and bowl on the washstand were plain, white, and chipped. Embers glowed in the narrow hearth, heroically casting a bit of warmth into the room. It was one she might have expected in a modest inn rather than the great Woodglen manor.

The only ornaments were two framed seascapes, neither large enough for its subject, neither of interest to Mia. "Dogs would have been better, at least," she muttered, setting the bundle on the desk. She hung her cloak next to Selina's on a wooden peg affixed to the wall for that purpose. She put her bonnet on the dresser.

"This must be the pokiest room at Woodglen. Like I'm some—" A cough interrupted Selina's complaint.

"She called this the guest wing. I suspect they don't get many." The room showed every sign of neglect. The curtains were dusty, the braided rug needed a beating, and the room smelled musty. Mia also suspected the floor below featured suites for prominent guests. This one likely served the lowest and the least—or the uninvited. She lit the lone candle, a tallow, using a spill lit from the hearth. It did little to improve the gloom.

Mia pressed a hand to her cousin's brow. "Not feverish," she said.

"But I could get one yet." The ninnyhammer sounded hopeful. Still, she huddled under the coverlet and was far more subdued than normal. She made one or two references to the duke's cousin, Mr. Tavernash, speculating about exactly where, in this great pile, he might be found.

When Selina dropped off to sleep, Mia was left with nothing to do. She sat on the window seat, peering out at a dismal inner courtyard, dark under the day's gray clouds. She wondered about the direction of the stables where they held Hector.

Soon Mia slept as well. An hour passed or perhaps two before she was awakened by the sound of the door opening. She blinked in the gloom to find Howard Gratis, Nether Abbas's only claim to medical care, and a frowning Mrs. Morrit, who ordered the footman accompanying them to wait in the hall. The physician set to work immediately.

Dr. Gratis pronounced Selina a "damned fool" but her chill genuine. He recommended she stay overnight and return home in the morning, "assuming she is no worse." When he ordered her to stay in bed until then, Selina managed only the weakest protest that she should come down to dinner, and Mia suspected her cousin was genuinely ill.

The grizzled physician scanned Mia's form too closely for comfort. "This 'un's healthy enough," he said, something in his eyes making her uncomfortable.

"John will show you down," Mrs. Morrit said pointedly, drawing his eyes from Mia.

He glanced back.

"Now," Mrs. Morrit said in a tone that brooked no argument.

"I can return in the morning," Mia told Selina after the footman had led the doctor out.

Her cousin grabbed her hand and whined, "Don't leave me here alone."

"Stay? But surely Mrs. Morrit—"

"We do not have time to cater to an uninvited guest. You will nurse your cousin, Miss Selwyn. We will send word to your uncle." Mrs. Morrit's tone allowed no objection or opinion. "I will have a pallet brought up and order dinner on trays." She paused as if weighing how little she could do. "You will fetch it, of course, Miss Selwyn. I will have someone show you the servants' stair." She turned on her heels and left.

At least I'll get out of this room, Mia thought.

A footman and maid arrived soon after. The footman flopped a pallet on the floor, leered at Selina, and left. There would be no help from that quarter.

The maid put two tallow candles on the washstand and dropped a bundle of wood near the hearth. Mia recognized her as the little gossip she had encountered at the tearoom in Nether Abbas.

"Mrs. Morrit sez as how you're to serve that 'un," the girl said, indicating Selina with a movement of her head. "I heard she walked here in the rain wearing a gown you could see through after she got soaked. The footmen were all buzzing around," she said. The maid picked up the water pitcher, a practical sort of vessel of thick white clay, and handed it to Mia before she could respond to the outrageous comment.

The maid paused, her avid eyes studying Selina, their cloaks, the bundle of clothing on the desk, and Mia. "I recognize you from the village. You're that poor relation that was forced on Viscount Clavering," she said.

Mia raised her chin and peered down her nose, grateful to be taller. "Miss Selwyn is a guest here. Dr. Gratis ordered her to stay over, and as her cousin, I've been asked to maintain propriety." Mia tried to hand the pitcher back, but the girl ignored her.

"That's the one I meant, the cousin." The little gossip shrugged. "Best come, then. I ought to warn you anyways."

"Warn me about what?" Mia said, following her down the hall.

The maid raised a hand to quiet her. As they neared the end of the passageway, she leaned toward the last door as if listening for something.

The corridor ended in a plain wooden door that led to a typical servants' stairway—narrow, shadowed, and steep. Just enough light filtered in through a vent above them to see.

When the door closed behind them, the maid whispered, "That last room is his. You best avoid it."

"Who?"

"The cripple, of course," the girl said. "I heard no decent woman is safe around him. Keep your door locked, especially at night. I heard he done foul things to his own stepmother. Other wimmen, too, but I never heard who. Fillmore had him dragged out and beaten good. Maudy over at the general goods store told me she heard two girls left town right after he did, and Harry at the—"

"What's your name?" Mia asked.

"I'm Mercy Miller," the girl said.

World-class gossip.

They reached the bottom and turned down a similarly hidden passageway. "How long have you worked here?" Mia asked.

"On two years. I come from Dorchester when my brother…when I heard they were hiring. Great monster of a place is

Woodglen. Takes a lot of folk to tend to it," the maid said.

"So neither you nor your family lived near here when Mr. Kendrick left years ago," Mia said.

"No, but people talk. I know what I'm saying," the girl went on. "Here's the kitchen. You kin find yer own way back." She flounced off.

Mia found the pump and filled her pitcher with fresh water. Upon her asking, a kitchen maid gave her two mugs with a grudgeful sneer. It took more prodding to get the approximate time for dinner.

She approached a passing footman and asked her most burning question. "Where can I find the library?"

He nodded vaguely at a door across the kitchen. "Halfway on the left, but it's for family only," he said, walking away.

Mia longed for something to read to get through the dreary afternoon, but her hands were too full as it was, and she had no way to carry a book. She trudged back the way she'd come, juggling the mugs in one hand, the heavy pitcher in the other. At least the passages were simple. She couldn't get lost.

GIDEON LEFT THE estate offices, walked along the grand central hallway toward the main block of Woodglen, and slipped through a little used withdrawing room and through a hidden door into the maze of servant hallways. He swallowed his pride whenever he did, but the passages led to narrower stairs he found more manageable than the wide marble stairs designed to show off graceful ladies and the fashionable fribbles. He was neither.

Gratis had departed. An uproar in the servants' hall over an attempt to molest one of the tweenies had sent him packing. *Thank God!* Nether Abbas's medical man was a selfish bastard with a sadistic streak, something Gideon had reason to know, and he had no desire to encounter him. He did, however, need to check on their unexpected guests' well-beings. He turned sharply right to climb the enclosed stairway, took two hurried steps, and bumped into the soft body of Euphemia Selwyn.

Their collision jarred her arm, and the pitcher of water she carried toppled from her hands and shattered on the steps below. Shards of clay spread across stair treads, a mug tumbled all the way down, and water flowed down the steps.

She turned, stumbling over anguished words. "I'm so sorry. I filled it too full, and it was too heavy for me."

"I—" The word came out a croak. His mouth went dry.

Water soaked the front of her gown through to the skin. The clearly visible skin. Even in the dim light of the stairwell, he could see more than he ought—the curve of her waist and the outlines of stays, pert breasts, and pebbled nipples.

Hot blood surged through him, shooting directly to an erection so hard he suspected she could also see more than she ought clearly outlined in his breeches. Feeling no better than Gratis, he opened his mouth—his suddenly very dry mouth—but no words came out.

Her face, Kendrick. Keep your eyes on her face.

She stood one step above him so that their faces were even, apology continuing to flow out of her. "I'm so sorry, Mr. Kendrick, I didn't hear you."

He pulled himself together. "And I obviously failed to see you. I am the one who should apologize. Perhaps you might—" His hands fluttered a gesture meant to suggest she turn around. "Go on up and dry yourself while I get someone to clean this up and bring you fresh water." He was gratified that he was able to speak sensibly. Her reaction sent him reeling. "Tears, Miss Selwyn? Please don't cry. I—"

She dabbed at her face with her palm, obviously distressed. She sank down to sit on a stair. "I'm sorry, I'm sorry," she moaned.

Gideon stepped lower as well, putting one foot two steps lower than the other. "You have nothing to be sorry for. I'm the clumsy one," he said, handing her a clean handkerchief.

She took it with a watery smile. He prayed she didn't notice the way his eyes darted to her glorious curves of their own volition. "It isn't your fault, Mr. Kendrick. I overfilled it, hoping to make fewer trips. I already dribbled water downstairs. Now this."

"Why didn't you ask a footman to fetch it?"

"Mrs. Morrit told me I was to fetch everything myself. She won't send anyone to clean this up, either, I'm sure of it. I don't know how I'll manage the supper tray." She wiped her eyes and dabbed at her gown, drawing his eyes downward again.

He cleared his throat. "That is unacceptable. You are a guest here. What floor are you on?"

"The fourth? Whichever one is the top one. I'm not to leave the guest floor except to fetch for Selina." She handed back his handkerchief.

He frowned fiercely. "Keep it, please," he said.

"I'm sorry," she murmured again, flinching at his frown.

School your expression, Kendrick. "Don't be. I will see to having someone clean up and fetch your supper tray as well. Let me escort you to your room." He put out a hand to help her rise, belatedly remembering neither wore gloves. She took it, and the warmth of her dainty hand in his added to his inappropriate reaction to her accident.

She turned, to his everlasting gratitude, but the narrowness of the stairs forced him to walk behind her, giving him a close view of the sway of her hips and rounded backside. He swallowed the lump in his dry throat and began to recite Caesar's soliloquy in his mind to chase away the images she invoked. *Friends, Romans, countrymen...*

She opened the door at the top floor, and light flooded in. Her gown clung to her waist, a gentle curve, one he wanted to trace with his hand. She stepped swiftly into the hallway as if she meant to dart off, but she turned to peer at the door on her left. His door. She darted a glance back at him, a peculiar expression on her face.

"What is it, Miss Selwyn?" he asked.

"They warned me…" Her face took on a deep rose color. "Why are you on this floor? I gather these aren't Woodglen's premier guest quarters."

A bitter laugh barked out before he could stop it. "Far from it." Her troubled gaze made his heart squeeze in his chest. "They warned you about me, did they?"

She nodded, turning even redder. "But you've behaved like a perfect gentleman, and I know better than to believe everything I'm told by gossips."

If only you knew what I'm thinking. Hardly gentlemanly.

As if she read his mind, she gazed down at herself, and she gasped, her eyes wide in horror. "I must change." She turned away from him and took a step away before adding, "I would be grateful if you could do as you said."

"I'll see to the mess and make certain someone else brings up your dinner tray. How is your cousin?" he asked belatedly.

She didn't turn to face him. "Sleeping. Chilled but not feverish. Dr. Gratis said she could go home in the morning. I fear she may worsen, though. She isn't herself. Thank you for your assistance." She hurried to a room at the other end of the hall and disappeared.

"You're welcome," he whispered, staring at the closed door, letting her words warm his heart as her body had warmed his more primitive parts.

But you've behaved like a perfect gentleman, and I know better than to believe everything…

He quite liked this Miss Selwyn. More than liked. He shook his head. He had no time for flirtation, much less dalliance—not that Euphemia Selwyn was a woman one dallied with—and certainly not here. The sooner he got to the bottom of Woodglen's finances, the sooner he could go home and shake the dust of the place from his feet. Unfortunately, the deeper he probed, the longer he was certain he would be there. He had found no major embezzlement, but something about the books was not quite right.

CHAPTER TEN

GRAY LIGHT FILTERED through the curtains when Mercy came to Selina's room without knocking and unceremoniously dumped a shuttle of coal at the hearth.

Mia groaned and rolled over. She rose on one elbow to glare at Mercy.

"Someone else best bring your tray. I'm not carrying it all the way up here again no matter what that Kendrick sez. Footmen fear him. They do as he says, even if Mrs. Morrit tells 'em different, so one of 'em will get to it." The maid left without another word.

It would no doubt be as it had been the night before when Mercy and a resentful potboy had brought a new water pitcher and supper on trays, complaining they'd been forced to clean her mess. Supper had been lukewarm and scanty, leftovers from the servants' meal.

Mia fell back and squeezed her eyes shut. She had spent most of the night sleepless on the thin pallet on the floor, uncomfortable and distressed by the previous day's events. Touched by Gideon Kendrick's kindness in this peculiar household and confused by the obvious heat in his eyes when they'd stood next to his bedroom door, she had tossed and turned well past midnight. Home at Selwyn Court, she'd have gotten up to read and calm her mind, but she had nothing to read here.

At least it was only one night. We'll be home today.

She rose and rolled up the pallet. The gown from the day before that she had laid over the chair to dry was wrinkled but wearable. She dressed quickly for fear the blasted footman would come sooner rather than later. Only then did she realize what was odd. Selina hadn't awoken even when the maid had made all that racket.

She studied her cousin, asleep in the bed, alarmed by the flush to her cheeks. The back of her hand to Selina's brow confirmed what she feared. Mia knew fevers from nursing her parents in their illness. This was quite high. Selina stirred, moaned, but didn't wake. *Damn.* She needed to fetch Mrs. Morrit.

A footman emerged from the stairs, carrying water, and put up a hand to scratch on Kendrick's door when she was halfway down the hall. "We have an emergency," she called. "I need Mrs. Morrit."

"She's in the housekeeper's office," he answered.

Mia glanced back to Selina's room. "My cousin has a high fever. I need help. I don't want to leave her."

The footman glowered at her. Before he could respond, the door opened. "What is it, Jem?" Gideon Kendrick stood in the doorway, clad only in breeches and a white shirt, open at the neck, with sleeves rolled up.

"This…lady wants me to fetch Mrs. Morrit." He managed to make it sound like her request was an insult.

Mia closed her mouth, which she feared had dropped open at the sight of Kendrick. Hair mussed, unshaven, and scandalously undressed, he took her breath away. Her expression must have alerted him, because he quickly closed his shirt at the neck and raised a staying hand.

"One moment," he said, ducking back into the room. He returned quickly wearing a waistcoat and shrugging into his coat. "Now. What is the problem?"

"She—" Jem started, earning a glare from Kendrick.

"Miss Selwyn? What is the problem?"

"My cousin, Mr. Kendrick. She didn't wake up even when Mercy made noise. She is burning with fever. I need Mrs. Morrit."

"Get on it, Jem. Fetch the woman," Kendrick barked, taking the pitcher of water the man carried. He stepped back, and she could see him put it on a rough table. His room was no finer than the one assigned to Selina. He tugged on the bellpull. If it was the same as theirs, a response, if any, would be slow.

When he turned back, he chewed his lower lip as if pondering a problem. "I would check on her myself, Miss Selwyn, but my presence in your room would compromise both of you. I will wait here for Mrs. Morrit or perhaps a maid to provide some protection."

"I don't need protection from you," Mia said. She wasn't certain how she knew that, but she did.

Sadness permeated his gentle smile. "Perhaps not from me, but from gossips most certainly. The place swarms with them."

Before she could walk away, he spoke again. "Is the room they gave you the same as mine?"

"Small and plain? Yes. There is only one bed. I have a pallet on the floor. I was grateful it was only for one night," she said.

He muttered what she suspected was a curse. "We can do better."

Of that she had no doubt. Hope flickered.

THE HOUSEKEEPER'S DISPLEASURE felt palpable. Mia refused to let it bully her. Selina needed help quickly. "I will require willow bark tea, soft cloths for wiping her, and—"

"I know the treatment for fevers, Miss Selwyn," Mrs. Morrit said, ice dripping from her words. "I will send for Dr. Gratis again."

"Must you?" Mia asked. "I'm not sure what he can add beyond bleeding her, and in my experience, it makes matters worse."

"You have nursing experience, Miss Selwyn?" Kendrick asked. He stood at the door as if reluctant to enter. On the other hand, the little room was already crowded.

"I nursed my parents until they died," she said. Glancing at Mrs. Morrit, she added, "They were bled."

"Very well. Mr. Kendrick is a witness that the decision is on you." The housekeeper swung back to the door.

Kendrick stood in the way of her exit. "It appears Miss Selwyn's cousin will need her ministrations for some time. They must be moved to a larger room. One with beds for both of them. One with better appointments." He held the housekeeper's eyes.

"Who are you to demand anything? I am housekeeper here, and I decide what is appropriate." Mrs. Morrit spat her words.

Mia watched a play of some unnamed emotion on Kendrick's face and saw the moment he appeared to come to a decision.

"Mr. Marshall has apparently not seen fit to enlighten you to my status," he said. "My brother has given me full authority over the duchy and all his holdings, including oversight of Woodglen and those employed here. I am to act in his stead in all matters. Marshall has had ample time to verify the credentials I brought, and I intend to act on them. You will consider my decisions as if coming from the duke himself."

"The duke is missing," the woman said hesitantly, her eyes wide with shock.

"He has gone away for reasons of his own and left me to oversee his affairs. I have been delegated full power. Since I have thriving businesses of my own, he believes me more than capable. Kindly see to a new room for the patient and her cousin."

"Rooms are all under holland covers. It will take time to clean. We haven't had guests here since the old duke passed," Mrs. Morrit temporized.

"Then get it done quickly. Since we're dispensing with the pretense about the nature of my presence here, I will take a room in the family wing so as not to compromise the young ladies' position in the guest wing."

He held her eyes long moments before the housekeeper nodded. "Will that be all?" she asked through pinched lips.

His eyes narrowed in thought. "First, care for our guests. Provide Miss Selwyn everything she requested while she waits to move. Send a message to her uncle about the situation here. Then manage my move. One more thing…" He waited for Mrs. Morrit's full attention. "It is already apparent there is much more here that needs my attention. If I'm to be here for several months, I will send for my children. Plan to prepare the nursery for them."

The housekeeper stared at him as if he had sprouted horns, or as if she didn't believe him capable of parenthood.

"There are three of them. Their governess will accompany them," he said without breaking eye contact.

"As you wish. I'll discuss the matter with Mr. Marshall." Mrs. Morrit lifted her chin as she spoke.

"You do that," he replied. He gazed at Mia. "Do you need anything else?"

Better food, larger room, respect… "Books," she said. "I need something to read while I sit with Selina."

"Make use of the library as you wish, ma'am," he replied.

Mia glanced at the housekeeper, who'd forbidden her to leave this floor. "Thank you. Perhaps once Selina is settled, I may do that."

Kendrick wasn't finished. "If you prefer to take your meals with family rather than in your room, let Mrs. Morrit know," he said.

She murmured thanks.

"If that is all, I'll leave you in Mrs. Morrit's undoubtedly skilled hands."

Mrs. Morrit, she noted, frowned even more deeply. The servants' quarters would be in an uproar. She swept out in his wake, however, without comment.

Goodness. He is rather magnificent when he takes command. And children! Who would have guessed? Another thought tugged at her. *These people do not make it easy for him.* She wondered if she had wandered into a civil war.

DINNER WITH TAVERNASH generally involved a long discourse about the nodcock's mother's opinions on everything from waistcoats to the Prince of Wales. Gideon endured it on principle rather than slinking up to a tray in his room. Tonight was no different.

"Fillmore told me there are young ladies in residence. Not the thing, bachelor establishment and all. M'mother would not approve." Tavernash frowned as if puzzling over that thought gave him a headache. "She says now I'm heir, chits will try to trap me. Don't plan to put my foot in parson's trap anytime soon. Pr'aps I ought to ask Mother about it." Cheered by that thought, he tucked into his mutton with enthusiasm.

"They've been housed in the guest wing on the other side of the house from family," Gideon said. Privately, he thought "family" a stretch in Tavernash's case, but he wouldn't say so.

Tavernash grunted.

"I will be moving to the family wing tonight as well. Jem is transporting my things now." Fillmore, he noted, looked as if he had swallowed a lemon, but then, he frequently appeared that way. Gideon had endured glances all day—both puzzled and alarmed. His confrontation with the housekeeper had likely been repeated word for word throughout the staff.

"Family wing? But you're—" Tavernash paused, his fork halfway to his mouth.

"Family," Gideon finished. "I am family. The duke, you will recall, is my brother. He sent me here."

"But my mother—"

"Will no doubt explain it to you," Gideon muttered. He

stabbed at his food, wishing Miss Selwyn had accepted his invitation to dine with family.

He left without eating his cake—Tavernash could undoubtedly devour Gideon's share. He expected Jem to fetch him when the room was ready. For now, he sought the peace of the library.

When he found it occupied, his feelings veered from disappointment to delight. He left the door open behind him and bowed. "Miss Selwyn. I'm glad you found your way here."

She dropped a curtsey that wouldn't be out of place in Mayfair. "Yes. Thank you, sir." She glanced at the open door and snatched up two books she'd been considering. "And thank you for having us moved. We are quite comfortable."

Relief flooded him. They'd been moved. He had feared he would have to follow up with a more aggressive demand.

"But you didn't join us at dinner."

"I—that is, Selina needs me. I must get back up. Besides, I have no proper clothing with me for dinner here. They are bringing broth for her and supper for me on a tray."

"I understand. How is she?" he asked, wondering if Mrs. Morrit remembered to ask the viscount to send clothing for his niece.

"Restless and feverish. She slept off and on all day and endured the move downstairs with some misery. Thank you for asking." She nodded to him again and was gone, taking both books.

He sat at the desk and started his own message to Viscount Clavering.

CHAPTER ELEVEN

UNCLE LUDLOW RARELY moved with anything resembling speed. Mia was therefore surprised when a footman—John, she thought—informed her that her uncle required her presence in the green drawing room the following afternoon. Her steps took her down a stately marble stairway that led her to the grand passage that ran the length of Woodglen's central block. When she reached the bottom, she turned toward a disturbance in the entranceway. She couldn't make out words clearly, but Fillmore appeared to be showing Eustace and his worthless friends out. The presence of a rather large footman suggested they were not going willingly. She swallowed a smile and allowed John to lead her to the green drawing room—Woodglen had several, and she would never have identified the correct one herself.

Mrs. Morrit exited the room as she approached and hurried away without acknowledging Mia. Curtis Marshall followed her out. He inclined his head. "Miss Selwyn. I trust your accommodations are comfortable?"

The pitch of his voice made Mia wonder if he expected an answer or merely intended some message to her uncle.

"Quite comfortable." *Now.*

"Good," he responded, obviously preoccupied. "I would stay to chat, but I have a clogged drainage ditch to see to." He hurried away.

Her uncle, grim faced, stood by the window with his hands behind his rigid back.

Mia dipped a curtsey. "Uncle, thank you for coming. You probably wish to see Selina." She gripped her hands tightly, fearing he planned to drag Dr. Gratis back to bleed the girl.

Uncle nodded. "The housekeeper reports she suffers from fever, albeit one brought on by her own hoydenish behavior."

"I fear Mrs. Morrit is correct. She suffers from catarrh of the head and throat. I see no sign of lung fever but—"

Uncle Ludlow sighed deeply. "Yes, yes, always a danger. Mrs. Morrit said Dr. Gratis ordered that she couldn't be moved if she worsened. Do you concur?"

Mia furrowed her brow and captured her lower lip in her teeth. "It does appear to be the best approach."

"And you refused a second visit from the physician?" he asked.

"It is my experience that bleeding only brings on weakness and worsens the condition. It is what he would try to do." They both knew the result of the quack's determination to bleed Aunt Harriet repeatedly. They had both been left to watch her fade away.

Uncle waved her words away. "Yes, yes, incompetent butchers, the lot of them. You know that more than most." His respect pleased as much as it startled. She had nursed her parents and then Aunt Harriet. Uncle Ludlow had left her to it but had never before indicated he thought well of her skills.

She let out a breath in relief. "Will you bring her home?"

"I thought you said it was not recommended."

"It isn't, but—"

"I fear I have no choice but to leave you here to care for my little girl, Euphemia. I cannot leave her here unprotected."

She couldn't account for the degree to which that pleased her. She was puzzled by her own motivations and complete lack of desire to leave.

"I am profoundly sorry to put you in this position." The viscount glanced at something in the far corner of the room.

"A wise decision, my lord." Mr. Kendrick's voice sent Mia's heart racing. She hadn't seen him. He stood with one arm on the ornate marble mantelpiece, casual yet confident. "Miss Euphemia Selwyn will see to Miss Selina Selwyn's illness with great care and ease your mind about the matter."

"It appears I owe you a debt, Mr.—Kendrick, is it? Marshall was horrified at the treatment our girls received in the hands of that Mrs. Morrit creature." Uncle Ludlow's lips pinched as if the words were forced out of him with great reluctance.

Mia's mind ran in circles. She was glad they would stay. Of course she cared about Selina, but more, she realized. She was to be free of her dreary existence at Selwyn Court and out of the path of Eustace and his horrid friends. She would be able to explore this magnificent house that she had long wondered about and perhaps even meet the would-be heir everyone spoke about.

"The problem has been resolved, I believe. Miss Selwyn, is all to your comfort now?" Mr. Kendrick asked.

A blush touched her cheek when she gazed at Mr. Kendrick. "Yes, sir, thanks to your intervention. The room is comfortable, and the servants are…"

"Respectful?" He raised one brow.

"I was going to say helpful," Mia responded.

Mr. Kendrick's slow smile made her toes curl. "That's all we can ask," he said.

She admitted to herself that the mysterious Mr. Kendrick intrigued her most of all. He was nothing like what people said about him, yet secrets lurked in his face and behavior. Curiosity was Mia's besetting sin, and this man brought it out in her more than was perhaps appropriate. What was it about him? Perhaps in time she'd figure it out.

Uncle Ludlow cleared his throat. "Take me to Selina, Euphemia, and then I'll take my leave." He made shooing gestures with his hands when Mia didn't move fast enough to suit him, and offered no polite nothings to Mr. Kendrick.

Mia led the way up the formal stairs. As they reached the floor and turned to the guest room, her uncle paused.

"A word of warning, Euphemia. I admit that man has better manners and speech than I expected, but he is not to be trusted."

"Mr. Kendrick has behaved as a perfect gentleman, Uncle. I have no fear."

"Don't be foolish, girl. Appearances can deceive. Too much has been said—by his own father, for one—for me to trust the man. Keep your distance from him. And bar Selina's door at night. Lock it if you have to step out briefly. Go to Marshall if you have fears."

"Yes, Uncle." *Could he be right?* Mia didn't think so. Still, caution wouldn't hurt.

GIDEON WAITED UNTIL they were gone before he lowered his left arm from the mantelpiece, groaned, and cursed his pride. Something about the viscount made him want to stand straighter. While the gesture brought his left shoulder even with his right, now it felt like the devil. *Stupid vanity. What was it about Clavering?*

He remembered Viscount Clavering as a man who'd fawned on his ducal neighbor, ever impressed by both the title and the house when invited to attend an event. Gideon did not recall that the viscount had ever attended Glenmoor's more private events, the dissolute ones that descended into debauchery of the worst kind, and that was to the man's credit. Clavering had tended toward awe where the duke was concerned, inclined to assume the title brought with it honor and character. He'd been blind to the duke's depravity, but he'd easily believed every word that dripped from Glenmoor's mouth, including the vile lies about Gideon himself. *More fool he.*

Gideon took no small satisfaction in toppling Clavering's expectations where he was concerned. Perhaps muscle aches were worth it, though he suspected his vanity had more to do with the fact that the viscount was Euphemia Selwyn's uncle than with the man himself.

Walking back to his office, Gideon considered Curtis Marshall. The steward's support for his dictates to Mrs. Morrit had come as a relief. How much of that support derived from the viscount's presence, he couldn't be certain. The two seemed to be on familiar terms.

Up until now Marshall had ignored Gideon to the extent possible. Surprisingly, he ignored Tavernash as well. A land steward for a duke carried respect, generally seen as the most respected untitled man in a shire, and in many households, such a man would join the family for dinner. Clearly Clavering held him in esteem. Yet Marshall kept his distance from Tavernash, even though he allowed the man to take up residence based on claims that had to appear shaky, even if the steward was unaware of the true state of the succession. *Why?*

Marshall hunched over papers at his desk when Gideon reached the work area. His expression suggested frustration. *No time like the present to ask...* He tapped the open door and stepped in.

Marshall frowned up at him, giving Gideon a moment to glance around the room. He wondered again where the family archives might be stored. *Here, perhaps?*

"Want something, Kendrick?" Marshall asked.

"I thought you had a drainage ditch to see to," Gideon said.

"I do." He waved a paper he had been fidgeting with. "We called in an engineer from Weymouth. Fool didn't seem to know the difference between a drainage ditch and a seaport. Left me this. Viscount gone?"

"Went up to see his daughter. He plans to leave them both here," Gideon replied.

The steward shook his head. "Mrs. Morrit will be more sour than usual. The footmen will be tripping over each other to fetch and carry to them."

"It is unfortunate they've been marooned in an all-male household."

"Aye. It is that. At least Tavernash hasn't taken an interest in them." Marshall scowled at the name.

"He's hiding because he thinks they plan to trap him into marriage, him being a duke's heir and all," Gideon said with a cynical twist to his lips.

Marshall let out a bark of laughter.

"Why didn't you send Tavernash packing as soon as he minced in here?" Gideon asked.

"He waltzed in acting all lord of the manor and announced he was 'heir presumptive' and that his cousin most likely is dead. I checked the relationship and found it true, so we couldn't just toss him on his ear. We give him room and food but keep the funds and the family papers under lock and key." Family papers. It was on the tip of Gideon's tongue to ask, but the moment passed.

Marshall studied him for a long moment. "Is His Grace really alive?"

"To the best of my knowledge, yes. He wrote to me in August about his scheme to send me here."

"Where the devil is he hiding?" Marshall asked.

"I have no idea. Paris, perhaps. He likes it there."

"I thought you two hated each other," Marshall said.

"No, that was my father—and Fillmore, his toady. You must have thought I was dead as my unlamented sire intended. His Grace did as well, up until a year ago," Gideon said. "We were happy we were able to reunite."

Marshall grunted. "The ways of the mighty…"

"Why don't you take dinner in the formal dining room?"

"With the 'family'?" Marshall gave the word a sarcastic twist. "I got tired of hearing what the man's mother thinks and how he plans to spend his coming windfall."

"I sympathize. I eat with him because he bears watching," Gideon said. "You might join us. I could use civil conversation.

I'm trying to convince Miss Selwyn to join us also."

Marshall cast an intrigued glance at Gideon and then picked up his pen. Gideon knew dismissal when he saw it. He turned to leave.

"Kendrick." At Marshall's word, Gideon paused in the doorway.

"You heard Clavering. Stay away from the niece." He rushed on as if embarrassed by the implication. "Sadler vouched for you. My man went up to London to see him face-to-face. He sent word I am to give you 'every courtesy.'"

"Kind of you to let me know," Gideon replied, biting back a laugh. He went on his way with a little lightness in his step, though only one burden had been lifted. There were plenty others.

CHAPTER TWELVE

"I REPEAT. BE on guard around that man," Uncle Ludlow hissed when they arrived on the upper floor. "I admit he was quite correct to demand proper accommodations for Selina, and he seems to have acquired the dress and manners of a gentleman in spite of deplorable origins, but I can't rest easy with you around him."

"His father was a duke, Uncle."

They reached the door to the guest room assigned to Mia and Selina.

"Don't be pert. He's a misbegotten American. The stories I've heard about him are not fit for a young lady's ears. Keep him far from Selina. Keep your door locked. Bar it at night."

Mia tried to picture Gideon Kendrick prowling the halls, wild-eyed, searching for a virgin to ravish. Her amusement must have shown on her face, because Uncle's glower deepened.

"Do as I say. Kerr will know what's up. You will follow her lead."

"Kerr?"

Uncle Ludlow ignored her gasp; his eyes swept over to Selina lying against white linens, pale and weak. He raised his hand as if to pat her or check her brow for fever, but he let it drop and took a step back. "Catarrh," he muttered. "At least."

He chucked Mia under the chin. "You are a good girl, Euphemia. Care for my princess well," he said, drawing away.

"But, Uncle, Selina is ill. Wouldn't it be better for Kerr to stay at Selwyn Court?" Mia asked, holding her breath.

"Nonsense. Kerr is a servant. She does what she's told. She'll come to lend respectability to the both of you." He didn't wait for an answer.

To cluck over Selina and bully me, more like. Mia sighed.

A few hours later, Mia sat on the window seat next to Selina's bed and watched Kerr bustle about the room, unpacking the great pile of gowns and linen she'd brought from Selwyn Court, with fierce efficiency and no little irritation. She had already rung for footmen twice.

Uncle Ludlow had been kind, Mia told herself. Well, he'd intended to be. Kind in his way. He'd had the sense to send Eustace and his hangers-on packing when they'd followed him. He had confirmed Selina's fever and cough for himself and rejected calling in Dr. Gratis again—for now. He had remembered to send Mia's clothes along with her cousin's.

At a moan from the bed, she leaned over to give Selina a sip of water.

Kerr hurried over. "Does my lady need something?"

Selina smiled wanly at the woman but didn't speak. When Mia wiped her brow, Selina closed her eyes and sighed.

"Tea," Kerr snapped. "My lady will be wanting tea."

Never mind we had tea two hours ago, and Selina took two sips and ate nothing.

"It is almost dinnertime," Mia reminded her.

"So it is. I should visit the kitchen and inform them of our requirements," Kerr said, head high and hands clasped firmly in front of her.

A decision snapped into place in Mia's beleaguered mind. "I will be taking dinner in the dining room if Selina doesn't object," Mia said. *I need a break from Kerr and the sickroom.*

Kerr opened her mouth to comment, but Selina blinked. "Do. Tell me all," Selina croaked.

"You want to know about the heir or the dinner?" Mia asked.

"All of it. I want to hear everything you learn," Selina said. A coughing fit followed.

Kerr glanced at Selina and back at Mia. "Very well. Do that. I will inform the kitchen," Kerr conceded.

The maid started to turn but stopped when Mia added, "You can help me dress when you return." Kerr glared at Selina but thought better of whatever she intended to say. She nodded and departed in a rustle of bombazine. Mia had no doubt Mrs. Morrit would be even more bad-tempered with them than she already was after Kerr visited the kitchen.

Whatever passed below stairs, Kerr managed to turn Mia out presentably and even fix her hair in a charming chignon before she all but pushed Mia out the door.

She likely wants her little darling all to herself. Mia stood at the top of the stairs, wondering why she hadn't begged to return to Selwyn Court. It would be several days before Selina could leave, and several days cooped up with Kerr loomed like purgatory. As she slowly descended, her heart sped up. She was about to have dinner in Woodglen's legendary dining room. She would see Gideon Kendrick again. Perhaps purgatory had its rewards.

Curtis Marshal hovered at the door. He wore a suit and cravat, a bit rumpled but rather finer than she'd seen on him before. He offered his arm to lead her in, leaning over when he did so. "I promised your uncle I would look after you," he whispered, casting a nervous glance at Gideon Kendrick standing at his place at the table.

Perhaps purgatory was simply complicated.

MISS SELWYN MET Gideon's gaze. *Is that a twinkle in her eye?* Gideon was certain it was. Marshall's protective hovering had amused him, and he suspected it amused Miss Selwyn also. She'd been warned about him by the maids, by her uncle, and unless he misunderstood Marshall's intent whispering in her ear, by the steward as well. Her amusement told him she believed none of it, God be praised.

"See here, what's this?" Tavernash demanded from the head of the table.

"Miss Euphemia Selwyn, may I make known to you Mr. Felton Tavernash. Tavernash, this is Miss Selwyn, our guest." Gideon emphasized the last word.

Miss Selwyn dipped her head. "I'm pleased to meet you, Mr. Tavernash." Pleased, not honored, Gideon noted.

Tavernash hesitated as if waiting for the deep curtsey due, in his mind, to a duke's heir. With a snort, he mumbled, "Uninvited guest," and sat.

Fillmore directed the serving of the first course, and Tavernash tucked in without so much as glancing at the others.

Gideon spoke into the awkward silence. "How is your cousin this evening? You were comfortable enough to leave her."

"She is no better. The fever persists, I fear. I left her in the care of Miss Kerr," Miss Selwyn answered.

"I heard your maid is a formidable woman," Marshall said.

Judging from Fillmore's fierce frown, the lady's maid had made an impression below stairs, Gideon thought. In many households, a lady's maid and dresser ranked just below the butler and housekeeper. She wouldn't be welcomed by the others.

"She is that! She adores Selina, though, and hovers like a mother hen." Miss Selwyn's expression seemed wary. Gideon noted she didn't say that Kerr doted on both of the young women, merely the daughter of the house.

"Have you found something enjoyable to read?" he asked.

She brightened at that. "I'm reading Sir Walter Scott's *Waverley* to Selina, and I enjoy it thoroughly. Selina listens when she's awake, but I fear she would prefer something by Mrs. Radcliffe."

"M'mother disapproves of novels for ladies," Tavernash interjected, glancing up from his food. "Wouldn't approve of young ladies cutting up a gentleman's peace, either."

Miss Selwyn put her fork down and appeared to struggle for a response to that. Gideon glanced over at Marshall. Marshall spoke first, glaring at Tavernash. "Unexpected visitors can be a burden," he said. "But we don't turn guests in need away from Woodglen."

"Indeed," Gideon added. "What would the shire think if poor Miss Selwyn were to die from her illness because we turned her out in the rain that morning?"

"M'mother…" Whatever pearl of wisdom Tavernash meant to dispense disappeared when servants arrived with the meat course and distracted him. His piggy eyes darted around the table periodically. Gideon wondered if the fool took in more than he let on.

"So do you prefer Scott to Radcliffe?" Gideon asked, turning the subject.

"Indeed. It takes me away to adventure and real history," Miss Selwyn said. "Quite stirring."

"Do you have Jacobite sympathies, Miss Selwyn?" Gideon teased.

"Sympathy for what happened to the highlanders, certainly," she replied. "But where do Mr. Scott's sympathies lie? His poor hero began in the English army and is now afloat in the highlands."

"I think perhaps he tries to have it both ways," Gideon said.

"Perhaps his sympathy is with suffering, the pain of divided loyalty, and the complexity of war and politics," she said.

"Well said, Miss Selwyn. Perhaps his domain is the human heart," Gideon answered.

"I'm not sure what is so complex about patriotism and loyalty," Marshall said. Soon the three of them were deep in a lively discussion of the Stuart succession and Jacobite ambitions. By the time a tasty pudding was served to end the meal, the three of them agreed, at least, that violent overthrow of government was a bad thing indeed.

Even Tavernash spoke up to endorse that idea. "People have to respect their God-given betters," he pronounced with a satisfied nod.

Miss Selwyn finished her pudding with relish and set down her spoon. "I best take my leave of you now," she said.

"I'll escort you safely up," Marshall said.

The gentlemen were halfway out of their seats when a footman came in with a message for Marshall.

"Crisis in the stables," he said. "Something every day is my lot. Can you find your room, Miss Selwyn?" he asked, casting a wary glance at Gideon.

"I am certain I can manage. The house is rather large and confusing, but I'm learning my way," she replied.

They watched Marshall leave.

"May I offer myself as a substitute?" Gideon asked over Tavernash demanding port at the far end of the table. Her smile was his reward. He ought to suggest that she have more care for her safety with men she hardly knew, but the trust he saw in her warmed his heart. He offered his arm.

"Where are the servants' stairs from here?" she asked when they exited the room. When he paused without answering, she added, "I recall it is easier for you than the great marble stairs."

Gideon stared into eyes as warm as they were deep blue. A man could lose himself in this woman's gracious care. He swallowed his pride. "You are correct." He turned them in the direction she requested.

A giggle escaped her. "Me, too, to be honest. A lady is meant to float, but I live in terror one slip will send me tumbling down them."

He led the way and took the stairs above her. It was the incorrect manner, a gentleman being required to go behind lest the lady take a tumble, but he remembered the impact of following her swaying body up before and thought it prudent to spare himself the view.

"That man is rather rude," she remarked when they started

up.

"Tavernash? Yes. Lord of the manor—or so he thinks."

"Even dukes are not exempt from basic manners, or shouldn't be. Is he actually the heir presumptive?"

No. Not even close. But what do you tell her, Kendrick? "Since my brother is very much alive, healthy, and young, Tavernash's ambitions are irrelevant."

"Is he truly? I'm glad. My cousin and his friends have been positively ghoulish about it," she said.

He stopped in his climb. "What do you mean, ghoulish?"

She described the sorts of nonsense foolish young men got up to. The betting books at White's neither surprised nor shocked. Her next words, however, sent him reeling.

"Eustace's latest nonsense is, 'What if the…' Oh my. His words about you are unkind," she said.

"I'm used to it. Finish what you meant to say."

"He and his disreputable friends have speculated no end of possible ends for the poor duke. The worst is that his brother murdered him to somehow get his hands on the estate."

"His brother." It wasn't a question.

"You," she whispered. "I told you they are horrid. It is nonsense of course, unkind but nonsense. Loose talk."

Gideon knew better than most the harm loose talk could have. Would anyone believe he killed Phillip? He prayed not. *Even if a few are gullible enough to believe it, how is that any worse than my current position? It can do no real damage.* At least, he hoped not.

As they continued on their way, Miss Selwyn expanded on her cousin's antics. "It's why they followed Uncle Ludlow here, of course. They hoped to get a look at Mr. Tavernash, and at you. They think clues will help them win bets."

He would have to keep an eye on young Selwyn and his friends before they caused real trouble. He fell silent, and Miss Selwyn darted concerned glances at him when they reached her floor.

"I'm sorry, Mr. Kendrick. I thought you ought to know," she

said.

"Young men get up to all sorts of foolishness, Miss Selwyn. I'm sorry they distress you," he replied. "Thank you for joining us for dinner tonight. The conversation was much improved."

She grinned at that. "If Felton Tavernash is your usual companion, any conversation would be an improvement."

He smiled back, lost in the gleam of eyes as blue as the lapis lazuli in Maera's wedding ring. The memory, a dart to his heart, brought him to his senses. *Why should that come to mind now?*

Her smile dimmed as if she felt his change in mood. "I'll bid you good night, then," she said.

He bowed, not taking her hand. "Sleep well, ma'am," he said. "Perhaps you'll join us again."

"Perhaps," she murmured before slipping into the room.

Walking back, he allowed the troubling memories of his marriage to surface. They hurt less than even a year or so before. She had been a good woman and a dutiful wife. He'd felt her loss keenly. Perhaps it was time to let his grief go, or perhaps he had just learned to live his life around it. In either case, he planned to enjoy dinners with Euphemia Selwyn as long as she was in residence. He'd allow himself that small pleasure at least.

BEFORE SEEKING HIS own rest, Gideon took a detour to the stables. He found Pritchard currying Hannibal. His old friend seemed to have appointed himself the horse's guardian angel. Purpose had given Pritchard a bit more energy. He even stood straighter.

"Do you have time for a chat?" Gideon asked as if empty time didn't hang heavily on the old groom.

Gideon's friend led him to a corner of the stables, where a kettle simmered over a brazier. "Keeps the beasties warm on the outside and the grooms warm in their innards. Kin I offer you some tea? Ain't fancy but…"

Gideon accepted a mug, and the two men sat, Gideon on a log raised up as a bench and Pritchard on an overturned bucket.

"Where are the other grooms?" Gideon asked.

"Called to help with the troublesome ditch, complaining every step." He shrugged the shoulder with the empty sleeve. "I'm not much use with digging, so they left me in charge." He laughed as if his being in charge was a perfect joke.

Miss Selwyn's hound bounded up to put his chin on Gideon's knee. "Has this monster been behaving?"

"That one is a perfect gentleman. Only time he misbehaved was the time he spied that lady. Longs for her, I think. She ought to pay him a visit. Meanwhile, I see he gets fed and has a good run every day."

Gideon nodded, making a mental note to tell Miss Selwyn. "Thank you," he said.

"I don't think you came out here to see about the dog, though."

"I came to ask what's being said about me," Gideon told him, scratching Hector's ears.

"What do you mean? There's the usual talk, filthy names, foul lies. Nothing you don't know," Pritchard said.

"Exactly the same as fourteen years ago?" Gideon asked cautiously. He had been twenty-three, dressed in servants' castoffs and publicly derided by his father. Fillmore, for one, acted as if nothing had changed. Others weren't in residence at Woodglen back then, though.

"You puzzle some, the ones with eyes. Not as deformed as they expected, smarter 'n they were told. They look for trouble, but they don't find any. Of course…"

"Go on."

"That is, folks warn parents to hide their daughters and ladies to bar their doors. They've heard the stories." Pritchard glanced at him sharply. "I'm not asking what really happened with Her Grace that night, but I never believed that story."

His loyalty put a lump in Gideon's throat. His hand stilled. "I need to ask you a favor, Pritchard."

"Ask me anything," the old groom said.

"I want you to visit the Cockcrow. I'll give you enough for your drinks and some to help loosen tongues. I want to know what's being said." He reached into his pocket and pulled out coins. "There'll be more. Will folks wonder where you came into money?"

"Let 'em," Pritchard chuckled, taking the coins. "This could be fun."

For one of us, perhaps. "I hope so," Gideon answered. He gave the dog another pat and left him.

Chapter Thirteen

"Tell me about him again." Selina's words ended in a coughing fit. Even feverish, with glazed eyes and cracked lips, Selina had one obsession, the heir. "Tell me," she rasped.

Two days had passed, and Selina had dined with the gentlemen both nights. Each time, Selina demanded to hear every detail of Tavernash's appearance, every word he said, every sumptuous adornment in the house. Mia avoided pointing out that the man was rotund, florid, opinionated, and overbearing by dint of simply providing facts and details, hoping Selina could draw her own conclusions. She seemed to find Mia's lack of interest in the dolt reassuring.

Kerr, Mia suspected, disapproved of the dinners and likely had been told to keep Mia to her room. She could deny her darling nothing, however. As long as Selina demanded Mia bring back description and stories, she was happy to encourage it.

When Selina drifted off, Kerr bustled over and put a hand to her brow, her expression worried.

"Her cough is worse," Mia said. "I've asked Mrs. Morrit for elderberry syrup. She says they have none, but the honey she sent helps a bit."

Kerr frowned down at the patient. "It has only been four days."

Only? "True. Perhaps things will improve tomorrow."

"Perhaps." Kerr did not seem hopeful.

"I promised Selina I would find the ballroom and bring back a description," Mia said.

"Go. She'll sleep for a while. Your little stories please her more than those books you read," Kerr responded.

Fillmore, stone faced and focused, passed the stairs as Mia descended, walking toward the formal entrance. She turned, curious about his mission, and saw a woman festooned in a cloud of feathers and purple ruffles advance on the butler, demanding attention.

Drawn toward the sight in spite of herself, she heard the lady demand to see her son. "…who will put worthless servants in their place as fast as can be." Her son? This must be Mr. Tavernash's famous mother. It was almost amusing until Mia remembered they would now have to deal with two of them. She sank against a wall between a column and a potted fern, silently fixated on the drama.

Fillmore sent a phalanx of footmen to alert Mr. Tavernash, gather luggage, order a bath, order tea… "And sandwiches. Make sure the bread isn't stale," the vision in purple demanded.

Moments later, the woman cruised by, a man-o'-war at full sail, led by a footman toward the stairs. Mia let out her breath when she passed, relieved to have avoided notice.

She breathed too soon. The woman swung around and pinned her with her gaze. "Is this one of the hussies attempting to snare my Felton? It won't fly, my girl. You and that other will decamp and soon. I know your type, and the little charade you're perpetrating will not stand." She didn't wait for a response; she simply sailed on by.

Mia, wide-eyed, met Fillmore's gaze. For a moment, he appeared almost sympathetic. "You best avoid that one if you know what's good for you," he said.

Mia nodded. "She's a sight to see, though." She thought for a moment how Mrs. Morrit would react to this newcomer. It could prove entertaining. Besides, Woodglen had its central block with the massive public spaces, two wings with parlors and drawing rooms, and by Mia's estimate, at least fifty bedrooms. In all that space, it ought to be easy to avoid the woman. At least, she hoped so.

For now, she went in search of the ballroom, sketch pad in hand.

LOOKING FOR FILLMORE, Gideon made his way down the central corridor past the ornate public rooms. He had a question about the wine expenses. He'd been told Fillmore was overseeing the settings in the formal dining room, but the old reprobate had not been there. He continued toward the front of the house, peeking into rooms one by one, though he thought it unlikely the butler would oversee the everlasting dusting even of the formal drawing rooms. He found most of them under holland covers, in any case.

He came upon the ballroom where it opened onto the central corridor at right angles before it stretched the length of the lower floor of the east wing. Gideon doubted it had been used in years, but he wouldn't put it past Fillmore to keep the thing in readiness. He opened the door and walked the ten steps to the balustrade overlooking the main floor. Curved stairs, designed to allow guests to make an impressive entrance, curled down to the right and to the left. The last thing he needed was to climb down and back up just to see if Fillmore hid in one of the alcoves along the wall.

He was about the turn when something caught his eye. Not Fillmore. A young woman sat directly beneath him on the floor, with her legs drawn up under her skirts.

"Miss Selwyn, what on earth are you doing?"

She tipped her head up and grinned. "Sketching the wonders of Woodglen," she replied. She rose to her feet in one remarkably graceful movement.

Gideon started down the steps, and she met him halfway. "Why would you do that?" he asked.

"For Selina. She longs to see everything."

"Has she asked you to count the silver?" he asked.

She responded with a musical laugh that vibrated through his heart and stirred his body. "Not yet. She's content with every morsel I can dribble out about Tavernash—or the heir—as she insists that I call him. I'm going to delight in telling her about his mother."

"From his description?" he asked.

"Why, Mr. Kendrick, don't you know? You have another guest. The grand dame herself floated in not an hour ago and has poor Fillmore in a taking."

"Formidable?"

"Oh yes. She will have the hussies pursuing her darling out of here in short order, and devil take any servant who doesn't do as they ought." Miss Selwyn made that pronouncement with good humor and no alarm whatsoever lurking in her eyes.

"God help us!"

"Indeed." She grinned at him. "What are you doing in the ballroom, Mr. Kendrick?"

"I've been searching for Fillmore, but now I see why I couldn't find him," he said. "He's probably hiding from Lady Tavernash."

Their eyes held, amusement drawing them together in perfect accord until Miss Selwyn blushed, and her gaze darted away. "I need to finish my sketch before she wakes up. I think I have a better view from here."

With that, she sat, her manner so unaffected that he hesitated only a moment before sitting down on the step above her. He shouldn't. He should leave. He couldn't help himself. Something about this young woman brightened his days; he didn't want to cut their conversation short.

"I saw Hector again today. I went out to visit Hannibal. Have you visited yet?" he asked.

"Once. Alas, poor Hector. It is difficult for me to get out there in the times I have free," she responded.

"Doesn't your cousin need a sketch of the stables?" he asked, raising a brow.

She turned to gaze at him skeptically. "Perhaps. It isn't her main interest. She wants the fine adornments and lush carpets."

"What about the estate? Wouldn't she like to see the extent of the place? How about the folly?" he suggested.

"Folly?"

It is on a hilltop overlooking the valley. I believe my… The former duke held parties there," he explained.

"She would probably love that," Miss Selwyn said.

"If you ride out, you would have an opportunity to visit Hector. He might want to lope along."

Intense longing overcame her expression, and Gideon felt a sudden need to make certain it happened. "Consult with this Kerr person and your cousin. I'm confident you can convince them you need to do it."

Her joy was palpable. "I'll do it!"

He rose to his feet, managing to suppress his groan. "And now I should go. Someone might find us here and draw improper conclusions. Finish your sketch and follow me later," he said.

Her expression as he walked away, trust comingled with hope, gave him a frisson of regret. The reports he'd had from Pritchard were alarming. Not only did the villagers believe him to be a ravisher of women but a murderer as well. Eustace Selwyn and his friends dined out on it. He shouldn't have offered to ride out with her. And yet he knew he would do it.

SUPPER THAT NIGHT proved as unpleasant as Mia expected. She had almost stayed away, but if she was to stay at Woodglen, she would face the dragon that was Lady Tavernash sooner or later.

Mia descended the stairs and went straight to the dining room. At no time had the odd mix of Woodglen residents practiced the custom of gathering in the drawing room first. There had been no point. Lady Tavernash had other ideas.

Marshall waited at the door for her. Behind him, the room was empty. "Where are the others?" she asked.

"In the chinois drawing room, the one that opens onto the dining room. The old woman is haranguing Kendrick about his presence here," he said.

Mia felt the blood drain from her face. The drawing room was steps away, and she could her the woman's strident tones.

"I need to join them before she tries to toss the lot of us out. Do you want to eat upstairs?" Marshall asked.

Mia stood up straight and raised her chin. "No. I refuse to hide from her."

Marshall smiled. "Good girl." He offered his arm and opened the door moments later.

"...and that isn't the worst of it. Now I'm hearing you murdered the poor duke in an attempt to take part of my Felton's heritage." The words brought Marshall to an abrupt halt. They made Mia sick to her stomach. Marshall's baffled frown made it clear he'd never heard Eustace's lies.

"Only a fool believes pub gossip," Mr. Kendrick retorted. "I hadn't thought you that sort, my lady."

"Felton, my vinaigrette quickly. This, this interloper insulted me." The woman collapsed onto the settee, one hand to her brow. Tavernash rushed over to pat her other hand. She spied Marshall and sat up abruptly. "You there. Marshall. I insist that you remove this creature from the house."

"I fear I cannot, my lady. Mr. Kendrick was specifically invited here by the duke."

Unlike some people, Mia thought ruefully.

"The duke is dead." Lady Tavernash almost shouted the words.

"Praise God, he is not," Kendrick retorted. "He wrote to me

and to his solicitors before he went away."

The woman made an unladylike noise.

"Mr. Kendrick has been given full authority over Woodglen, my lady. He acts in the duke's stead. I have verified the paperwork. For now, he's the duke in all but name." Marshall tossed Kendrick a speaking glance as if to say, *And you can damn well deal with these two troublemakers.* Kendrick didn't respond, so Marshall went on. "Perhaps under the circumstances, it might be better for the two of you to go back home to await word about the duke's whereabouts."

"Nonsense! We will stay right here until we hear from the dear duke," Tavernash's mother said, glaring at Kendrick. "Or until his body is found."

Mia swallowed to hold back a hysterical laugh. The entire conversation had the air of melodrama—or farce.

Fillmore opened the doors to the dining room at that moment and announced dinner. Mia's shoulders relaxed. At least the bizarre conversation came to an end. Lady Tavernash demanded her son's arm and sailed out first as was her due.

Marshall leaned toward Kendrick and muttered, "You could order them removed."

Kendrick shook his head. "So could you, but not yet, at least. Let's see what the shrew is up to." When he leaned toward Marshall, Mia heard only something about family papers.

Whatever was said, Marshall seemed to agree before offering his arm to Mia. She had no time to tell Kendrick she'd been unable to ask Selina about riding out. She let the steward lead her in to dinner. One thing was certain: when the gentlemen got their port, she would return to her room posthaste. She wouldn't risk letting the old witch get her alone.

CHAPTER FOURTEEN

G IDEON WENT DIRECTLY to Marshall's office in the early morning before seeing to his own work. Something about the Tavernash pair made the issue of inheritance more urgent.

A letter had surfaced the year before that called Phillip's legitimacy into question. It implied that Gideon was in fact the legitimate son, in spite of what their father had said. If Gideon's mother had been legally married to their father, Phillip's mother's marriage was bigamous. In that case, Gideon ought to have inherited the title. Gideon didn't care, except Phillip was determined that Gideon's son inherit next, restoring the legitimate succession. He'd tried to ignore it, but the sight of Felton Tavernash gorging himself at the duke's table every night gave Gideon a fierce desire to save the succession for his son—or for his brother's, if it proved to be legitimately his.

The question was clear, and Phillip believed it, but there was no proof. Surely he must have gone through the family papers. Did he find the proof? Was that what sent him running away?

"You're anxious this morning," Marshall said, his greeting curt as usual.

"You agreed to show me the Glenmoor archives," Gideon said.

Marshall heaved a sigh. "After the old woman made the same demand, I thought I better show you." He opened a drawer and hit a lever to open a hidden compartment. He removed an antique key, heavy iron and several inches long. He held it up. "This belongs to the dukes only—but you're one in all but name, they say."

He handed the key to Gideon and led him down the corridor past workrooms and Gideon's own office to a door at the far end. It opened easily, causing Gideon to glance at the key in his hand. It opened into a stone-walled room lined with shelves and a counter covered with herbs.

"The stillroom?" Gideon asked.

Marshall smirked. He reached for a wall sconce and twisted it. One stone wall opened a crack. Marshall had to push it open. "Need to oil this. It is opened rarely."

"When was it opened last?" Gideon asked.

"The duke came here in January. Rooted about and left right after."

So not just before he absconded. Curious.

Another door, ancient and heavy, lay behind the stone. Gideon put the key to the lock, and it clicked open. He took the lantern Marshall offered and peered in at the records of his ancestors. He raised the lantern high. The space appeared to be twelve or more feet deep. Shelves lined three walls, and another shelf up the center divided the room in two. Ledgers and/or journals, their bindings in various states of repair, lined the top shelves. A large book with a cracked leather binding, likely a bible, occupied a bottom shelf. One wall had cubbyholes filled with rolls of documents. To his right, boxes—a newer sort of storage, he thought—were neatly stacked. It amounted to massive amounts of information. Anyone seeking to research the history of the Dukes of Glenmoor and the Tavernash family would face months, if not years, of work.

"Which of these are the most recent? I'm interested only in the current duke and his immediate predecessor," Gideon said. "Is there some order?"

"I have no idea," Marshall said.

"Can you make out what that says?" Gideon asked, pointing to a paper nailed to the end of the central shelves.

Marshall squinted at it. "No. Too faint."

Gideon tucked the key into his pocket and shuffled closer to the stacked boxes. He brought the lantern in close. "Look, you can read the dates."

Marshall squinted down at them. "Hard to make out," he said.

Gideon started to wonder if the man had vision problems. He ran the lantern along the row toward the end, where a stack had been disturbed and there was much less dust. He handed Marshall the lantern and reached for the least dusty, a box a foot and a half long and several inches deep. He carried it to the stillroom and locked the archives. Marshall hung the lantern and sent the stone wall back into place. In the better light, Gideon confirmed the date: 1780–1790, the years that covered Gideon's birth. The lack of thick dust made him certain now that Phillip had checked it.

Marshall went on his way. He didn't ask Gideon to return the key.

Gideon considered putting the box in his office, thought better of it, and carried it up to his suite. When he entered, he found Jem, who made a great show of organizing a drawer in the dressing room.

Gideon cursed to himself. The make-bait had been snooping. Gideon had suspected it before but had never caught him at it. Now he stood there holding something he preferred to keep private. He put the box on the table in the sitting room.

"Do you need something, Jem?" he asked.

"I was just fetching some shirts. Need ironing." His eyes darted to the box. "Do you need anything, sir?"

"I do not." Gideon folded his arms. It was an obvious dismissal, but Jem still lingered a moment before grabbing a shirt from the drawer and leaving.

Gideon raised his eyes to heaven before peering about for a place to put the box he preferred to keep from prying eyes. Still,

Jem was Marshall's creature, and Marshall already knew he had it. He slid the box under his bed. The massive iron key bore protecting. He found his valise in the dressing room and opened the false bottom. A hundred pounds in cash lay there safely. He added the key and went on to his office to work.

ANY THOUGHT OF riding about the estate with Gideon Kendrick died in the night. Selina's cough deepened, coming in great racking waves, and her fever spiked. When Mia had come up from dinner, Selina had no interest in the goings on for the first time. By morning she was incoherent.

"We must call Dr. Gratis. The viscount instructed me that if she got worse, we're to call him in no matter what you say to me," Kerr said, holding a wet cloth to Selina's brow. "You don't seem to have any other ideas."

Mia didn't. Willow bark worked to a degree but never for long. She feared a lung fever had developed, and she was terrified for her cousin.

"Go," Kerr snapped. "Find that snooty butler and order him to send word."

Mia nodded, pulling on simple stays and a plain morning gown that buttoned in the front. Her hair, still braided and coming loose, would have to do.

"Let me write a quick note for Uncle first," Mia said, putting action to her words. She folded the missive and set out in search of someone she could rely on to act quickly. She took the servants' stairs, thinking they might lead to the butler's pantry, but she couldn't find Fillmore. She confronted Mrs. Morrit instead.

"Send for Dr. Gratis?" Mrs. Morrit sneered. "He'll come faster for Marshall." She directed Mia to the estate offices. "I'll warn the maids to stay away."

Mia hurried toward the offices and almost bumped into Gideon Kendrick in the connecting passage. He grasped her with one hand on each arm. "You're upset. What is it?"

"Selina is worse. We need to send for Dr. Gratis," Mia said.

"That toad? He's worthless. Less than," Mr. Kendrick replied.

Mia fought tears. "He'll want to leech or bleed her. It will only weaken her."

"Then why send for him?"

"I don't know what else to do. She's out of her head with fever. Uncle will insist, in any case."

A door opened, and Marshall joined them. Mia explained the issue. "Best send for the doctor. I'll see to it," he said.

"You do that, and I'll see if I can get someone else from Shaftesbury—or even Dorchester," Mr. Kendrick said.

"Who will you send?" Marshall asked.

"I'll go myself. If I find someone in Shaftsbury, I can be back by dark or soon after," Mr. Kendrick said.

Marshall nodded. "Do that. We should warn Clavering."

"I've written something for my uncle. Can you send it over, please?" Mia said.

Marshall took it with a nod, but neither man paid her further attention. Mr. Kendrick had already lurched off toward the stables, and Marshall was calling for the footmen.

GIDEON LED HANNIBAL into the stables in the gloaming, also leading the horse the Shaftsbury physician had ridden, grateful it was not yet full dark. The man appeared young, but he seemed sensible enough, understood lung fever, and answered Gideon's questions sensibly. He suspected, however, that the word *Woodglen* attracted the man's interest, and he might have agreed to anything.

He dismounted, leaned his head against the great horse's

neck, and spoke words to soothe himself as much as his mount. Hector hurried up at the sound of his voice, but Gideon had time for the briefest ear scratch, anxious as he was to discover how matters sat since he'd left. All thought of the box of papers under his bed had gone from his mind entirely.

He reached the Selwyns' room more quickly than he might have a month before. Woodglen's expansive floors forced him to walk more than he had to at home, and the exercise had strengthened his back muscles, one small blessing in his mission there.

The housekeeper stood at the door, frowning. Dr. Standish, the new man, hovered over the bed, his back to them, while Euphemia Selwyn stood across from the bed, looking worried and fearful. Their maid stood at the foot.

"Did Gratis bleed her?" Gideon asked Mrs. Morrit quietly.

"Miss Euphemia tried to stop him, but Kerr insisted the viscount would wish it," Mrs. Morrit retorted. "Doesn't appear to have helped."

Of course not. Daft practice. "Have we heard from Clavering himself?"

"Aye. He said we should call the doctor, as if we didn't know that already. He's staying safely away," Mrs. Morrit replied sourly. "We're to bear the brunt here. I don't want my maids catching a fever."

They waited in silence until the physician rose from his study of the patient and had earnest words with Euphemia Selwyn, who responded in kind, glancing over once toward Gideon and the housekeeper. Standish and Miss Selwyn approached, while Kerr wiped the patient's brow and murmured words of encouragement.

"Your guest suffers from influenza, I fear," Standish said. "There has been some in Shaftsbury and, I heard, the seaside towns."

Mrs. Morrit paled. "I will keep my maids away from this room."

"Wise. They can leave meals on trays by the door," Gideon said. Mrs. Morrit stared at him before giving a sharp nod, as close as she came to agreement on anything.

"Yes. It is best if only Miss Euphemia and their maid remain in this room. They will need water regularly and tea as well—tisanes of willow bark, echinacea, or slippery elm—elderberry is ideal if you have it. Fluids are vital. Do you have ice?"

Mrs. Morrit blinked as if mentally reviewing inventory. "Aye. Some remains in the icehouse. I'm afraid our stillroom has been allowed to deplete, what with the duke gone."

"Please send to Selwyn Court for slippery elm and willow bark to refresh your stores. I keep it well supplied there. Also, there are elderberries along the east pasture. Send someone to see if any berries remain. If found, I'll need sugar to create syrup." Miss Selwyn spoke with the confidence of a woman used to managing a household. Gideon wondered again about her role in Clavering's house.

Standish beamed at her. "Good choices, Miss Selwyn."

Mrs. Morrit, who had been absorbed in thought, glanced up at Gideon. "Will you still be wanting that nursery for your children?"

The children! Thank God he had not yet sent for them. "No. Not as long as there is contagion in the house." Mrs. Morrit appeared relieved, but it was Miss Selwyn's sad sympathy that touched his heart.

"One more thing, Kendrick, if I may suggest it. The patient would be more comfortable if she were raised up a bit, either by several pillows or, better, if the mattress were raised slightly."

"I'm not sending footmen in there!" Mrs. Morrit snapped.

"I'll do it. Will you please prepare a room for this gentleman, Mrs. Morrit? He's had a long ride and won't be returning tonight," Gideon said.

"I will warn Mr. Tavernash and his lady mother. Will you warn Marshall?" Mrs. Morrit asked. Gideon nodded, relieved she took on the Tavernash pair. The entire household needed to be warned away.

Standish went off with the housekeeper, and Gideon took Miss Selwyn's hand. "I'm sorry this burden falls to you, but you seem to know what you are about."

"I nursed both my parents through their final illness and Selina's mother as well. I know how to make a patient comfortable as can be, but I'm terrified I don't know how to make them survive."

The urge to take this courageous young woman into his arms, to comfort her, almost felled Gideon. He couldn't. He shouldn't. But one hand came out as if of its own volution, and he touched her cheek tenderly. "I have confidence in you," he whispered. Their eyes held, and he didn't remove his hand for long moments. Even in a plain, slightly rumpled gown with her honey-brown hair coming loose from her braid, her beauty touched him. He broke the connection reluctantly, common sense coming to the fore. "Now let's see about that bed."

He spoke to the patient soothingly before giving the mattress a great heave. "Rest easy, Miss Selwyn. This will only take a moment." He held it while Mia and Kerr slid bolsters and, he noted, the pillows from Mia Selwyn's bed under it. He directed them to arrange them for the most stable position before gently lowering the patient, who succumbed to a coughing fit. Kerr immediately rushed to give the girl a sip of water.

"Miss Selwyn, perhaps you could write to your uncle with your needs from Selwyn Court. I'll wait outside for it."

Moments later she handed him a folded piece of vellum through the door. He tucked it in his coat and took her hand in his once more, rubbing his thumb across the top of it. "If you need anything you aren't getting—anything at all—send for me," he said.

Her face, worried but determined, embedded itself in his mind as he made his way, candle in hand, to the estate offices in search of Marshall. The steward's office was closed when he got there. He gave it a tap and opened it without waiting for a reply.

Jem sat in the steward's chair in a pool of candlelight, pen in hand, a ledger book open in front of him. His mouth gaped, and he put the pen down and rose hurriedly. "I... I was just leaving a message for Marshall," he stuttered.

Gideon took in the open ledger, the ink bottle, and pen. *Spying? Altering the accounts? If so, why?* It was a conundrum for another day.

"Where is Marshall?" Gideon asked.

"Out in the fields."

"In the dark?" *You can do better than that, Jem.* How often did Marshall's toady make free with the office? Did he have access to the key to the archives? The family papers?

Gideon filed his thoughts away while Jem babbled. "Oh yeah. I remember. Poachers. He rode out to the woodlot."

"The one that borders Selwyn Court?" Gideon asked.

Jem nodded. "He, ah, he should be back. You need him?"

"Yes. I need to warn him. You, too, I expect. The sick woman has influenza. Staff is to stay away from that room."

Jem paled. "That took my gran. Well one day, gone in a week. You best tell Marshall. He may, ah, be back. Try the stables."

"I'll do that. Are you finished with your message?" Gideon held the door open.

"Oh, aye." Jem quickly covered the ink, blew out the candle, and wiped the pen before scurrying out the door and back toward the kitchen.

Gideon paused at his own office, raising the candle to check the room. Nothing appeared disturbed.

He reached the stables to find Marshall deep in convivial conversation with two of the grooms. Whatever was being said, laughter prevailed. Of a recently ridden horse or saddle, he saw nothing.

"Marshall, I need a word," he said. At the sound of his voice, Hector bounded toward him. He might have knocked Gideon down, but a firm, "Hector. Down," stopped him. The great hound halted at Gideon's feet, peering up hopefully. Gideon rewarded him with a scratch to his ears.

The grooms stared in astonishment. "That monster listens to you," Marshall said.

"He's a big, shaggy beast, but he's well trained," Gideon replied, hand on the dog's head. "Where is Pritchard?"

"Down at the pub with Peter and Frank. Taking to drink lately is our Pritchard," the youngest groom said, snickering.

"What do you need? I heard you brought in a new doctor." Marshall gestured to the door and waved at the grooms.

Gideon followed. He only had to tell Hector once to stay put. "I came to warn you. The sick woman has influenza. Mrs. Morrit is warning her people to stay away from the sickroom. All deliveries are to be left out in the hall."

Marshall cursed under his breath. "Bad stuff. Few of my people would have cause, but I'll warn them all away. What about Tavernash? Maybe they'll leave," he said hopefully.

"Mrs. Morrit said she would warn them," Gideon replied.

They walked back toward the house in what, with another man, might have been companionable silence. Marshall kept his pace to Gideon's, a small courtesy that surprised him.

"I also need to warn you about something else," Gideon said.

Marshall dipped his head up with a raised brow. "What about?"

"Found Jem sitting at your desk. He appeared to be interfering with your current books."

Marshall grunted. He took several steps before replying. "I'll take a look at it. Thank you for telling me." Whatever was going on, he didn't seem alarmed by it.

Gideon went on to bed with much to ponder. He found Jem waiting in his room and let the man undress him. He didn't want a valet, but this night, he was even more glad then usual he had decided to keep him close. "Do you help Marshall often?"

Jem reared up from where he was folding Gideon's waistcoat. "Now and again. I do what I'm asked."

That, Gideon suspected, was the truth, at least. The valet left, and Gideon sank into his bed. Much to ponder indeed. But when he closed his eyes, it wasn't the puzzle of Marshall and Jem, or worry for Pritchard down at the Cockcrow, that absorbed him. Euphemia Selwyn's lovely face, her fear overlaid with determination and courage, loose tendrils of honey-brown hair encircling it like a halo, took over and saw him off to sleep.

CHAPTER FIFTEEN

MIA'S DAYS QUICKLY fell into a pattern, as if her life had been severed into four-hour blocks around the clock. Sleep. Eat. Care for Selina. Get up and do it again. Not that there was a great deal of sleeping or eating, but she tried to keep her strength up. After some tension, Kerr quietly fell into the same pattern, alternating with Mia. They spoke little.

Meals, simple but adequate, were left at their doorstep along with regular deliveries of water, tea, clean linens, and sometimes—God be praised—ice. In turn they left dirty dishes, soiled linens, and chamber pots to be carried away.

On the second day, a message from Selwyn Court and a package were left next to a pitcher of water. The message, in Uncle Ludlow's scrawl, informed her that her cousin Eustace and the Not-So-Honorable Richard Bettinton had fallen ill with influenza, caught, Uncle believed, at the Cockcrow. Two grooms were ill as well. Sir Harvey Rowlinson seemed to be spared. He had hightailed it back to London. Mia wondered if Eustace's useless friends had infected Selina so that her adventure in the rain brought it on. Or perhaps she'd encountered the grooms when she'd gone to release Hector.

The next bit startled her. *That young physician Mr. Gideon Kendrick sent over left us with a list of things we're to do. Mr.* Kendrick's kindness didn't surprise her, but Uncle's acceptance of it did. The note went on, *We could use you here, Euphemia, I can tell you that. The staff is at sixes and sevens. But my girl needs you. I charge you to stay where you are and do your best for her.*

"I'm doing that, Uncle," she whispered under her breath. She wondered what he would do if her best wasn't good enough.

The package contained a fair amount of the herbals she had requested, though his letter indicated they had held some back for their own sickroom. She was particularly happy with the slippery elm and quart of honey. No one had found the elderberries she'd requested.

One bright light on the second day occurred when Mr. Kendrick knocked. He stood well back from the door to inquire about Selina, but his concern gave Mia a bit of strength. She needed it. His news, however, was not good. He reinforced Uncle Ludlow's belief that the Cockcrow was a source of contagion. Three of the grooms who frequented it were ill with influenza, including Mr. Pritchard. Mr. Kendrick's worry for his friend was obvious. He had come, in fact, for Mia's advice.

"Who is nursing them?" she asked.

"I am, as much as anyone. The other grooms are afraid of contagion." He shook his head. "Two others are ill but not as bad. Pritchard is frail."

His grim expression tore her heart. She wished she could reach over and put a hand on his arm. "I'm sorry about your friend."

"It's my fault. I sent him to the pub," he said, eyes downcast.

"You can't have known there was influenza there," she said, puzzling over his words. "Why would you send him to the pub?"

"There's been talk. About me. Turning uglier than usual. I needed warning," he said.

"Eustace's nonsense? How can anyone believe that you—"

"Would kill my brother? The good people of Nether Abbas have been primed to believe the worst of me since I was a boy. Talk spreads and grows in the telling. I of all people know that. But it wasn't worth Pritchard's life," he said.

"Don't speak as if it is hopeless!"

He smiled sadly. "Thank you. Hope matters, doesn't it?"

The warmth of his eyes filled her. "In the sickroom, always." She sent him on his way with some of her precious supply of slippery elm and instructions for the kitchen. He left her to her struggles, feeling the loss of his presence, his support, his warmth.

Day slipped into night, and Mia slept in her clothes, once sitting up, once leaning over Selina's bed. The following morning, she and Kerr changed Selina's bed linens. Their patient groaned.

"You were always cruel, Fee. Can't you see I hurt? My head is…," Selina murmured, squeezing her eyes shut. Mia glanced across to see a similar expression on Kerr's face as if the maid's head pounded in sympathy. Mia was too tired to think about it.

The day passed as the previous ones had, in a daze. Late on the afternoon of the third day, Mia noticed Kerr's hand shook when she picked up the water pitcher to replenish Selina's cup. "You're chilled!"

"No, I—" The maid's teeth chattered, making speech difficult.

Mia put a hand to Kerr's brow. "You're burning up! Willow bark for you, and a lie down."

Kerr shook her head. "Save it for my miss." She didn't object when Mia took a counterpane from Kerr's pallet and bundled her in it and into a chair.

"You can't care for Selina if you don't care for yourself. You'll be no good to her ill. Take this," Mia insisted. The willow bark tea was lukewarm, there being no way to keep their tea hot, but Kerr took it.

"I ache everywhere," Kerr admitted.

"How long has that been going on?" Mia asked.

"Since morning."

"Sit and finish your tea," Mia said. The woman's meek acceptance frightened her more than anything. She was obviously ill.

"Fee, what is it?" a weak voice from the bed called.

Mia wiped sweaty hair back from her cousin's face. "Not to

worry, dear. Kerr is feeling poorly."

Tears appeared in Selina's eyes. "My fault. All this. Take care lest you are next, Fee."

By nightfall, Kerr took to her pallet and didn't rise. Mia, left alone, had two patients.

"Awake, are you?" Gideon asked. "Then get some of this willow bark in you."

"Can't. Hurts. Throat," Pritchard said, his breath coming shallow and fast.

Gideon dipped a clean rag in the tea and dribbled it in the old man's mouth, but even that made him choke and cough. He turned his shoulder away.

Hector, camped at his side, whimpered, and the old man fell back. Pritchard dropped his one hand over the edge of his cot, laying it on Hector's head. The hound licked it and leaned his head against the cot.

"The beastie," Pritchard said, his voice a faded rasp, "…keeps me."

Gideon wet the old man's lips and laid the cloth across his brow. The rheumy old eyes fluttered shut, his breath shallow and wheezy.

The dog peered up at Gideon as if to ask if the old man would live. "You stay close, old fellow. I'm going to check on the others."

Two grooms, those who'd avoided the pub, also avoided the ones who were ill. They had taken to sleeping down in the stalls. Peter and Frank, the pub regulars, had come down with fevers soon after the night Gideon had found Marshall in the stables. Their fellows brought them food and water up in the grooms' dormitory but stayed far away. *For the best*, he thought. For Gideon himself, it was too late for caution. He had been in the

Selwyn cousins' sickroom and at Pritchard's bedside in his little hovel at the back of the stables.

The sounds of voices greeted him when he climbed the stairs to the dormitory and, as he reached the top, laughter. *They'll do,* he thought. Disease was never fair, attacking as it did the old and the weak. And children. *Thank God mine are far from here.*

Others, he thought, had few ill effects. "Is all well here? How do you feel?"

"Been better. Frank here has the constitution of an ox, though. Not much gets him down," one said. Peter, he guessed.

"Look who's talking. He's the one that fetches what they put on the steps," Frank said.

"Do you need anything? Are they bringing you enough?"

"Water plenty, and the foods no worse 'n usual," Frank said.

"Could use some hot tea now 'n again," Peter said.

"Could use some good stout ale for me throat," Frank added, and they both laughed.

Gideon chuckled along with them. "I'll see what I can do about the tea. I'm thinking you'll be up in no time and can fetch your own ale."

"Wait!" Frank squinted at Gideon. "Aren't you the one what killed the duke?"

Gideon froze, half turned toward the stairs. "Only a fool believes loose talk," he said through tight lips. Their murmurs followed him down the steps.

Probably planning how to defend themselves when I come to murder them in their beds. Disgust roiled his belly. He wouldn't be back.

The other grooms and Jem grew silent as he walked by, watching him, he thought, for signs of madness. Jem at least ought to have known better. Gideon turned toward them and watched the young one's eyes grow large. "You lot. Fetch some hot tea up the stairs to your fellows," he said. He went up to the house—carefully avoiding people,—reached his room, and washed up. He changed his shirt and linens before returning to the stables.

He stopped in the door at the far end of the kitchen near the estate offices first, requested a crock of broth for Pritchard and a sandwich for himself. There was water aplenty by the stables. Mrs. Demming, the cook, studied him from across the room but ordered her kitchen maid to do his bidding. They sent the potboy to bring him what he requested. The boy set it on a counter to Gideon's left and ran back.

To his ongoing battle to lay the half-wit cripple to rest, he had added fear of the sickroom.

He found Standish in the stables, waiting for him. He had lingered in the area, finding plenty of need. The influenza had abated in Nether Abbas. There were three dead, however, including Rogers the tavern keeper's elderly mother. "You called for me? These fellows tell me we have two sick grooms."

"Those two are recovering quickly. I want you to look in on an old friend." He led the physician through the stable block and tack room to Pritchard's hovel, not much more than an A-frame leaning against the wall.

Hector, who had been lying by the cot, rose to his feet and pressed himself against Gideon, whining while Standish examined the patient. It didn't take long.

"I'm too late." The doctor glanced back over his shoulder, saw Gideon's expression, and spoke gently. "It comes on fast sometimes in the elderly. I'm sorry."

Gideon knelt by the bed and put a hand on Pritchard's chest, still where it had labored before. "I should have stayed by him," he murmured.

"You can't have known. I'll just check on the grooms," Standish said with the brisk tone of a medical man here to serve the living, not the dead.

Gideon stood. "Have you seen Miss Selwyn?"

"This morning. The cousin is giving her excellent care. I think she'll recover. I'm less sanguine about the maid."

"The maid?"

"Aye. Kerr is her name? She fell ill two days ago."

"Euphemia is alone," Gideon murmured without thinking.

Standish raised a brow. "Can't be helped. I'm on my way. Get some sleep, Kendrick. So far, the house staff has stayed well; I don't need another one down."

He left Gideon to his grief. The only man here who'd ever believed in him, the last one he'd trusted at Woodglen, had just died, and he had no one to share his grief except a shaggy mountain of a dog. He lay his head on the bed, one hand clutching thick fur, and gave in to tears for Pritchard, for his brother, Phillip, on whatever godforsaken trek their father's perfidy had driven him, and for the boy that he had been, derided, abused, and driven from this place.

The unfamiliar lapse concluded, and he stood. Determination stiffened his spine. This illness would pass. He'd give Euphemia Selwyn as much help as she needed until it did. Then he would unravel the peculiarities in the management of Woodglen if he had to throttle Marshall to do it. While he was at it, he would search the family papers for proof that his father's marriage to Phillip's mother was—or was not—bigamous. That it would also prove his own mother was—or was not—the vile old man's legal wife, he brushed aside. Phillip deserved to know for certain. Then he would go home where he belonged. To Wales. Away from foolish gossip and ignorant speculation.

CHAPTER SIXTEEN

SUNLIGHT AND THE sound of her cousin's voice woke Mia in the chair where she had fallen asleep. She had no idea how long she had slept, nor did she know how many days had passed. She stretched her back, tipped her neck to ease her aches, and wrinkled her nose against the smells of sickness and unwashed bodies. The weather had been too foul to even open the windows. Sun this morning didn't mean warm, but she might check.

"Fee?" Selina's thready voice called again.

She hurried to the bedside.

"I'm cold, Fee," Selina said, her voice quivering but clear and coherent. Sweat beaded on her face and soaked her pillow. Mia raised the covers.

"Your nightgown is soaking wet. I think your fever broke." A hand to Selina's brow confirmed the fever had gone. She tucked the covers around her. "God be praised for his mercy. We'll have to change you in a bit. How do you feel? Well enough to sit?"

"Miserable but less. Is there tea?"

Last night's tea would be stone cold. "I'll see if they brought hot water," Mia responded. She had heard no knock, but she might have slept too soundly, so bone weary she could no longer help it.

She opened the door, pleased to see a large teapot wrapped in a cozy. Next to it a towel covered a plate of toast and boiled eggs, both lukewarm at best. She brought them to the table and used the water—blessedly still hot—to put willow bark to steep. There was enough left to make two cups of tea, reusing leaves from the day before or perhaps the one before that.

She brought the weak tea to Selina, slipped a hand under her shoulders, and helped her drink. She drank well, but it exhausted her.

Mia laid her down gently. "I need to see to Kerr," she said. Selina nodded and closed her eyes.

A firm knock startled her. Had they brought more?

The sight that greeted her sent her heart racing. Gideon Kendrick leaned against the doorframe. "How is Miss Selwyn?" he asked.

"Better, thank you, but I fear Kerr is worse," she replied, cataloging details of his appearance. Coarse black hair rumpled. A day's growth of beard. Shadows in his dark eyes. Cravat loosely fastened. Yet properly dressed.

He must have examined her appearance as well. "You are exhausted. When did you sleep last?"

"I just woke up," she replied. At his skeptical expression, she admitted, "I fell asleep in the chair. I don't know how long I slept."

He studied her so long she squirmed under his scrutiny. His gaze drifted away. "Pritchard died," he said without preamble.

Mia reached out without thinking and put her hand over his heart. "Oh! I am so sorry. I know he was your friend."

He peered at her again as if weighing some serious matter. She saw when he reached a decision. "You need to sleep. I'll care for your patients."

"No! You mustn't expose yourself," Mia said.

He stepped forward, forcing her to give way, and closed the door behind him. "It's too late for that. Besides, no one else will come in to help you. Let's get you to bed."

She felt her face flame. He meant sleep, but the mention of

bed…

"This situation is long past the point you can afford to be missish." He pushed her toward her own bed, unoccupied in the corner. He pulled back the covers, and she fell on it.

Gentle hands removed her shoes, covers came over her, and she felt sleep closing in. Mrs. Morrit will have apoplexy," she murmured.

MRS. MORRIT WON'T *be the only one. The Tavernash dragon is likely to be overcome with glee, and I don't dare consider what her uncle will say.* Gideon swallowed a frisson of guilt.

Miss Selwyn's reputation wouldn't survive this. But there was no help for it. If Euphemia Selwyn fell ill, there would be no one to care for any of them. He would deal with the scandal afterward.

He would have to make the honorable offer. If they all survived. He'd never planned to take another wife, but he would if necessary. It would be one more burden from this misbegotten journey inflicted on him by his brother, but he would do it. Of course he would. Staring at her hair against the sheets, he thought it might not be so terrible. His foolish body certainly reacted to her, and he'd come to admire her. Her reaction to a forced marriage was the painful question.

He examined the washstand she used to prepare tisanes and tea and added his remaining stock of slippery elm to her much-depleted reserves. There appeared to be plenty of honey, but willow bark ran low.

A lady's desk was tucked next to Miss Selwyn's bed. He took pen and paper, casting surreptitious glances at the lady, pleased to see the gentle rise and fall of her breathing. He scribbled a quick note requesting willow bark, tea, and additional linens. He stared at it long and hard before scrawling his signature at the bottom. There was no point in being coy. His presence in the room would be all over Woodglen by noon. He left the note in the hall along with some dirty linens.

"Fee? Is that you?" Selina Selwyn must indeed be better, from the sound of her voice.

When he approached her bed, her eyes flew wide, and she grabbed the covers, pulling them to her chin. "You mustn't be here!"

"I'm sorry. Believe me, there was no other choice," he told her.

"What have you done with Fee?"

"Miss Euphemia is sleeping the sleep of the just. She was exhausted and on the brink of collapse. She'll be no help to you if that happens, Miss Selwyn," he said gently.

She leaned up to glance at Mia's bed and fell back as if the effort wore her out. "If you've harmed her, my father will see you hung," she said. Her expression was defiant, but fear lurked behind it.

Gideon hadn't considered what she might have been told. He was supposed to be the stuff of a young woman's nightmares. He ignored it, a strategy he generally found effective. "There appears to be marmalade with the toast. Are you able to eat some?" he asked.

She blinked at him. He thought she meant to refuse, but hunger won out. "Fee meant to care for Kerr," she said between bites.

"Ah yes, the redoubtable Miss Kerr."

"Her pallet is in the dressing room," Miss Selina told him.

He poured a tisane in a cup and located the dressing room through an open door.

Pale and shrunken, the woman on the pallet did not seem so fearsome. Her skin burned, and a ragged, dry cough seemed to be torn from her throat. When she gazed up at him vaguely and accepted a swallow of liquid without attempting to send him on his way, he was certain she was ill indeed. He took time encouraging as much of the tisane into her as he could and then brought a wet cloth for her head. Her eyes drifted shut, and he sank back on his knees. *This one is fading away.*

He removed the dry linen cloth next to her head, obviously left from the night before. She lay flat on the floor and had no pillow. *Because we put them all under the other patient.* That could be corrected.

"There is a cup of hot tea on the washstand. Would you like it?" he asked Miss Selwyn.

"That must be Fee's. I drank mine." Her eyes darted to her sleeping cousin. "It will only get cold. I may as well have it."

"Would you like to sit in a chair? It would be easier to drink," he said.

"I can't. I—"

"Dizzy?"

"No. It is personal."

"Don't be missish. This is a sickroom," he insisted.

"I'm soaking wet under here. Fee said that I got sweats when my fever broke. She's meant to change me." She made it sound like an accusation.

"She is obviously in no position to do it now," he said. "I don't suppose…"

"Absolutely not! I will wait." She glared at him.

Good idea, Miss Selwyn. He handed the tea toward her, and she pushed herself up on one elbow to take it. She took two sips and handed it back. "I'll wait for Fee. Then you can leave."

"Perhaps you should sleep as well. Sleep is healing."

"I will not! You bear watching, sir, and I intend to do it."

Dear God, his well-intended—and necessary—intervention compromised both cousins. He damned well couldn't marry both of them. He hoped he was wrong. Perhaps no one had seen him. Perhaps Mrs. Morrit would believe his note was from Miss Selwyn. Perhaps the servants wouldn't gossip. Perhaps pigs would fly.

Time passed swiftly. He alternated between regular attempts to get fluids into Kerr and efforts to sooth the fretful Miss Selina

Selwyn. When luncheon arrived, he assisted the latter in eating and managed to coax a mere spoonful of broth into Kerr before her head lolled sideways, the woman senseless and uncooperative.

Miss Euphemia, as she had become to him, didn't awaken until the sun had dipped to the horizon and light through the window dimmed. She sat up, stretched, and rubbed her eyes. "What—" He watched memory return. She gasped and jumped to her feet. "Mr. Kendrick, I—"

He put aside the book he'd been reading to her cousin. "You slept soundly. How do you feel?"

She put a hand to her head. "I—Better, I think." She glanced at the window. "How long did I sleep?"

"All day, Fee. You slept for hours." Miss Selina Selwyn's tone left no doubt it was meant as condemnation. "This man has been—"

Miss Euphemia's eyes flew wide. She glanced from one to the other.

"Oh, very well," the cousin said with pouting lips. "He's behaved like a gentleman. We're finishing *Rob Roy*, which, I may say, is more interesting than *Waverly*. There's no luncheon left. We ate it all."

Gideon poured a glass of water. "The hot water is gone as well. We put the pot out for a refill, but I have no tea to offer."

She took the water and sipped, staring at her cousin. The fog of sleep appeared to clear. "You are much better today." Memory surfaced. "Kerr!"

"Not as well," Gideon said. "I have been able to get her to drink little."

"Did you try dripping it into her mouth?" Miss Euphemia asked, wide awake now.

"Yes. I tried that. We had a bit of ice at noon. I could get a few chips in her, but her fever remains high."

She took the water with her to the dressing room, to attempt to give it to the maid, no doubt. She returned moments later, worry etched in every line of her lovely face. "She didn't respond. How often did you try?"

"Every thirty minutes," he said.

She squeezed her eyes shut, shook off her worry, and forced a smile for her cousin. "It is good to see you better," she said.

"You promised to help me change," the patient whined.

Miss Euphemia glanced at Gideon.

"She's been waiting for you." He shrugged.

Gideon retreated to the dressing room after Miss Euphemia retrieved clean linens, and sat with Miss Kerr, soothing her with cool cloths while Miss Euphemia took care of Miss Selina's personal needs.

He found the cousin—who had been dressed in a clean night-gown, trussed up in a wrapper, and covered with a blanket—sitting in a chair. A pile of sheets lay by the door, and clean ones had been put on the bed. Miss Euphemia knelt before her, holding her cousin's hands and speaking earnestly to her. Miss Selina glanced up at him speculatively but didn't speak.

"Miss Selwyn—" he began.

"Yes?" Euphemia responded, rising to her feet.

"Yes?" Selina said simultaneously.

Both cousins laughed, forcing Gideon to do the same. "Miss Euphemia Selwyn, I meant."

Her brilliant smile lit his world. "This won't do. Not if we're to live in close quarters. May I call you by your Christian name?" he asked.

The other Miss Selwyn gasped. "Not I. I will be Miss Selwyn to you, if you please."

He didn't look at the cousin in the chair; his gaze never wavered from Euphemia. He took her hand in his. "I would be honored to make free with your name, at least in private, which we most assuredly will be as long as we're in this room. Euphemia is rather a mouthful, though. Your cousin calls you 'Fee,'" he said.

"Not that!"

He chuckled. "Do you have a middle name?"

She glanced at her toes, one of which made a pattern on the floor. "Forbearance," she murmured, making him laugh harder.

"What, then?"

"Mia. My mother called me Mia."

"May I ask you to do me the same honor? My name is Gideon."

Her trembling smile shot like a dart to his heart. "Thank you. Gideon."

"My father will not be pleased," Miss Selwyn said, and the invisible connection he felt with Mia faded away under cold reality, making him wonder if he'd actually felt it.

"And you look terrible, Fee. You ought to tidy yourself," the irritable cousin went on.

Mia blushed a delicious deep rose and peered down at the clothes she had slept in. "If you could read to my cousin for a while, perhaps I can freshen up in the dressing room."

Gideon bowed and gestured to the basin and water pitcher. "May I carry it in for you?"

At her nod, he filled the basin, stopping halfway to save their precious water, before putting a towel over his arm and carrying it into the dressing room. A shelf over drawers with a mirror above made a sort of vanity in the room. He placed the basin and linen on it. The candle they kept lit to care for Kerr sat in the corner of it and reflected light from the mirror. He paused to check on Kerr, who moaned in her sleep, her jaw tight as if she was in pain. He took the cloth from her brow, dipped a corner of it into the water he'd just brought, and wiped the maid's face before placing the cloth back on her brow.

"Do you think she will recover?" Mia stood in the doorway, staring at the woman, a well of sorrow in her expression.

He thought of Pritchard. The similarities were too great to overlook. "Perhaps. We have to remain hopeful," he said. He considered sending for Standish. It might help Miss Selwyn, but he doubted it would do Kerr any good.

Mia made way so he could exit the dressing room.

"When you return, perhaps we can remove a pillow or two from Miss Selwyn's bed to make Kerr more comfortable," he said.

She nodded, a sad smile on her face, and closed the door behind her, leaving him once again with Miss Selwyn, whose unwavering gaze bore into him.

"Shall we read some more?" he asked.

"He won't let you marry me," she said.

Gideon blinked. *Dear God, I hope not.* He couldn't imagine being shackled to this spoiled miss. "Your father?"

"Yes. He wants better for me. I may yet fix the attention of the heir." She tossed her head as if loose curls hung down, though her hair was in fact bound in the back.

"When you meet Tavernash and his mother, you may think better of it," he said. "Besides, my brother will return, leaving the man high and dry." He picked up the book and sat on a stool next to her.

Her certainty wavered. "Do you truly believe so?" Her eyes glittered with calculation.

A duke is a much bigger prize than a possible heir. "I know so. The duke will return."

"Mia is ruined now, locked in here with you. I've been ill and don't count. My father will—"

"Miss Selwyn, we shall see what happens. For now, we have a book to finish." With that, he began to read.

His thoughts wandered even as the words on the page slipped effortlessly from his lips. He could see Mia in his home in Wales. His children would welcome her. Would she be happy there? Would he? The answer, he increasingly thought, was yes.

CHAPTER SEVENTEEN

KERR LIVED ANOTHER day and passed deep into the second night. Mia found a note from Gideon, who had been on duty. He had covered the woman's face with the coverlet, left the note, and slipped away.

In the early morning light, while Selina slept soundly, Mia went into the dressing room to pray for Kerr. The woman had been unkind to Mia, but she couldn't hold resentment, not after this. She scribbled a note about Kerr's death to Mrs. Morrit and set it in the hall.

She washed her face and hands, went to sit by Selina, and reread Gideon's note twice. It was best, he said, to leave when there would be few about to witness it. She supposed that was true to a point, but she knew full well the entire manor already knew he'd been with them for two days.

A scratch at the door announced breakfast. She found a teapot in its cozy and a tray with three bowls of porridge. Word hadn't reached the kitchen, she could see. She ate her porridge and poured a cup of tea, waiting for Selina to awaken.

A firmer knock came before she did, and Mia found Mrs. Morrit standing as far across the hall as she could. The gaze she cast on Mia held neither disapproval nor reproof. There was instead, Mia feared, pity in the woman's eyes.

"Are you well, Miss Selwyn?" the housekeeper asked.

"Yes, thank you. I seem to be immune to the disease," Mia replied.

"I know that man was here. Did he—I just—" She'd never seen the housekeeper quite so flustered.

"Mr. Kendrick heroically stepped in when I reached the end of my strength, Mrs. Morrit. He was a perfect gentleman. He is gone."

Mrs. Morrit's skepticism was palpable. "He informed us that Miss Kerr is no longer among the living."

Of course he did. He thinks of everything. Mia nodded sadly. "We left her in the dressing room. I didn't know what to do."

"The dead are being kept in the icehouse. Mr. Kendrick directed me to send footmen to move her remains. Will that be acceptable?" Mrs. Morrit asked.

"I would be most grateful. I suppose my uncle would know if she has family and where she ought to be buried," Mia replied.

"He has been notified," the housekeeper said crisply. Mia wondered what all he had been told but didn't dare ask.

"Fee?" They'd woken Selina. Her voice sounded weak and thready.

"How is the other Miss Selwyn?" Mrs. Morrit asked.

"My cousin is very weak but mending. Thank you for asking. Her fever is gone," Mia said.

"That will put my footmen's minds at rest. Prepare her for their entry," Mrs. Morrit said.

Mia went to get Selina up but first had to tell her about Kerr.

Selina squeezed her eyes shut as she listened. They were moist when she opened them. "But, Fee, who will take care of my clothes or fix my hair? Papa will have to hire a new ladies' maid. He won't be happy."

Mia breathed in deeply. *So much for depth of grief for the poor woman.*

She soon had Selina wrapped and in the chair, feeding her porridge when the men arrived to carry Kerr out wrapped in a sheet. She thanked God and Mr. Kendrick that she had the strength to do so. The footmen cast a glance or two Selina's way, but neither spoke. They worked quickly and were on their way.

Selina fretted and fussed. She hated porridge and refused to face any more. Sitting up for any time wore her out, and she had to be helped back to bed. She demanded that Mia read and then that she stop. "Mr. Kendrick reads better than you do," she whined. She demanded tea, then left half of it. She asked for willow bark and then complained that it did no good.

Shortly before noon, in the midst of another attempt at the book, Selina murmured, "Why did Kerr have to die...," and turned her face to the wall. Her words touched Mia, who was relieved to know the woman's death affected her cousin after all.

Mia left her there. She scooted her chair into a patch of sunlight from the window, her head aching from rioting thoughts and confusion over the events of yesterday and that morning. She could do nothing for Kerr and nothing about the result of Gideon's presence in her room. In a moment of blinding honesty, she realized she wanted him to come back. She missed his comforting presence. With a faint smile over that thought, she fell asleep in the chair.

⟫⟫⟫×⟪⟪⟪

THE SUN HAD barely reached its zenith at midday when Jem woke Gideon to inform him that Viscount Clavering had arrived and was in a "powerful anger," demanding Marshall, the housekeeper, and above all, Gideon.

"You best dress in your finest to face him, Mr. Kendrick," Jem said. It was good advice, and besides, the footman kept the cheeky amusement lurking in his eyes to himself.

Gideon washed briefly and let himself be dressed. Jem stared openly when he was shirtless. For the first time, he commented on the vicious curve in Gideon's spine. "The amazing thing is, it doesn't seem so bad when yer dressed."

Gideon didn't respond. "Wait while I shave." He still didn't trust the footman completely, though his relationship with Marshall had softened. Jem seemed to find that amusing as well. The footman finished him off with an elaborate cravat and pronounced him ready to "visit the old lion in his den."

"The green drawing room?"

"Aye."

His lurching gait took him to the family stairs, the formal marble stairway that swept down to the central hall. He squared his shoulders to the extent he could and descended slowly. He found Fillmore in the hall, arguing with Felton Tavernash and his mother. The two interlopers hadn't run from the contagion after all.

"If Viscount Clavering has come to visit, my son ought to be the one to greet him, not some horde of servants!" Lady Tavernash's strident voice echoed off the walls.

"As I'm certain Fillmore has informed you, madam, it is not a social call," Gideon declared. He turned his back on the lot of them, left her sputtering, and closed the door to the green drawing room behind him.

"You!" Clavering roared, rising from his chair to glare at Gideon.

Gideon made a proper bow. "Good afternoon, Clavering. I apologize if you've had cause to worry. Your daughter is much improved, and your niece is no longer on the brink of collapse."

Outside of Clavering's line of sight, Marshall raised his brows and gave a cocky salute. Mrs. Morrit stood in one corner, hands clasped, knuckles white, mouth in a tight line.

"You—You—" Clavering sputtered.

"I assure you neither young woman came to any harm," Gideon responded.

"So this woman told me," he said, pointing at Mrs. Morrit. "But your reputation will do them no end of harm. What's being said—"

"Has there been gossip about Miss Selwyn—either of them?"

Gideon asked.

"Not yet, but—"

"May I suggest you speak with them yourself?" Gideon said. "Mrs. Morrit, would you please ask Miss Euphemia Selwyn to join us? Her cousin is well enough to be left alone for a few moments. Then I'd like a private word with the viscount."

Mrs. Morrit and Marshall left with all haste.

Clavering glared at him, studying Gideon as if searching for the horns he expected to see sprouting from his head. He looked like a man working up to an explosion.

Gideon swallowed and took a deep breath. "I'm prepared to offer for Miss Euphemia Selwyn, with your permission, if and only if the lady herself is willing."

"Not my Selina?" Clavering demanded.

"I realize it wasn't quite proper to enter the sickroom, but your daughter was perfectly safe with her cousin to guard her. She also had Kerr." It wasn't exactly a lie, though Kerr had been in no position to guard anyone's reputation.

Judging from Clavering's expression, he wasn't mollified. A miserable frown replaced his fury. "But you. The things I've heard. The duke—"

"I am well aware of the lies my father told and the malicious gossip. I gather the festering stories have taken wing since I arrived. That doesn't make them true. My brother doesn't believe them."

"What proof do you have?" the viscount demanded.

"None, and the situation is not ideal. But Miss Euphemia's reputation and power to contract a marriage have suffered. I owe her recompense," Gideon said.

"Euphemia has a maternal great-aunt. A Methodist prune of a woman. She'd probably take her," Clavering said, misery pooling in his eyes.

What a horrible fate! "If you send her away, you'll confirm that there is shame. Talk will flourish about both of the Misses Selwyn. On the other hand, no one will think anything about

Miss Selina, if Miss Euphemia contracts a respectable marriage with the supposed villain of this farce." *I hope.*

"Out of the pan, into the fire?" Clavering said.

"She ought to at least be given an opportunity to decide for herself which fate may be the least distasteful. You may ask her about my behavior. If she is repulsed or reluctant, she shouldn't be forced." Gideon wouldn't have her bullied or abused by some maiden aunt.

"What kind of life can you possibly give her?" the viscount demanded.

"You may find this surprising, my lord, but I'm a wealthy man. I own three mines, and I have a comfortable home. My brother sent me here because he respects my business acumen." He didn't actually know if that was true, but it should have been. Did Phillip have financial sense? He was beginning to think he might.

Clavering's expression altered sharply, shrewdness driving out misery. "My niece has no dowry. I was prepared to find some funds, but now…"

Now you don't feel obliged, you old skinflint. The viscount might have recoiled from submitting his niece to someone who might do her harm, but he was still cheap.

There was a soft knock, and Fillmore announced Miss Euphemia Selwyn. She glanced into the room and quickly focused on Gideon with a soft smile. She was rumpled and weary so that any fool could see the days of caring for her cousin had left her exhausted. He smiled back, trying to reassure, but he dared not take her in his arms to comfort her. He wished he might at least stay to intervene between uncle and niece but thought better of it. He bowed to Clavering. "I will leave you and your niece privacy," he said.

Mia opened her mouth to object, glanced at her uncle, and shut it again. A smile was all he had to leave with her.

✦ ⟨❦⟩ ✦

CHAPTER EIGHTEEN

ALONE WITH HER uncle, Mia couldn't be certain if his ferocious frown meant fury or simple worry. She groped for something to say. "I'm surprised to see you, Uncle. It appears you were spared the influenza. How is my cousin Eustace?"

"On the mend, they tell me. Unlike that worthless friend of his, Bettinton, who died," Uncle Ludlow grumbled.

Mia had few emotional resources to extend to the rakehell. "I wasn't fond of The Honorable Mr. Bettinton, but I didn't wish him ill. His poor parents."

"Raised a ramshackle son, the damned fools, didn't they? But don't distract me, girl. What were you thinking, allowing that man to insert himself into my Selina's care?" Uncle Ludlow demanded.

Fury, then. "I'm sorry to cause concern, Uncle, but Mr. Kendrick stopped to inquire after Selina and found me ready to collapse. He had been treating the grooms who had fallen ill, and felt he was in no greater danger entering. Without sleep, I might have succumbed and left poor Selina bereft of care." Mia tamped down irritation that the man had yet to ask about her own well-being. There was little point in antagonizing him.

"I'm told she is better," the viscount said.

Mia brightened. "Much better. Her fever has gone. I believe it is safe for you to visit her. Mr. Kendrick sent for Dr. Standish yesterday, and he pronounced the worst over but ordered another week or more of bedrest until she fully recovers."

"That doctor knows you were alone with him?" Horror transfixed her uncle's stiff posture as much as his face. "The entire county will hear of it! How long was Kendrick alone with you?" Uncle Ludlow paced furiously, spun on his heels, and waved a hand as if to brush something away. "It doesn't matter. Your reputation is shattered. No decent man will marry you now, and you've tainted my Selina as well. You'll have to marry him."

"Three days, two nights," Mia whispered, answering the question he waved away. "And we weren't alone. Selina and I—"

"Selina was incapacitated and can be held harmless," he insisted. She wondered if he was attempting to convince himself.

"You can't force him to marry me," she said more emphatically. "He did nothing wrong."

"It doesn't matter what he did. It matters what people think. No gentleman will have you now, and I'll not have you haunt my house as some fading spinster for decades. I won't have it. Eustace will marry, and his wife will manage Selwyn Court. Marry Kendrick or go live with your Great-Aunt Hortensia."

The breath left Mia's chest. Uncle Ludlow had never been particularly unkind, but he'd always made it clear she was a burden he wished to dispense with, the product of his impecunious brother's unwise marriage to a dissenting preacher's daughter. After his wife had died, Mia had ceased having any use to him. She shouldn't feel as shocked as she did, yet a weight had settled in her stomach.

A ruined reputation would leave her at the mercy of the worst of the gossips. She'd seen what vicious talk had done to Gideon. It could mean she would never marry, never have children of her own. The thought of living as Eustace's impecunious dependent made her stomach curdle. Great-Aunt Hortensia would be only marginally better. Worst of all, however, Gideon was to have a wife forced on him. He didn't deserve that. She opened her mouth to say something but could not.

Uncle ignored her shock. She realized he'd continued speaking. She tried to listen.

"…worst of it probably isn't true, but to be fair, you need to know a girl went missing in the village last week."

"What are you talking about?"

"Aren't you listening? The blacksmith's girl, Lizzy something or other, thirteen years old," he said.

"Lizzy Carter?"

"That's the one. She went out to fetch milk and never came home. Woodglen's dairy sells milk, you know, and—" Uncle's color rose along with his voice.

"What a horrible thing! But what does it have to do with me?"

"Don't be dense, Mia. I'm not saying Kendrick did it, but folks are saying that sort of thing happened when he was here before, and now it is happening again." The viscount glared down at her.

"He would never! That is nonsense," Mia shouted.

"If you're that worried about him, marry the man, then. It won't hurt his reputation none and might help it. Its best for my Selina if you marry the villain. I ought to force you, but he said—"

"What did he say?" Mia demanded.

"He offered for you; I'll give him that. He said he wouldn't have you bullied, though. Now you talk to him. Ask him about the village girl. Ask him about the duke. Dukes don't just disappear. You're well to remember that. But think of what's good for Selina—for our family. I'll be with Marshall."

He left her there, alone and confused. She sank onto the settee, unable to sort through her muddled thoughts.

Moments later Gideon entered, shut the door quietly, and drew a chair up to sit in front of her.

"Did he berate you horribly?" he asked.

His kindness upended her already confused feelings. To her horror, tears threatened. She breathed in lest she dissolve in a puddle of them. "A bit," she said, forcing a wobbly smile.

"Did he threaten?"

"No. Unless you consider Great-Aunt Hortensia a threat. She's a kind enough old woman. I can—"

"But you don't have to. There is my poor self as an alternative." He took her hand in his. "Unless the thought of taking me as a husband horrifies you."

"You had no intention of taking a wife. I will not have you forced into a marriage not of your choosing!"

HER BLEAK EXPRESSION at the mention of the aunt told Gideon everything he needed to know. Yet she faced misfortune with admirable courage, painfully young though she was. How old was she? Not a schoolroom miss but certainly no more than twenty, much too young to be thrust into marriage to a deformed man at least seventeen years her senior. And yet her concern was all for him. He squeezed her hand. Courage and strength—she had both.

"Leave me to my own decision, Mia, but before you make yours, there are some things you should know." It struck him how little they actually knew each other. How much could he share in the midst of the urgent situation in front of them? He cleared his throat. "First of all, I can well afford a wife. I own three prosperous mines. I have a large home, one I believe to be comfortable and well appointed. It is, however, in the mountains of Wales."

He waited for her to react in horror to the remote location. "Are they as beautiful as people say, your mountains?" she asked. It struck him again how very young she was.

"Every bit." He smiled at the thought before continuing. "I come with baggage, however. To begin with, I have three children."

She smiled at him. "You mentioned them before. Children are blessings, not baggage."

Grateful to have one hurdle crossed, he briefly considered describing his twisted back and rejected the idea. She could see some of it for herself and would have to face the worst of it when the time came. He felt a twinge of uncertainty. What if his body repulsed her? It couldn't be helped. "We need to discuss the stories you may have heard."

"You're certainly far from the 'half-wit cripple' folks liked to call you. I cannot believe anyone who lives or works at Woodglen believes any such thing any longer."

"Thank you. Far worse rumors spread about the night I was sent away. You need to hear the truth of that." *Damn it, Kendrick. This woman is an innocent. Choose your words carefully.*

"Is it why people have warned me it isn't safe for a young woman to be near you?" Mia appeared amused rather than horrified. "That's something else I know to be untrue."

"That I'm a danger to you is certainly untrue. However, I was in fact found in my stepmother's room that night, just not for the reasons my sire put out. I went to warn her. He had plans involving his cronies and Madelyn that I won't sully you by describing other than to say they were debauched and evil. I wanted her to bar her door. He went into a rage when he found me there and had me beaten, trussed up like a Christmas goose, and shipped to his mines in Wales. I never doubted he meant me to die there."

Her watery smile, filled with compassion, moved him. She leaned forward. "Vile man," she whispered.

"Indeed. The stories don't go away, however. If you choose to marry me, you need to know such stories follow me, especially here in Dorset. Are those the only rumors you've heard?"

A veil of confusion came over Mia's expression, as if she was remembering something, uncertain what to say. "Tell me," he prodded.

"Lizzy Carter, the blacksmith's daughter."

He had no idea what she meant. "What about her?"

"Uncle said that she has disappeared. She is only thirteen, a decent girl," Mia said sadly.

He cursed under his breath. "That sort of thing should be reported to the magistrate, but who that is with my brother gone, I don't know."

"People are accusing you," she said.

"Of course they are. That is exactly what I meant. Can you bear it?"

"Vicious gossip is best ignored!" she said, her determined chin jutting up. She may be young, but her backbone and character rivaled anyone's.

"What else did your uncle say?" For a man in a hurry to marry her off, the old man certainly tried to sow seeds of doubt.

"He told me to ask you about the duke, but I already know the duke is alive and well somewhere, and I heard Eustace create rumors to the contrary out of thin air myself." Mia's direct gaze gave him confidence. "Did the duke really send you here?"

"He did, over my objections. He wishes me to be well acquainted with the duchy."

"It is part of your heritage, too, is it not?" she asked innocently.

The complication of illegitimacy and an invalid inheritance was another subject too convoluted for this conversation, though he ought to explain it to her before they married. There would be time later. "You know my father called me a bastard."

She shook her head impatiently. "Such an ugly word. It says more about your parents than about you."

If he had been seeking a wife, she was the sort of woman, one who matched beauty with strength and intelligence, that he might have sought. He dismissed the seventeen-year age difference. Other successful marriages flourished in spite of such a gap. He captured her other hand and gave them both a tug. "In that case, Miss Euphemia Selwyn, I believe we will do well together. Would you do me the great honor of marrying me?"

They sat opposite each other, hands clasped between their knees, leaning forward so they were within inches of each other.

She studied his face as if she might find the secret to the meaning of life there. Perhaps she could. "But this is being forced on you," she whispered.

"Do I strike you as a man who allows himself to be forced to do something he doesn't choose to do?"

Her sweet lips spread in a smile. "I think not."

"I would have your answer, Miss Selwyn."

"Yes," she breathed. "I'll marry you."

A surge of joy startled him, but it felt right. "May I kiss you?"

Her eyes widened, and he feared she would deny him, but the lids drifted shut as she leaned closer to receive him. His mouth touched hers in a gentle salute, one he found wholly inadequate. He stood, bringing her to her feet with him, and kissed her again, gently at first. He leaned back, searched her eyes for denial, and kissed her yet again, taking her mouth with fierce possession.

Mine, he thought, *from this moment on.*

CHAPTER NINETEEN

"MRS. MORRIT SAYS you must rest as much as you like, but that other Miss Selwyn is demanding that you come, and Mr. Kendrick keeps asking after you," Mercy said.

Mia sat up in bed with a tray in front of her and gave free rein to her suddenly ravenous hunger. She glanced around the strange room Gideon had insisted she needed if she was to get enough sleep. It wasn't as large as the one she'd shared with Selina but much better than the tiny one they'd first been given. She'd been too tired the night before to argue or take in details.

The confrontation with her uncle had left her drained and weak at the knees. Only Gideon's hand at her elbow and, once, around her waist gave her strength. The entire episode felt unreal, yet she knew it had happened. She was to marry Gideon Kendrick. She'd said yes and then—that kiss! She filled with heat at the memory of his mouth, hot and searching, on hers. It had been… Overwhelming. Engulfing. Wonderful. It had been wonderful. He'd gazed at her as if he'd expected her to be shocked afterward. The only shocking thing had been her reaction. She hadn't wanted him to stop.

"Right unhappy is your cousin." Mercy puttered about, hanging clothes in the press and folding personal linens. She'd fetched them from the sickroom soon after she'd arrived with the breakfast tray.

A change would have been enough. I'll go back to Selina today, won't I? "I'll go to her directly," Mia said.

"Mr. Kendrick may want to see you first. I almost forgot," the maid said. She reached into a pocket sewn in her skirt and handed a crumpled piece of paper to Mia.

Mia examined the message and glanced at Mercy, who tried to appear innocent. Mia was more surprised the girl could read than that she had snooped.

"I'm pleased you are able to sleep in peace. I beg leave to speak with you as soon as you awaken. Gideon."

Gideon. My fiancé.

She sipped her chocolate and tried to sort her feelings about what had happened. Relief, certainly. Uncle could have done much worse. Humiliation at being forced on a good man who had done her no harm. Even more humiliation over Uncle's insistence she had no dowry. Other feelings gnawed at her belly. Not fear. He'd never hurt her. Worry, perhaps. Uncertainty about many things. She could manage a house, but would his children accept her? He didn't love her, and she wasn't the wife of his choice. Would he come to resent her?

He wants to speak to me. Has he changed his mind?

Mercy watched her avidly. Storing up tidbits of gossip, no doubt. Fodder for talk below stairs.

"Help me dress quickly. When we're finished, notify Mr. Kendrick that I will meet him in the…library. In the library," she said.

Mercy suggested her green morning gown, an excellent choice, one she believed flattered her. The maid had little skill with hair, however. Mia managed to coax her hair into a nest of braids at her nape with a bit of help from the girl.

"Now off with you to let Mr. Kendrick know I'm up. Do you remember what to tell him?"

"Y'll meet him in the library."

"Correct! I should be there shortly, once I've confirmed my cousin's care."

Mercy paused in the doorway, blocking Mia's exit. "But, Miss, he wants to see you right away. Him being your betrothed and all! Old Mrs. Morrit has one of the upstairs maids with that cousin of yours."

An unaccustomed confusion muddled Mia. Care for Selina had absorbed her for days. Was her first duty now to the man she was to marry? Whatever the answer, it wasn't Mercy's place to point it out. She raised her chin and said, "Just do as you're told. Tell him I'll meet him in the library shortly. Only that."

She swept forward, forcing Mercy to move, and on down the hall. She had to pass Selina's room. *It won't hurt to peek in, briefly, will it? Just to be sure all is well.*

Her feet slowed. She realized with sudden honesty that she was reluctant to face Gideon. What had passed between them was still too raw, her uncertainties too many. And that kiss! She both worried he'd do it again and feared he wouldn't.

She shook off her confusion. *Stop being a ninny, Mia!* She found Selina's door open and peered in, and the breath left her body.

Gideon sat in the chair beside the bed, bathed in light from the window, a book in his hands. Her heart skipped a beat.

AS THE DAY had gone on and Mia hadn't sent word, Gideon had grown anxious. Now she suddenly appeared, looking like a frightened deer and lovelier than ever.

He rose so quickly he dropped the book he'd been reading to her cousin. "Mia, you're here."

Stating the obvious, nodcock? What will she think of you? He scrambled to pick up the book, hardly taking his eyes from Mia.

"Fee! At last. I can't imagine where you've been. You never sleep the day away. If Mr. Kendrick hadn't come, I'd have perished of boredom. As it is, Papa will disapprove of his being here. Even if he is betrothed to my cousin and there is a maid to lend me consequence." Selina rose on one elbow and rattled on behind Gideon.

Her words washed over him while he filled his senses with the sight of Mia, rested and refreshed, clad in a green gown that caressed her curves in ways that would give any man ideas. She gazed back at him, uncertain and dazed.

"Don't stand there, Fee. Now you're here, you can help me brush my hair and—" Selina continued to prattle, paying no attention to Mia's nervous expression.

Mia approached and stood at his side, giving him a whiff of something earthy. Lavender, perhaps. "You seem better, Selina," she said.

"Well, I'm not," her cousin whined. "I'm weak as a kitten and can't do for myself. There's no one here to help me save this maid—who knows naught about serving a lady." She sank down on her pillow and glowered at them.

"Alas, Miss Selwyn, my betrothed and I have much to discuss, as you can imagine," Gideon said.

"I can't think what. It isn't as if you have some grand wedding to plan. Papa said you best marry quickly." Selina glared at Gideon.

The pinched expression on Mia's face in reaction to that bold statement infuriated him. He struggled not the lash out at the spoiled cousin.

Mia sank to the chair and spoke softly. "Dr. Standish said you are to rest for another week. You must do as he says, if you want to recover enough to come down to dinner with Mr. Tavernash. Sleep today. Tomorrow we'll wash your hair and get you into the chair for a while."

Mention of Tavernash distracted the chit. Mia stood back up before her cousin could spit out another complaint. She took Gideon's arm and let him lead her from the room.

"Kerr left me, and now you will, too," Selina cried from the bed.

Mia wobbled a step at those words but didn't turn around. She didn't speak as he closed the door; neither did she look at him. He put his knuckle under her chin and lifted her face to his. "Are you afraid of me, Mia?"

"No. Never," she said vehemently, gazing at him directly for a moment before her eyes darted away. "It is just…change. Too much, so little time to do it." She returned her gaze to his, pleading for understanding.

Her entire life was being upended. He would at least return to his familiar home when this was done. This woman—this very young woman—would leave everything she knew. "Would you like to visit Hector?" he asked.

Pure joy rewarded him. "Above all things, but—"

"No 'but.' We can talk while we walk. Gather your cloak and bonnet. I'll meet you downstairs by the estate offices. A footman can direct you there."

His own hat and coat hung in his office. He found Marshall and Jem in conversation when he made his way there. An odd glance passed between them, and Jem departed with a bow. Gideon watched him go and turned to find Marshall studying him, his posture rigid as if bracing himself for a blow.

"How is your audit coming? You've said nary a word," Marshall said.

He responded with the bald truth. "I found the first seven sloppy. Your writing is difficult to decipher, and the numbers are sometimes off but never by much. More careless than fraudulent. I began with the ledgers from nine years ago. I'm working forward and just started the books from three years ago. It is more of the same."

Marshall squirmed a bit. "Let me know if you have questions," he muttered.

Gideon hadn't lied about the 1815 ledger. The first pages were more of what he had been seeing. However, a month into it, a different hand had taken over, one that was tidy, neat, and invariably correct. Odd, that. Gideon wasn't ready to confront

Marshall, but the books had obviously been turned over to someone else—probably Jem. He needed time to study them more carefully.

"You have company," Marshall said with an inclination of his head.

Gideon added promptness to his growing list of virtues in his future bride.

"May I offer my good wishes on your betrothal, Miss Selwyn," Marshall said.

"Thank you, Mr. Marshall. I'm not yet used to it," she said.

"Your uncle was rel—pleased with your announcement," Marshall said. "He tells me the wedding will be soon."

Relieved, no doubt. Anxious to give up all responsibility for her. "We have not yet settled on a day," Gideon said before retrieving his hat and coat.

The path that led from the manor to the stables passed through hedges and a few trees, providing some privacy.

"That is twice someone has announced we're to hurry our wedding. Perhaps we should settle that first. Is that what you want?" he asked.

"Is there a choice?" she asked.

"Always. It will be your wedding; you should decide. If marrying quickly is your choice, I could ride to London for a special license and be back in three days, and we could marry in private the hour I return. Or I could ride to Bristol and obtain a common license from the bishop there, and we could be married at Saint Peter in eight or nine days—two for travel and seven for the mandatory wait. But it will be less private. Or we could ask the vicar to call the banns, it being your home parish, and be married in three weeks." His own choice was to do it as soon as possible, removing her from Clavering's authority and his spoiled daughter's demands.

Walking at his side, she bit her lower lip, mulling over his words.

A young woman dreams of a fine wedding, not a rushed hole-and-

corner affair. "Would you prefer to take a few months to court properly?" he asked. "It would give you time to plan the wedding you want."

"There would be scandal if we did that," she replied.

"Perhaps." *No doubt.* "You would move back to Selwyn Court in that case." From what he'd heard of Selina's brother and his friends, he hated that idea.

"If we wait, you could bring your children here for the wedding. Would you want that?" she asked.

It was his turn to consider the possibilities. "I would like it but perhaps not enough to weigh against other considerations." He found that he wanted to take her under his protection—to make her his—as soon as it could be arranged. He paused in the privacy of the walkway and told her so.

"This marriage is being forced on you, Gideon. If you prefer to get it over with quickly, then that is what we will do," she said.

"I would rather keep you at Woodglen, frankly," he admitted. "The wedding itself matters little to me."

"Won't we live in Wales? How long do you plan to stay here?"

Good question. "I thought I would be here a month. It has taken much longer. Now there's this business of Lizzy Carter to consider. We need to get to the bottom of that. I'm not easy about the Tavernash pair camping out in my brother's house, either. There is more I need to share with you." He needed to examine those family papers.

She peered at him. "You mean to find Lizzy?"

"Someone must investigate it. She could be in danger, and rumor and innuendo won't fix it."

"I agree," she said fiercely. "Perhaps I can be a help to you. With all of it."

He rather liked the sound of that. They walked on toward the stables. "Gideon, one other thing."

"Yes, Mia?"

"Send for your children. You shouldn't be apart so long."

CHAPTER TWENTY

HECTOR AMBLED ALONG beside them as they walked arm in arm toward Woodglen's wood. Sun took the nip out of November's chill, and Gideon took heart that he and his soon-to-be wife were able to agree on the wedding as smoothly as they had. In the end, they'd decided on a common license and a wedding one week hence. That was soon enough, but it would give Mia some room to come to terms with the arrangement and to think about her gown and fripperies, things that mattered to a bride.

"Tell me about your family," he said. It seemed as good a place to start as any.

"There isn't much to tell. My father was Viscount Clavering's younger son. A bit of a scholar. Impractical and idealistic. He married my mother over his father's objections and his brother's stern disapproval. We were frequently out of funds, and Grandfather's assistance always came with a lecture on foolish young men."

"Why did they object?" Gideon asked.

"My mother's family were dissenters. Her father, Amos Hodge, was a chapel preacher, Methodist of the radical sort. Bible and brimstone." She grinned. "I take my middle name from Grandmother Hodge. They are gone now."

"Except for the great-aunt."

"Except for Aunt Hortensia, yes. She sends me regular warnings about the dangers lurking in society and living in a viscount's house. Woodglen would give her apoplexy."

Gideon chuckled. "I sometimes feel the same."

"But you grew up here." She gazed up at him, confusion and no little compassion in her voice.

Perhaps the best place to introduce his complex heritage was the beginning. "I was born in South Carolina," he said.

Her eyes flew wide open at that. "You're an American?"

"I am, at least in part. My father was an officer in the king's army during the American rebellion. He was a grandson, and his father was a younger son. He didn't expect to inherit. He met my mother when they captured Charleston. Her name was Mary Jessop."

"Go on! Don't stop now."

"My maternal grandfather owned a small inn, more public house than hotel but respectable. During the occupation, British troops frequented it. He met her there." The words came slowly. It wasn't a story Gideon told often.

Her brows drew together, forming a deep line between them. "Did he… Did he take you with him when he left?"

"Hardly. I grew up in Grandfather's public house. My mother inherited it when he died. I cleaned floors, helped do dishes, and later, waited tables and learned to tally the take. Good business training, that."

"How old were you when you came here?" she asked.

"Twelve. When my mam died, her brother took the business and hurried me onto a boat with a letter for His Grace," he said. "I expected to discover my father was a groom at a ducal estate. Imagine my shock."

"He acknowledged you." It wasn't a question.

"Oddly, yes, if cursing the arrival of a son who spoke with a strange accent, had a twisted spine, and questioned authority is acknowledgment, then yes, he did," he said.

"How horrid for you, and you only a boy. I've heard the

names. Did they come from him?"

He nodded, giving her time to think.

"Yet he took you in. Guilt because he never married your mother?" Her innocent question churned up other issues he wasn't sure he was ready to address.

They had reached a path that led up to a ridge just above them. He knew from his time here before there would be a bench at the top. "Shall we take in the view?"

"Can you manage the climb?" she asked.

A brief smile came to his lips. "It isn't far, and I'm stronger than I appear to be."

"So I've noticed," she said. Hector barreled up the path ahead of them, stopping periodically to snuffle for rabbits.

The climb made conversation difficult and gave Gideon time to come to a decision. The bench stood where he remembered, and they sank onto it gratefully.

"Is the drop safe for Hector?" she asked, leaning forward to peer at it.

"The slope is more gradual than it appears. He'll manage." The great beast was happily exploring already.

Gideon put a hand to Mia's cheek. She blinked up at him expectantly. "I'm going to tell you some things about my birth. About the duke. Things you have a right to know as my future wife. What I tell you must be kept in absolute confidence. You must repeat it to no one. Not one person."

"I would never betray you," she murmured, meeting his direct gaze.

"The information might not hurt you and me, but it could do my brother harm." He had her absolute attention. "Most of my life, I accepted what the world believed. My father impregnated my mother and abandoned her in the way of some soldiers when the troops moved out. Some called me Mary's bastard boy. I just accepted that reality as long as I had Grandfather and Mam's love, though neither of them ever used that word. When she died and I discovered the army officer had become a duke, I was shocked.

That he found me cause for shame and disgust was my lot here at Woodglen. Then he sent me to his mines in Wales and told everyone I was dead. Phillip inherited, believing it."

Mia nodded solemnly. "All of Nether Abbas thought you were dead. But you said 'most.' You said 'most of your life.' What happened?"

"Not quite two years ago, my mother's brother turned up searching for me. He expected me to be Duke of Glenmoor. He was furious when he was shown in and found Phillip."

"How could he think that? Didn't he understand that only a legitimate heir can inherit?"

He gave her a moment to think about it, entranced by the emotions flitting across her face as she sorted it. She glanced up sharply. "He believed they were married!"

"He did. Isaiah Jessop was a vile man hoping to extort money. He stalked Phillip and my stepmother, Madelyn, then still the dowager duchess."

"Couldn't the duke have had him jailed or deported?"

"There's more. Remember, Phillip and Madelyn believed I was dead, but Madelyn, it turned out, had her own secrets. She had discovered the letter that had come with me from South Carolina. She hid it away and used it to blackmail the old duke."

"For her own safety, from what you've told me. What a horrid man your father was. You have much to forgive," she murmured.

"Forgive? Is that the Methodist forbears talking?" he said, genuinely startled by the word. It had certainly never occurred to him.

She nodded, studying her feet. "What was in the letter?" she asked.

"It said, 'Your wife is dead. I'm sending you your son.' The dating was enough to call into question the old duke's marriage to Phillip's mother. She left it alone. If I was dead, she thought, it didn't matter."

Mia stared out at the magnificent panorama of Dorset countryside for long moments. "But you aren't," she murmured. She gazed back at him. "And it means that you are his legitimate oldest son. Is that it? You're the true duke."

"Phillip is the duke. His title was confirmed on him by committee of Parliament, and they won't rescind it, but the ensuing scandal would be horrible. He is determined to make it right in the next generation, with the title falling to my son Daniel rather than any son of his," he said. "He's left documents with his solicitor laying it out." He grimaced.

"But how did you find out?" she asked.

"Madelyn knew my father to be a liar. My uncle's words reminded her of the letter. She decided she needed to unearth the truth about my fate, and Phillip joined her. Imagine the surprise when they found me alive, well, and prospering. The reunion was welcome. The letter was not."

Mia nodded, lost in thought. "You love your brother."

"I do. I always did. None of this is his fault—except for running away to lick his wounds and leaving me to manage." He gave her hand a squeeze. "The thing is, that letter is not proof. Phillip believes it, and my sire's determination to get the son he despised out of the way lends credence."

"Do you care?"

"I didn't think I did. But the thought of Felton Tavernash inheriting changed my mind. I've begun to search the family papers for proof one way or the other. Perhaps if I set Phillip's mind at ease, he'll come home and sire his own damned heir. Pardon my language."

"I can help. I'm good with papers. I helped Uncle Ludlow sort his," she said.

He raised her hand and kissed her knuckles through her glove. "A partner?"

She beamed at him. "I like that idea."

The need to kiss her drove out rational thought. He leaned forward until breaths mingled and her herbal scent sent waves of heat to his most precious parts.

Hector bounded up at that and plopped at her feet, gazing up expectantly and breaking the spell. She turned her attention to the beast's pleasure, leaving Gideon with frustrated longing, one thought in his mind. *Soon. We'll marry soon.*

They were quiet on the way back, exhausted from the flood of words that passed between them. As they approached the stables, she spoke.

"I know someone who will not be happy when this information surfaces," she said.

"Who?"

"Felton Tavernash."

GIDEON HAD DECIDED to ride into Bristol that very afternoon to consult with the bishop or archdeacon who could provide a common license. Once it was obtained, they would speak with the vicar and schedule use of the church. Mia smiled at him. "A week will do for me, I think. Marriage! I don't need any great show."

The shadows and smells of the stable, earthy and familiar, put Mia in mind of horse and hound. She went instinctively to Hannibal's stall, and the horse responded to the sound of her voice with a whinny and bright eyes.

"Sorry, old friend. I have nothing for you today. Next time I'll remember. For now, your master needs you," she said, soothing his neck.

A cry from the tack room broke into her reverie and sent her running while a string of curses fouled the air. She found Gideon in a rage and could see why. His beautiful custom saddle lay on the ground, in pieces.

"You, boy. What is your name?" he snarled at the youngest groom.

"I'm Bert. Yer funny gear must have fallen from the sawhorse, gov," the boy said, backing away.

"No fall caused this much destruction!" Gideon shouted. He knelt on the ground to examine the damage. "This thing cost me a fortune." Mia had never seen him shout before; cold authority had always been effective.

"Kin you use a regular saddle?" Bert asked.

Gideon ignored him. "How did this happen? No more nonsense about it simply falling."

"I dunno! Truly."

"Who was in here? Who had access to the tack room?" Gideon demanded.

"Frank and Peter are still in bed. Harv and I are the only ones. He and I were cleaning out stalls after."

"After what?"

"After that high and mighty who thinks he's a duke got saddled up for a hack out. Keeps us running, he does. Wouldn't have time to think about the tack room," the boy said.

Tavernash. Mia couldn't see him vandalizing Gideon's saddle. *Thinking it, yes. Bestirring himself to do it, no.*

"No one else was here in the past few hours?" Gideon asked.

Bert shrugged. "Marshall stops in. Jem came for coffee and left. Dint see anyone else. Who'd want to wreck your gear?"

"Good question," Gideon said. He glanced at Mia.

Another mystery to solve. "Can you and your friend Harv repair it?" she asked.

"Never saw the like, but Harv can fix most things."

She glanced up at Gideon, who stared at the ruins of his tack.

"There's a sovereign in it if he succeeds," he muttered. "For now, hitch the tilbury for me. I have an errand in Bristol."

Mia waited impatiently for Gideon to return; she spent her time entertaining her increasingly restive cousin. When she came down to breakfast two days after he'd left and found him there ahead of her, she felt both relief and delight, even more so because for once, there was no sign of Lady Tavernash.

"Success!" he said. "I'm going to visit the vicar this morning and arrange use of Saint Peter's for Friday next," he said.

"I'm coming with you," Mia said. Gideon glanced up and blinked. She went on. "We need to talk, and I can assure the vicar of my well-being. I should have considered it before," she said. He didn't argue.

This time, Bert hurried to do as he had been ordered and hitch the tilbury. The stable reminded Mia of the destruction of Gideon's gear, and they waited in a tense silence while Gideon fought to rein in his anger. They tooled out of the stable minutes later.

"I apologize for my temper the other day, Mia. I don't often lose control," Gideon said.

"I know that. I'm guessing the saddle was constructed to accommodate your back. Can it be replaced?" she asked.

"Not easily, but yes, it can be replaced. Pritchard would have—" He took a shivering breath. "It was Pritchard who created the first one, who gave me the confidence to ride even short distances."

She reached over and put her hand on his thigh, sorrow for his losses filling her. "I can't see what anyone gains from doing such a thing. Was it pure malice?"

"Perhaps, but why now? I might have expected it when I first came here—drive the monster out."

"What has changed?" Mia mused. She could think of nothing. Only one thing was clear to her. She was to marry this man. His sorrows were now her sorrows, his mysteries hers as well.

GIDEON KEPT HIS hands on the reins, though the warmth of her dainty hand on his thigh sent into his heated imagination a rush of other ideas of ways he could use his hands. It helped that his future wife brought a brilliant mind with her tempting body. He kept his eyes on the road as well, considering her question, her clever, very excellent question.

What has changed?

"We're betrothed," he said. "That's one change."

"Do they want to keep you from arranging the wedding? That doesn't make sense. Lady Tavernash's arrival?" she suggested.

"She's spiteful. I'll give you that. If they meant to harm me, though, they would have sabotaged it rather than destroying it," he said. Grim thought. His little bride-to-be didn't shrink from painful possibilities, though. "Perhaps I'm closing in on something in the finances."

"Or your family papers," she murmured.

"Only Marshall knows I'm investigating those."

"Still, why destroy something? That's an act of pure malice," she said.

He had no answers for her. He took the reins in his left hand and covered hers with his. "We'll just have to take care and watch."

She turned her hand over, entwined their fingers, and gave a squeeze. "'We.' I like that," she said.

God help him, so did he. *What have I gotten her into?*

CHAPTER TWENTY-ONE

MIA INSISTED ON spending mornings with her cousin the entire week, although Gideon knew it had to be tedious for her. He was left to puzzle on his own over the strange handwriting he'd discovered and some discrepancies that had appeared soon after. He looked forward to the day Mia's blasted cousin went home and he could take Mia up on her promise to help. Another set of eyes might help him make sense of it.

Lack of focus certainly made it difficult to work, his mind being on the wedding—more specifically the wedding night. Bedding a virgin would require care, but the more thought he gave it, the more his growing arousal made him worry he would be less careful than he should be. He had been without a woman for too long.

To his joy, Mia joined him for a walk every afternoon while her cousin napped. No more vandalism had occurred, and the darkness it had caused dissipated. At her insistence, he had sent for his children, though he warned her they couldn't possibly arrive on time for the wedding. Their conversation focused on the wedding or Mia's flood of questions about her future home. His comfort with this unanticipated decision to marry grew daily.

Evenings, they continued to take dinner in the formal dining room in spite of the repetitious diatribes from the Tavernash pair. A few harsh words from Gideon put a stop to Lady Tavernash's verbal darts aimed at Mia the night they announced their betrothal. To her credit and his pride, she kept her backbone straight and her chin up in the face of it.

When Selina, dressed and coifed, announced she was ready to join them two days before the wedding, he escorted both Selwyn ladies down. The Tavernash woman pointedly ignored both of them. Felton Tavernash, as was his habit, gave his food more attention than he gave anyone.

Climbing the stairs, leaning heavily on Gideon's arm, after dinner, Selina appeared both exhausted and disappointed. "He's old and fat," she whined. Mia's lips twitched, and he suspected she bit back a smug *I told you so.*

"I'll help you into bed, dear heart," Mia said to her cousin, taking her arm and letting Selina sag against her shoulder. She glanced at him, a gleam of promise in her eyes. He nodded. He would wait as he had every night when she bid the spoiled chit sleep well, eager for a good-night kiss. The intimacy of those kisses had grown daily, becoming longer, deeper, and more passionate every evening.

She took less time than he expected, coming to him breathless, with heat in her eyes that matched the warmth flooding him in anticipation. He took her hand, kissed her knuckles, and led her toward the room he had insisted she keep, the one she didn't have to share with her cousin.

"How was she?" he asked.

"Asleep as soon as I got her into bed."

"What did you decide about a gown?" he asked. She hadn't mentioned it in the afternoon, but he knew Selina had peppered her with comments earlier in the week.

"Selwyn Court sent over Selina's cerulean silk. With a bit of updating, it will do nicely. It flatters me, and Selina is positive it will harmonize nicely with the jonquil lustering she plans to wear."

She put a finger to his lips before he could object to Selina's self-centered interference. "It is a lovely dress, truly, and her determination that the Selwyn ladies make a good showing in spite of 'the taint of scandal' has given her incentive to heal. I'm confident she'll be able to stand up with me."

"I will buy you a new wardrobe as soon as we are married," Gideon said, kissing the convenient finger. He put an arm around her waist to bring her close. She rose to meet him in a tender kiss and then another. When he took possession of her lips, open-mouthed and hot, she didn't object. His breathing grew ragged as he kissed a line to her ear and down her chin, to her neck, driven mad by the way she leaned trustingly against him. His hand came up to cup her breast through her gown, and she stiffened, reminding him of her inexperience. And yet...

How can we go from a few chaste kisses to a pleasurable wedding night in one step?

She settled back against him and kissed his chin, an invitation if ever he'd had one. He took her mouth in his, this time moving farther to the modest decolletage of her gown. Did he dare unfasten it and pull it down?

"Mia..."

She peered up at him, eyes dark with passion, and her trust humbled him. He recalled belatedly that his young bride had no mother to confide in.

"Has anyone spoken to you about the marriage bed?"

She dropped her forehead to his chest.

He lifted her chin and forced her to meet his eyes. "Do you have any idea what will happen?"

"Only whispers. Some of it sounds unlikely."

He could imagine what she might have heard her cousin Eustace and his vile friends say. "Does it worry you?" he whispered.

She thought about that, his serious-minded bride. "A bit. I don't know what I'll be expected to do."

He kissed her tenderly. "No expectations. Let me lead, and do what feels comfortable. Tell me if you dislike anything."

He captured her mouth again and let passion swell. Certainly, carrying their lovemaking a bit farther wouldn't hurt. He reached behind her and opened the door to her room. *Just a bit more. Just for a brief—*

"Oh, miss! Oh, sir." The little maid, Mercy, dropped the nightgown she was folding across the bed and scurried to the door. Gideon and Mia jumped apart, and Mercy ran down the hall.

Mia clamped a hand over her mouth. He felt sick that he'd embarrassed and upset her, but when she dropped her hands, she was convulsed with silent laughter. "There goes the biggest gossip at Woodglen and in all of Nether Abbas," she choked out. She lay her head on his chest and laughed until he joined her.

"That's our lesson in indiscretion," he said with a grin. He gave her one more smacking kiss. "Until Friday, then."

HER WEDDING DAY dawned gray and stormy. It wasn't a good omen. Lady Tavernash had resumed her sniping attacks at dinner the night before after Gideon had been called to the stables to see to a problem with Hannibal. She'd waited up for him to come to her that night, but he had not.

Now she stood on the covered hexastyle at Woodglen's formal entry, dressed in a borrowed gown with a simple veiled bonnet, and watched the Selwyn carriage lumber up the road. Fillmore stood nearby with an umbrella, while Selina complained about her hair, the weather, the hour, and "that horrid mother of dear Tavernash." How he'd gone from "fat and old" to "dear" was beyond Mia at the moment. All of it was beyond her. She wanted to run back up to her room.

A footman jumped down and stood ready to open the carriage door. Selina stepped toward Fillmore, but the old gentleman surprised them both. "The bride goes first today of all days, Miss Selwyn," he announced. He walked Mia to the carriage and went back for Selina.

Uncle Ludlow, who sat in the rear-facing seat, greeted her with a stern expression. "Well, girl, you dragged your feet, but I'm glad to see you are prepared to do your duty."

Dragged my feet? It had been eight days since he'd given her a choice of marriage or exile to her great-aunt.

Selina climbed in fretting about the impact of rain on ladies' hair. Through the window, Mia was stunned to see Fillmore and his umbrella climb up to the box with as much dignity as the starchy butler could manage.

When they reached the church, she understood why. All of Nether Abbas appeared to have crowded into the church, eager no doubt for the sight of the independent Miss Selwyn wedding the Glenmoor bastard. These weren't well-wishers. They were gawkers hoping for spectacle.

She swallowed back bile, wishing the common license would have permitted a private ceremony at home. Fillmore stood at the door with his ever-present umbrella, holding out a hand. She didn't expect the sympathy in his eyes, but whether it rose from the attitude of the village or from her forced marriage to a man he continued to view as a colonial interloper—at best—she couldn't be sure.

Uncle Ludlow and Selina, who had gone before, met her in the back of the church. Fillmore closed his umbrella and made his way to a pew halfway down occupied by Marshall and Mrs. Morrit, who wore a plain gray gown—one Mia suspected was her Sunday best—and a sour expression. She was surprised to see Mrs. Demming, the Woodglen cook, next to them.

Every seat in the church was occupied, and people stood in the side aisles—villagers, servants from Selwyn Court, and others from Woodglen. She scanned the crowd with growing panic until Gideon stepped into the center aisle, his eyes fixed on her. She breathed in one shuddering breath, and peace settled over her. It was Gideon. All would be well.

CHAPTER TWENTY-TWO

C LAVERING SEEMED DETERMINED to fete every person of substance in Nether Abbas and surrounds—and some of no substance at all—as if to prove his family had nothing to hide. Gideon couldn't blame him, but he hated it just the same. Selwyn Court's dining room and central hall had been cleared of furniture to accommodate a crowd, and the wedding breakfast droned on while people nibbled dainty sandwiches and swilled punch served from trays by harried-looking footmen.

Gideon stood near the mantel in the front drawing room, forced to endure the greetings of the vicar, Hinson the grocer, a grim-faced Carter the blacksmith, Duger the balding apothecary and his skinny wife, several Selwyn Court tenants, and God help him, Adcock the stationer and Gratis, not one of whom had ever extended him courtesy before. He felt like the clown in a mime, all eyes watching to see if he made a fool of himself. He hated that Mia, standing at his side, had to hear sly innuendo and witness sidelong glances. Her cousin Eustace had been among the worst of them. Her grim expression left no doubt that she enjoyed it all as little as he did.

When at last the parade of spectators stopped, he took her hand in his, and they made their way through the throng in the hall, nodding to Marshall and Mrs. Morrit. Selina, long-faced at the failure of either Tavernash to put in an appearance, sat surrounded by local swains and left them alone. Clavering himself held court in a massive chair at the end of the dining room, telling all and sundry who would listen how proud he was that his niece had married the duke's brother. *The old hypocrite.*

With Mia's hand firmly in his, Gideon continued on into the servants' hall, drawing stares there as well but blessedly no comments. He walked her to a window. "The rain has not returned." They'd been grateful it had ceased before they'd left the church and were bundled into the Selwyn Court carriage. The brief ride had been their only time alone.

"So it has." She glanced up. "Dare we do it?"

His new bride was a quick one. "Why not?" he grinned.

She sent a young and obviously adoring footman to fetch cloaks, hat, and bonnet. The lad seemed eager to demonstrate stealth.

A dash to the stables and the services of a groom eager to get his own view of the notorious couple had Hannibal saddled in short order.

"You rode?" she gasped. "How did he get here?"

He lifted her to the great horse's back. "I had grooms bring him. I can manage short distances in a standard saddle. I didn't want to be at the mercy of either household's carriage, for this very reason," he grinned.

He heaved himself up behind her and wrapped her warm body against his. Hannibal had hardly left the stable yard when Gideon saw the French doors in the dining room open. "Shall we flee, Mrs. Kendrick?" he asked. He didn't wait for an answer. He urged Hannibal to a gallop.

Mia glanced up at Gideon. Her husband. As he walked toward the big house, his rolling gait was more pronounced than usual. She kept her pace to his, concerned about his back.

They had rushed to the stable at Selwyn Court like naughty schoolboys and galloped off on a laugh. Gideon hadn't been laughing when they had surprised the Woodglen grooms, but he hadn't asked for help dismounting. She was certain he'd winced when he lifted her down, but his swift kiss on the end of her nose had reassured her, and she didn't comment.

She longed to ask him if he was in pain, if he had overdone it, if he needed help. She did none of that, uncertain whether he would welcome it. She suspected not. The ways she might cause hurt were many; there was much she didn't know.

"Shall we take the servants' stairs? It will be faster," she said. *Also easier for him and more private.*

"Eager, Mrs. Kendrick?" he asked.

Her face heated. "I—That is, I assumed. I—oh, bother."

His wicked smile turned her insides to mush. He tugged her hand toward the servants' passage. When they passed the kitchen, he startled the lazing kitchen maid by requesting a cold collation. "Tea?" he asked, gazing at Mia.

She nodded. "Where?" she asked.

"My quarters, of course," he said.

"Of course," she whispered, her face even hotter.

Progress on the stairs was slow. He had wrenched his back; she was sure of it. She stopped. She'd held back long enough. "Gideon, would a hot bath help?"

She thought for a moment he wouldn't answer her. He sighed. "It would."

"I'll go back and order it. You continue on. I'll be right up." She didn't wait for an answer. She hurried to the kitchen and left firm instructions to bring a tub and hot water—hot not lukewarm. "We'll require a kettle and spirit lamp as well." It would enable them to heat their own tea in privacy. That they needed privacy, she had no doubt.

Breathless when she reached what she hoped was the correct floor in the family wing, she was relieved to see one door ajar. She peeked in to see Gideon standing by the window of a comfortably furnished sitting room.

"Shouldn't you be seated?" she asked.

"If I do that, I'll have to get myself up. I see your eyes darting around. Wouldn't you like to explore our quarters?"

Our! She did, but she couldn't hold back a skeptical frown. He ignored it.

The sitting room boasted an array of windows that let in light even on a day as dreary as this one was. A remarkable chiffonier, a small cabinet with inlaid wood in the Italian style, lay against one wall, a set of crystal glasses and a spectacular bouquet of flowers on top. Paintings of dogs and horses covered the walls as might be expected in a gentleman's room. Mia smiled.

"You like the paintings?" Gideon asked.

"I like animals. I prefer these to landscapes!"

The room also boasted a table with straight-backed chairs and two plush ones arranged by the hearth. Smaller nosegays of flowers had been placed on the table, the mantel, and the window seat. To the left of the hearth, there was a door. With a glance over her shoulder, Mia opened it to find a cozy bedroom holding a four-poster bed with a flowered coverlet. Flowers on the porcelain washing set matched it. Her own brush and mirror lay on a dainty vanity next to yet more flowers, and her trunk had been brought from her room. Even the book she'd been reading lay on the bedside table. Someone had gone to great care, but one thing worried her. "It is a bit small," she said.

He didn't ask her what she meant. "This is yours. My room is across the way."

Her unexpected rush of disappointment left her feeling foolish. She hung her cloak and bonnet on pegs by the door and crossed the sitting room to a door next to the chiffonier in a rush. It opened onto a very different bedroom with deep-blue hangings and heavy furniture, as masculine as the other was feminine. They each had a dressing room beyond. "It—It's very fine."

"The bed is larger." She hadn't heard him come up behind her. His breath, warm on her neck, sent shivers through her. Or perhaps his words did.

A scratch at the door presaged the arrival of their food, and he moved away. The maid laid a platter, two empty plates, two cups, and a bowl of sugar out on the table. A footman carried a tray with a kettle, a teapot, and the spirit lamp. Mia had him arrange it all on the chiffonier, moving the bouquet to the window seat. "Water is heating for your bath," the little maid said with a blush before curtseying out.

Mia discovered the teapot was already full and hot. She brought it to the table.

He gestured to the table. "Shall we eat while we wait? I know you didn't eat a bite at the wedding breakfast."

She sat and gazed up at him. When he grimaced while taking his seat, she stared at the platter to keep from commenting. "Cheese, ham, and fruit. Shall I pour?" Her hand was on the teapot.

"If you wish."

"Were you hoping for something stronger?"

He glanced at the chiffonier. "Probably."

He didn't try to rise when she went to the beautiful cabinet and opened the door on a selection of wine and spirits. She returned with a bottle of brandy and a crystal glass. She set them in front of him and poured herself tea. He had put a selection of foods on her plate, and her stomach clenched at the sight; she was certain she couldn't eat a bite.

"Are you well, Mia?"

"I'm sorry to be so nervous. It is just all so strange."

"And it came on you too fast. Have a bit of this; it may help." He tipped a tot of spirits into her tea. "Go on. Try it."

She took a sip, frowned, and added sugar. The next sip went down comfortably "Better. Good, in fact," she said.

"You don't need to be nervous around me, Mia. I won't hurt you."

Uncle and her father barked at mistakes. Would her husband treat her the same? "It's just that I don't know what is expected of me, or how to go on."

"Act however comes naturally. If you're uncertain, ask me whatever you like."

"There is one thing, Gideon. I don't mean to pry, but I need to know about your back. Did you injure it riding here?"

"Injure? No. The reason I have a custom saddle is that it enables me to sit upright without straining muscles. In a standard saddle, it takes all I have to keep from sliding to one side because my posture is uneven. The ride from Selwyn Court took more out of me than I expected, and I pulled a muscle in my back. Hot water—which you wisely ordered—should do the trick."

Mia swallowed and plucked up her courage. "How bad is your back? How did it happen?"

"I was born this way. It is a sharp curvature in my spine they call scoliosis. It is why my shoulders lean and why I walk the way I do."

"It is why your father scorned you."

"One of the reasons," he said tightly. He waved that away with one hand. "It has never hindered me from doing what needs to be done."

"I suspect you are too determined to let it, even if it ties you in knots." Her next question slipped out before she could stop. "May I see?" she breathed.

His gaze intensified. "You don't have to. I can—"

A commotion in the hall and a knock at the door cut his words short. Two footmen and Bert the groom came in with a copper tub and buckets of steaming water.

"Where do you want it, guv?" Bert asked.

"The dressing room," Gideon said.

"I'll show you." Mia rose and led them to his dressing room.

"More is coming!" Bert said cheerfully.

They stood at the door to his bedroom. As soon as the servants left to bring the rest of the water, Gideon turned to her. "Don't do that."

"Do what?"

"Leap up to fetch, show servants where to set things, or otherwise do for me what I'm perfectly capable of doing for myself."

Irritation made his words harsh. She had offended him. The tears that threatened would have made her humiliation complete, if she had allowed them. "I'm sorry. Is it not what a wife does? I simply don't know what is expected in marriage. I won't do it again."

He sucked in a breath. "Mia, I—" His shoulders sagged, and a gentle smile softened his expression. Her tension seeped away at the sight.

"Yes, you will," he said. "Helping people is what you do. And I will learn to let you. That is indeed how marriage works, each giving a bit."

The army of servants returned, filled the tub, and lingered to cast a few sly glances Gideon's way.

"That will be all, thank you," she said primly. "We'll ring if we need anything."

The door shut with a solid click. Mia felt Gideon's breath on the back of her neck, breathed in the scent of pine woods, and leaned back with a sigh.

"Well, Mrs. Kendrick, will you help me out of my clothes and into my bath?" His deep voice, close to her ear, rumbled through her. Was her galloping heart responding with panic or eager anticipation?

CHAPTER TWENTY-THREE

G IDEON REGRETTED HIS complaint as soon as it left his mouth. His young wife wished to help. Of course she did. Naturally she wished to see his back. *You've been alone too long.*

He turned her around to face him, took her hand, and entwined their fingers. "Come."

The tub, he saw through the door to the dressing room, took up most of that space. He paused by the bed, shrugged out of his coat, and loosened his cravat.

She hesitated, confusion in her brown eyes, before reaching up to unbutton his waistcoat. He laid it on the bed next to his coat, holding her eyes, hoping his expression appeared more encouraging than he felt.

"Your shirt?" she asked.

He nodded. This was the moment. He prayed she wasn't repulsed, waiting for her to take the initiative.

She tugged on his shirt, pulling it from his trousers, while he untied it at the neck. He started to lift it, but she got there first as if to spare him raising his arms. He slid it over his head and turned, giving her his back.

"Oh my," she breathed.

He shuddered when one finger touched the spot just below his neck and began to trace his spine.

She paused. "Does that hurt?"

"Not in the slightest." The little finger continued its trail down the curve of his backbone, to the spot where it disappeared beneath his trousers. He loosened his falls and let the trousers slip to his hips so she could finish her exploration all the way to the spot above the cleft in his buttocks. Her calm deliberation and her soft touch soothed his fears and inflamed him at the same time. By the time she finished, he was fully engorged, fully aroused. He needed to get a grip on his lust if he had any hope of giving her the gentle attention she deserved.

Before he could move or even speak, her mouth replaced her finger as she kissed across the worst of the curvature. His arousal increased, and he couldn't hold back a moan. "Mia…"

"Is it your shoulder muscles that hurt because of our ride?" She kneaded the places she meant. Gideon was beyond speech. Her hands moved down his side, and he could hear her murmuring to herself.

"Oh, tight here on the side, I can feel the knots. You have…a muscular back." She choked the words.

He longed to turn and read the expression on her face but couldn't bring himself to interrupt the touch of her hands.

She cleared her throat. "I can massage those sore muscles later. We need to get you into the bath," she said.

The tub. Yes, the tub.

He turned then, and her eyes dropped down, following the line of dark hair to the place just below his navel where his trousers caught on his hips and his swollen member. She couldn't help but see the bulge clearly visible even though the trousers had been loosened.

She glanced up at his face and back down.

"Mia—"

Before he could choke out words to comfort or reassure, she reached for the buttons on his fall and undid the rest of them. His trousers dropped to his knees. Mia stared at the erection she'd revealed.

"I—Goodness, Gideon." She glanced up, wide-eyed and rosy-cheeked.

He couldn't speak. He watched her swallow, her graceful neck moving with it.

She dropped her eyes again, moving across his chest and slowly down. "I had no idea. You are beautiful."

Her words staggered him, and his knees almost gave out. His twisted body had been called many things, but no one—not even Maera—had ever called him beautiful. He reached for her to steady himself, surely only that.

She took it as an invitation and went into his arms. "I've embarked on an adventure, haven't I?" she murmured, her words hot against the bare skin of his chest.

His hands caught in her hair, sending pins flying and her glorious honey-colored locks free before he crushed his mouth to hers.

Easy, Kendrick. Remember her innocence. He eased the kiss, tenderly nibbling her lips. When she responded in kind, he urged her open, reveling in the sense of her blossoming passion. It wasn't enough.

His fingers found the neckline of her gown, gently probing. He reached for the ties at the back and unfastened the first few.

She stepped back then, questions in her eyes.

"I need to see you, too," he said.

"But your bath?" He expected discomfort. What he saw was concern.

"The bath can wait." He kissed her tenderly. "Unless you want me to."

She turned her back. "I can't reach the ties."

He had them undone in a trice and untied her stays, tossing the blasted garment to a chair before turning her, now only in her chemise and stockings, to face him. He studied what he'd revealed before sitting on the bed and yanking off his boots and stockings so he could remove his trousers.

She took them from his hands and folded them, a sweet, wifely gesture that touched something deep in his soul. He kept himself under rigid control while he watched her take his clothing and her own to the chair. Then—joy beyond words—she came back to him, standing inches from his parted legs.

"Now what?" she whispered.

He reached down and took the hem of her chemise, sliding it over her legs, her hips, her breast until she raised her arms and he tossed it to the floor. His eyes burned into hers. "Now we get you ready to receive me."

She asked no questions, nor did she hesitate. When she walked into his arms, her trust humbled him. They stayed for a while, Gideon on the bed, Mia between his legs, her body against his, their mouths joined in exploration, his hands roaming across her back and bottom. She followed his lead, touching and exploring his shoulders, sides, and hips.

He loosened his embrace and smiled, studying her face for signs of distress and finding none. He kissed her again, this time below her ear, down her neck, and finally on the tops of her breasts. He took them in his hands then, gently kneading and caressing her nipples.

When her breathing became ragged and her hands restless, he put both hands beneath her rounded bottom and lifted her to the bed. He went up on his knees and laid her on her back.

"Gideon, what is it? You are looking at me so strangely. As if you're amazed."

"I'm in awe, Mia. You are so lovely. What did I do to deserve such a gift?"

"Gift," she whispered. "My gift to you and yours to me."

He touched her cheek with a trembling hand and moved with unhurried reverence, caressing every sensitive spot, touching her everywhere, down her body until he reached her most intimate places. When she opened for him without needing to be asked, he found her ready, to his delight.

He gazed back up to find her eyes closed, her breathing coming rapidly. As if she felt his gaze, she opened her eyes to peer back at him. "This is splendid, Gideon. You are splendid."

That almost undid him. "There's more," he said.

She laughed. "I know. Now. Please." She reached over to touch his erection, but he caught her hand, fearful he would come too soon.

"Next time, Mia. Next time you explore." He hurried to obey her insistent command to take her now, and the adventure she sought began in earnest.

The bath was forgotten.

MIA CAME AWAKE slowly the morning after her wedding. Warmth and peace filled her as they hadn't in days—perhaps ever. A smile grew as memory returned slowly and with it, joy. She opened her eyes to strange bedcovers. Gideon's bed. But where was he? She rolled over and buried her head in the empty pillow next to hers, breathing in something earthy, faintly redolent of the out of doors, utterly Gideon. The undertones brought more memories, and her face heated. Adventure indeed. It had lasted much of the night.

She slipped from the bed and searched about for her chemise. She found it over a chair, and a very masculine wrapper next to it. She put on the chemise and bundled herself into the wrapper before opening the door to the sitting room.

Mia found Gideon sitting at the table in his shirtsleeves and frowning over papers and the content of an open box. At the sound of her, he stood, and a warm smile transformed his features into a picture of welcome and happy anticipation. This was the man who had led her to places unknown the night before, the one who had left her feeling cherished and safe.

He opened his arms, and she ran into them. "Good morning, wife. How do you feel?"

Loved. "Well cared for," she said.

He touched her face tenderly. "Good. I want that for you

always." His kiss was tender as well and his hold gentle, as though he worried she might break. She ran her hands up his back, feeling the now familiar lines and ripples through his fine lawn shirt.

He stood away, retaining one hand. "I'll ring for breakfast. In the meantime, I believe the tea is still hot," he said, indicating the pot under its cozy on the Italian chiffonier. He urged her to sit, and put action to words.

He handed her tea and straightened the papers. She reached over and lay a hand on his to stop him. "What are you doing?"

"This box is from the family archives."

She pulled her hand back and glanced at the side of the box. "Seventeen hundred and eighty to seventeen hundred and ninety? That covers the year of your birth, doesn't it? Have you found anything?"

"Not yet."

"You were frowning when I came in. Something made you unhappy," she said.

He grunted and scooped the papers up again.

"Wait, do you have them in order?"

"No, it doesn't matter. Things are simply tossed in here. It can be organized later. I was frowning, dear wife, because someone has been in here," he said.

"You think your brother already went through it?" she asked.

"Probably, even likely, but not this week. I can't be certain, but it appears that someone has been in here since I brought it up."

Her mouth fell open. She recovered from the unladylike reaction immediately. "Who would do that—and why?"

Gideon leaned over and kissed her nose. "You ask excellent questions, do you know that? Drink your tea, and we'll talk," he said. He put all the papers in the box and placed it on the window seat.

Their conversation was interrupted by the servants with breakfast. "They must have been waiting for us," she said.

Platters of coddled eggs, toast, and roasted ham were accompanied by berry scones and ginger biscuits. Gideon, delighted his new wife shared his tastes, sent the plate of kippers back. Pots of coffee and fresh tea completed the feast. "Marriage to you has enriched me already," he murmured.

"How so?" she demanded.

"Woodglen's kitchens aren't this generous with me, or at least, they weren't before." He grinned.

"Me, either. Perhaps it's the wedding. We certainly entertained them all," she said.

He rolled his eyes and confided his feeling the day before of being a clown on stage. She agreed and began, with an impish grin, to imitate some of the most intrusive guests. Breakfast passed with laughter and sharing.

"What shall we do today?" she asked, heat coming up at the possibilities.

An answering heat blazed in his eyes. "I thought I would go work in the estate office. The sooner I get to the bottom of what I came to do, the sooner we can go home."

At "office," her heart fell, and she couldn't keep the disappointment from her expression.

He peered at her earnestly. "I adore your eagerness for the marriage bed, Mia, but last night was your first, and I came to you twice. Can you tell me you aren't sore?"

"I—Well, perhaps. A little."

"I'm glad it is little. It will pass, but a day to heal will make the next time better," he said, rising.

Next time… "How can it be better?"

He chuckled. "I anticipate exploring all the ways with you. For now, let's get people up here for these dishes and request fresh bathwater for you."

"That does sound lovely," she said. "But do you have to go?"

He hesitated a moment. "If I stay, I won't be able to keep my hands off you. I'm determined to give you today."

She studied her toes beneath his wrapper. "In that case, I'll work, too. I'll sort those papers."

"Sort?"

"I'll put them in a sensible order," she said. "We'll organize it in such a way we can tell if someone disturbs it."

"You, my dear, are a treasure beyond pearls," he said, kissing the top of her head.

CHAPTER TWENTY-FOUR

W HO WOULD HAVE *an interest in the papers? Marshall? Hard to see why. Tavernash, perhaps. It is difficult to envision him bestirring himself from his smug beliefs. Who, then?*

Gideon had no idea. It was one more mystery. His battered saddle. Ledgers that didn't add up. The blacksmith's missing daughter.

He passed Jem coming from the estate offices. He did that far too often for Gideon's taste. His presence there was another mystery. The would-be valet inclined his head. "Am I needed upstairs? I thought you wouldn't require me for a spell." His speculative expression, Jem obviously wondering what a newly wedded man was doing coming to the office the day after the ceremony, irritated Gideon.

"I'll leave my boots in the hall for you after supper," Gideon said. "We'll see about tomorrow." He didn't want the man anywhere near Mia, a complication of marriage he hadn't anticipated. He didn't want him near the box of family papers, either.

"Allow me to add my congratulations, sir. I hope all was in order when you returned from the wedding breakfast yesterday," Jem said. Gideon couldn't say what lurked in Jem's eyes that bothered him, but something did. He let the man pass.

One more damned mystery. He paused in his tracks. Of them

all, the disappearance of Lizzy Carter must be the most important, more than the never-ending ledgers waiting for him. The blacksmith had cornered him about the girl in the middle of his wedding breakfast.

"Who's gonna do something with the duke in charge and him gone?" Carter had demanded. "Does anyone up at that big house give a damn about my girl?" His voice had grown harsh until the vicar had intervened.

Who indeed? Gideon thought. *No one, if I don't.* He knew little enough. He would have to go into Nether Abbas and face the gossips to ask questions, but that was too much for today.

The one thing he knew was that the girl had been on her way to the Woodglen dairy. The dairy lay southwest of the manor, behind a stand of trees that separated pasture land from the artificial lake and landscaped grounds of the manor, two miles or so above the village. She'd have taken the walking path that led to Nether Abbas. He ought to examine her route and question the dairy maids. He walked right on past his office and the pile of ledgers waiting for him. He could do that last part, at least.

Getting there would be easier if his tack had been fixed. He walked the quarter mile to the stables, hoping it was so. He'd gone a quarter mile in the opposite direction if not.

He found Marshall leaning against the hay bin, chatting with Bert and Frank.

"Good morning, gentlemen," Gideon said.

The three of them glanced up, and brows rose. More speculative glances, whispers, and a nudge between Frank and Bert.

Gideon sighed and gave a wry grin. "The lady deserves her rest, I fear." That put speculation to an end and earned him respect with the younger ones, at least.

"Feeling better, Frank?" Gideon asked. At the sound of his voice, Hector loped over for a pat.

"Summut." Frank grinned. "Peter's still malingering."

"Bert and Harv are glad to have them back, I can tell you," Marshall said. The steward always seemed more at home in the stables than he did in his office.

"Where's Harv? He agreed to fix my saddle," Gideon said, gazing pointedly at Marshall.

"Just finishing it, as it happens." Marshall followed him to the tack room, and Bert trailed along. So did Mia's dog.

"Pity about that," Marshall said.

"It is that," Harv said, glancing up and inclining his head to Gideon. "Beautiful piece of work, this was. Is again, if I do say so."

Gideon breathed a sigh of relief. If he hadn't seen it in pieces, he wouldn't have known it was damaged.

"Luckily the vandal kept the bigger pieces intact. I couldn't have done much if the fancy leatherwork was wrecked," Harv said, running his hand against the fine-tooled leaves and flowers along the back piece. Similar decoration went along the sides.

"I can't think why anyone would do this," Marshall said.

"Someone wants me to know I'm unwelcome," Gideon replied. All the while, he examined the work, seeing nothing to complain about.

"If they knew you, they'd know you don't back down easily," Marshall said with a shrewd grin. "It doesn't make sense to me."

"He raked us all over the coals about it," Bert added, nodding toward Marshall, "even Frank and Peter, as if they would climb down and get into mischief. None of us saw anything."

Marshall shook his head. "I can't think who in the village would come all this way just to tear something up, even if, begging your pardon, they don't like you much down there."

Their eyes met. *Who did that leave?* Tavernash had neither motive nor capability, and Gideon was sure Marshall thought the same. As to Marshall himself, why eliminate other suspects if he had reason to deflect blame?

"At least I have it back," Gideon said. He reached in an inside coat pocket, took out a sovereign, and flipped it to Harv, who caught it in the air. "As promised," he said, rubbing his hands along the saddle and giving a firm tug on the back. It held fast.

"Gawl, Harv. Teach me how to do leather work," Bert said. "Want I should saddle that great beast of yours, Mr. Kendrick?"

A short time later, Gideon stood at the stable door with Marshall, Hector content at their feet, while Bert led Hannibal out.

"You're nothing like what they said," Marshall said.

Gideon hoisted himself into the saddle with one mighty heave. "I never was," he said, taking the reins.

Bert shook his head as if the sight continued to amaze him. "On that horse, you look different, begging your pardon, Mr. Kendrick. You don't limp."

"That I don't," Gideon said with a chuckle. *On horseback, I'm almost normal.*

Marshall gazed at him curiously. "Where are you off to, today of all days?" The faces of the grooms added their own curiosity.

Gideon grinned. "To the dairy," he said. Marshall's knowing gaze gave him pause.

"Might be interesting," the steward said. "Come see me when you get a chance."

Gideon nodded. "Come, Hector!" On horseback, with the dog loping along beside, he reached the dairy in twenty minutes.

The dairymaids were between milkings, working in the cheese room.

Mrs. Millbrook came over to greet him. "Did Marshall send you over to fetch my monthly report? It's on my desk."

He let her believe that. "I'll take it to him," he said. He followed her out past the milking room to a small desk in the corner. Pen and ink had been placed against the wall and a neat stack of paper in the corner. She picked up the report and handed it over.

He glanced at the neat writing and tiny column of numbers and had to respect the woman. Literacy wasn't as common as it should be, and in her case, it enhanced her value to the estate.

"Thank you, ma'am. I'll see that it gets delivered."

She studied him cautiously. "Will there be anything else?"

"Being here reminded me of something. What do you know

about Lizzy Carter?"

Her gaze intensified. "Some folks think you took her."

"Some folks think any number of untrue things about me, Mrs. Millbrook. I didn't take you for one of them," he said steadily. "Did she come here often?"

The woman's posture unbent a fraction. "More than she needed to. I think she came to get away from that father of hers. She claimed she hoped to be hired on, but she was too young and flighty."

"My wife described her as a sweet, decent girl," he said. "Why would she want to get away from her father? He seems devastated by her going missing."

"Decent enough girl but worn to the bone. Bill Carter hates to lose a free cook and housemaid since his wife died. Carter's a mean drunk, and I don't doubt Lizzy caught some of his temper."

"She never made it here the day she went missing?" he asked.

"Carter came roaring up at about dusk, demanding to know why his dinner wasn't on the table. I told him she never came, but he charged through the whole place, searching for her. He even stormed into the girls' dormitory like she'd be hiding under the bed," Mrs. Millbrook said.

"It sounds like he suspected she ran away," he mused.

"That it did." She pursed her lips in distaste.

"Did he report it to anyone?"

"A magistrate, you mean? With the duke gone, nearest one is the next shire. Viscount Clavering has no interest in such things."

He got no more information out of her. A male friend was unlikely. Public coaches didn't stop in Nether Abbas.

He left Hector in the stables, and his steps picked up the pace on his way to the manor. He had a wife waiting for him in his rooms. He couldn't keep from smiling.

MIA LEANED OVER the table, trying to concentrate on the papers in front of her. Her bath that morning had been heavenly, once the army of footmen had managed to empty and fill the tub. Mia had hidden in the other bedroom—her room—watching Mercy pretend to hang her clothes while talking a mile a minute, fishing for gossip. Mia confined her responses to monosyllables and orders regarding the clothing. She'd chased them all out and sank against the wall, reveling in blessed silence, before adding her own special lavender soap to the water and settling in for a long soak.

She had lingered in the tub, reliving the night before and growing hot from both the water and her memories, lost in a dream world, wishing Gideon hadn't left. Eventually reality had returned in the form of cooling water.

Now she worked her way through the box of what Gideon described as family papers and that proved to be a jumble of contracts, receipts, letters, and other odd bits. After fits and starts of various ways of dealing with it, she settled on date order.

She withdrew a receipt for boots. London, 1783. She placed it in that year's pile. Next she picked up an order with specifications for a new carriage in 1785. She squinted at a scribbled note on the bottom: *delivery rejected, Glenmoor.* She put it there. A vellum packet bearing a heavy seal came next. *Letter Patent...* She opened it, taking care not to damage the elaborate broken seal and read.

> *...do hereby acknowledge Randolph Tavernash, Duke of Glenmoor, and do confer on him the rank, style, title, and privileges of that estate. And We do affirm his sole and exclusive right to bear the following Arms by Letters Patent, to wit...*

She scanned to the bottom quickly. The signature belonged to His Majesty, George III, and it was dated April 10, 1785. This, she thought, was why there was a family archive, not some piddly boot receipt! There must be one for the current duke, but that would be in a different box.

She set the letter patent aside, wondering what other treasures she might find. Did Gideon expect to locate a document like the patent? Probably. Her mind pictured him sitting across from her, going over the papers. She pictured him doing other things, too.

The door clicked open, and there he stood as if she'd summoned him with a mere thought, and her face heated. She rose to her feet and took two steps, realizing some worry or frustration marred his face.

"What's wrong? You're early," she said.

His gentle smile relieved her. "I needed to see my new wife," he said.

When he started forward, she dashed up, about to throw herself at the poor man, but she stopped, suddenly shy. "I'm glad. I was thinking about you."

He reached out and touched her cheek, and she went into his arms, delighted when he kissed the top of her head. "What's all this, then?" he asked. She followed his line of sight to the piles on the table.

"Sorting! Everything is in a jumble. But I found a treasure. Come and see." She tugged him by the hand.

Gideon applauded her methods and took his time reading the patent. "I was four years old and already sweeping in my grandfather's tavern when that was issued," he said. "Anything else of interest?"

"Not yet, but a timeline may help. If you were born in 1781, we may need to go back a few years. We may need the other box," she said.

"Well done. I'll see to it another table is brought up so we have a place to eat." He sobered suddenly. "We may want to eat downstairs, though."

"Eventually, I suspect. Is that what you prefer?"

He smiled ruefully. "I rather prefer our private meals. But if you aren't seen below stairs, rumors may start that I've done you in."

She made a rude noise. "Mercy was up here half the morning

fishing for gossip. She'll know I'm perfectly fine."

He took her by the hand to the settee by the window and drew her into his lap. "That's better. We need to hire a maid for you. Someone with no loyalties in this house. We may have to send to London," he mused, stroking her hair.

"Pishposh. I can do for myself. I did most of the time anyway while Kerr made herself busy with my cousin. You don't have a valet, do you?"

He told her about Jem and his suspicions. "The whole situation is odd."

"You think he's diddling the books?"

"I've begun to think he's the actual bookkeeper. It would help if I could get a sample of his handwriting. If he is, he's stealing. Small discrepancies started eight months after the ledger entries changed to a new hand."

"If he works for Marshall, why isn't Marshall catching it?"

"That's another odd thing. I brought Mrs. Millbrook's report from the dairy. I asked him what he thought of it, and he made some vague comment about her being efficient. I'm sure he didn't read it, and that isn't the first time. I've begun to wonder if he just can't read."

"A steward that can't read would be a problem. He'd want to hide that. He's certainly intelligent enough. I wonder...," Mia mused.

He moved his head to peer down at her. "You wonder what?"

"There was a man like that in Yorkshire, a friend of my father. He had a successful business, could hold his own in any conversation, and yet could not read. My father was convinced something prevented it. Papa admired him. He told me he coped by having his son read everything for him—that, and he had a prodigious memory. Marshall may have the same problem." Something he'd said struck her. "What were you doing with the dairy's report?"

"She assumed I'd come for it, and I allowed her to think it. I actually rode over to ask about Lizzy Carter. Hector trotted along with me, by the way. He seems to be thriving."

"What did you learn?"

"Not much." He repeated everything Mrs. Millbrook had told him.

"I can see that she might want to get away from her father. I don't see her going off with a man, however. I wonder if she thought she could find employment in a larger town, the foolish mite."

"Would you mind riding over to the village with me tomorrow?" he asked.

"So that they know I still have all my body parts?" she teased, inhaling deeply. He smelled of horse and effort but also of pine forest and the out of doors.

"That. But mostly to see what people know about Bill Carter."

She rubbed her nose on his neck, enjoying the scent of him. He kissed her then, a soft, possessive kiss that heated quickly.

"I think we'll stay private here for one more evening. What do you think?" he asked against her ear.

She didn't respond. She was too busy kissing the spot above his neckcloth.

CHAPTER TWENTY-FIVE

AS IT TURNED out, it was well after breakfast on the third day after the wedding when they decided to ride into Nether Abbas. They didn't leave their suite the night after Gideon returned from his visit to the dairy, or the following day, either. The box of family papers lay forgotten on the table where it had been when Mia opened it—there being much more pleasurable pursuits to be had for a newly married pair. They made do with trays by the fire—or in bed. That suited Mia down to her toes. Days had been growing colder, their bed warmer.

"Do you suppose we scandalized the grooms?" Mia asked with a sidelong glance at Gideon. She rode a sweet little mare named Buttercup, one she was pleased to find lively for her age. Marshall had dredged up an ancient sidesaddle when she'd asked for one.

"I hope so. A flood of gossip about how sweetly you blush when I make suggestive remarks might counteract the other kind," he answered.

"In that case, we'll have to continue to tease in Nether Abbas. Perhaps I can make you blush instead," she retorted, drawing an affectionate chuckle.

She could almost feel the eyes on the back of her neck when they rode into the village and stopped in front of the apothecary, a store she knew to be a hotbed of village gossip. "Odd, I know," she had explained to her husband, "but Mrs. Duger is the sister of the wife of the green grocer and the linen goods owner. They're the central pipeline for talk."

Gideon had pointed out that the Cockcrow also seethed with talk. She didn't dispute that but had insisted that in the end, it was the ladies' opinions that mattered, and the ladies were more likely full of intelligence about Lizzy Carter.

"Good morning, Mrs. Duger," she chirped when the entered the store. "I hope you have that French lavender I so adore. After days of nursing my cousin and…other things, my supply has quite evaporated." She let "other things" hang in the air. Mia felt so totally loved she wondered if she actually glowed. She smiled expectantly.

Mrs. Duger, a pinched, wiry sort of woman, blinked, her eyes darting between Mia and Gideon.

Cataloging juicy tidbits to spread, no doubt, Mia thought. Of Mr. Duger there was no sign, but then, there never was. Mia assumed he sat at his usual table at the Cockcrow. Uncle Ludlow had told her the husband was the chemist who elevated Evelyn Duger's little herbal business to the glorified name of apothecary when he'd married her, one more sign of the sad state of professional medicine in Nether Abbas.

"Right away, Miss Selwyn, or should I say, Mrs. Kendrick. And may I co…" She reached up for a jar of lavender, hesitating over her words. "…congratulate you over your marriage." Mia guessed "commiserate" was her original intention.

"Thank you, Mrs. Duger. Was ever a bride so lucky?" Mia asked, smiling soulfully up at her husband, who played his part by feigning a besotted expression. At least, she assumed it was feigned. After yesterday she wasn't sure.

"Would you like something with that? I have some fine lavender cream today," the woman said.

"Do you have soaps as well?" Mia asked. Soon they had a whole array of goods on the counter, different scents, multiple herbs, and some woodsy products. Studying them with every sign of absorption, Mia casually said, "The talk of Lizzy Carter's disappearance devastated me. How could such a girl simply vanish? Is there any news?" She glanced up at Mrs. Duger innocently.

Duger glanced at Gideon and back at Mia. "Rumors, yes, but no news. Someone said they saw her in Shaftsbury, but that has to be nonsense. How'd a chit that size walk there?"

"It sounds like she was a sweet, innocent girl." Gideon spoke for the first time, injecting his words with sympathy.

Mrs. Duger gave him a penetrating glance. "Dunno who told you that; she's anything but. Too smart for her own good, that one. Always up to something. Chases boys, too." She leaned across the counter and lowered her voice. "I saw her making sheep eyes at Charlie Davis over at the Cockcrow, and him betrothed to Hilda Watson."

"What do you think happened to her, then?" he asked softly.

She blinked, opened her mouth, and shut it again, darting a glance between Mia and Gideon. "I'm sure I don't know," she said primly.

"Who has searched for her?" Mia asked.

"Her da went up to the dairy, where she said she was going. No sign of her."

"Has anyone searched the woods and fields between here and there?" Gideon asked.

"Carter and the vicar got some of the men to search. They didn't find nothing," the woman said. Mia wondered how thoroughly they'd hunted.

Gideon nodded, absorbed in thought. "I've been wondering something, Mrs. Duger. The ladies at the dairy said she asked them about work. Has she ever asked you something similar?"

"Goodness, no. I shooed the chit out as soon as she came in."

They bought Mia's lavender, some skin cream, and some fine soaps—lavender- and pine-scented. "Perfect for the bath," Gideon murmured, making Mia blush. As they walked to the door, he turned back. "One more thing, Mrs. Duger. What do you think of

Bill Carter?"

She snorted. "That one? Nasty piece of work."

Back on the street, Mia ignored the stares of ladies passing on the other side. "We didn't learn much."

"Some. If a man had been stalking her, do you think Mrs. Duger would have said?"

"I have no doubt she would. She couldn't resist that piece of tattle." Mia shook her head. "I doubt if that's the case."

"Shall we move on to linen goods?" he asked.

"You look like you are enjoying this," Mia said.

"Not Lizzy's disappearance, no. But this is the first time I've ever tried to cause gossip before, and that, my darling wife, is fun."

AGNES PETTIFER, THE linen draper's wife, who resembled Mrs. Duger in appearance and behavior so much as to leave no doubt they were sisters, was no more help. They moved on after purchasing a bolt of muslin as yellow as a buttercup that Mia thought might make a particularly delightful morning gown.

The green grocer ran his own store, but his wife, the third sister, managed a few tables in an alcove to the side that had the pretense of being a tearoom. They took a seat at one of the linen-covered tables bedecked with a nosegay in the center, and Mia placed her bundles on an extra chair.

"Good enough for Nether Abbas," Gideon muttered.

Mia cast him a quelling glance. He doubted she'd seen many truly fine tearooms, a deficiency he would have to correct.

She introduced the woman who bustled out from the back room as Martha Hinson, the grocer's wife. Unlike her sisters, this woman was a cheerful as she was plump but, if Mia was correct and the woman's avid gaze was any indication, equally a gossip. He reached over, put his hand over his wife's, and cast her an adoring smile.

"I understand you have the best biscuits in Nether Abbas," he said, smiling at the woman. "Might we have some with our tea?"

"Ginger biscuits today, and I have a good China black." The woman wrung her hands nervously, studying him carefully. He wondered if she searched for the ghoulish dwarf she'd been led to expect. She spoke cautiously. "I made up ham sandwiches fresh. Would you care for some, it being after midday and all?"

"That would be lovely, Mrs. Hinson."

The woman beamed at him now, praise for her food overcoming old talk, before bustling away.

"We should come to the village more often. Keep making up to Martha Hinson and they'll all have you up for canonization," Mia teased.

He snorted at that. "They're as likely to burn me at the stake."

Martha returned with a tray and set down a pot of tea. "Let it steep a bit, lovies. I'll be back with your food," she said, depositing cups, sugar, and a pitcher of cream. She left before they could say anything.

They were sipping strong tea when she returned, laying out napkins, plates, and a platter for wedge-shaped sandwiches. She added a basket of ginger cookies with the flourish of a magician. What she lacked in resources, she made up for in enthusiasm, he thought.

"Thank you, ma'am. This looks delicious." And it was certainly more than palatable, though he found the bread a bit dry. Still, the mustard and pickle made up for it. He eyed Mia, waiting for an opening while their server hovered, studying them avidly.

"What is new up at Woodglen?" Martha asked. "Aside from you getting hitched."

Mia wiped her mouth and put her serviette in her lap. "We've been a bit preoccupied," she said, blushing prettily. "But I can tell you that my cousin is back at Selwyn Court."

"I heard she never got to have dinner with that Mr. Tavernash who's camped there," the woman said.

"Not true. She had dinner with him one night." She leaned conspiratorially, the image of Mrs. Duger earlier that day. "He ignored her completely, and that mother of his did, too."

The gossip leaned closer as well. "Is it true the woman acts like she owns the place?"

"Why, no, of course not. She acts like *her son* owns the place," Mia said with an impish grin and a wink. "When the duke returns, they are in for a shock."

"But the duke is… That is, I heard…," Martha sputtered, casting a nervous glance at Gideon.

"What is the newest rumor about my brother, ma'am?" Gideon asked, acting more serene than he felt. *Control your temper. We're here for information about the Carter girl.*

"They think—that is, there was talk down at the public house that someone did him in, poor man."

"Thank you for your concern," Gideon said smoothly. "It may cheer you to know my brother is quite well. He wrote to me in August. It is he who sent me here."

"Well. Well, that's good, then," she replied, wringing her hands. "Can I get you anything else?"

Gideon had finished his sandwich and reached for a biscuit. "These must be the pride of Nether Abbas," he said, pouring on oil to soothe the sting of contradicting rumors.

Their server rocked back on her heels, preening. "I think so."

"Martha," Mia said as if the idea just happened to occur to her. "We heard an odd rumor about Lizzy Carter. We heard she'd been asking for people to give her work. Did she ever try that here?"

"She did, the cheeky miss. My Alvin let her sweep up the back for a while. Her father put up an awful fuss, so we had to let her go. She put up a howl about the final wages due, too, but then she then up and disappeared. She never came back to collect. Alvin gave the pennies to Bill."

Gideon had begun to believe she ran away, but not returning

for coins owed made that unlikely. "How do people know she was going to the dairy that day? Did someone see her?"

"My sister said the vicar's wife told her that Milly Adcock saw her heading that way that afternoon with a milk bucket. That's what they told Bill Carter, and that's what he believes."

"Then it must be so," he said.

Martha Hinson did not appear to recognize sarcasm when she heard it.

"Did Milly Adcock tell the vicar's wife whether anyone was with her?"

"She were alone," Martha said emphatically.

"There's one more stop we need to make," he told Mia when they were out on the street. At her raised brow, he said, "The blacksmith's forge."

They found Bill Carter hot and sweating despite the bitter November day—a hazard of his profession, no doubt. He pounded on an iron wheel bent over a form, hammering it into shape. "What do y' want? Have y' found my Lizzy?" he demanded. He stalked toward Gideon, sledgehammer in hand.

"No, sir, we have not," Gideon said. "After hearing your concern at the wedding, I decided someone needed to investigate."

He studied Gideon from his heels to his hair. "Asked you to see what you'd say. There's folks who think you did it," he snarled, raising his hammer.

Mia grabbed Gideon's hand.

"There are folks who believe many things that aren't true. People at the dairy think you hit her. Did you?" Gideon replied without backing up.

"Not unless she deserved it," Bill said, wiping his face with his free hand and smearing grime.

"Do you think she ran off with a man?" Mia asked.

"My Lizzy were a good girl, and I'll kill the man that says otherwise!" Bill shouted.

"We heard she was seeking to earn money. Do you know

why?"

"No. She'd a roof over her head and food in her belly. I needed her home looking after things, not running the street."

"Did anyone send to the magistrate in Shaftsbury? Could she have gone there to work?" Gideon asked.

Bill Carter exploded. "Someone took her on her way to the dairy. You know it, and I know it. You better find out who done it before folks here take it into their heads it was you."

It was a threat, pure and simple. Gideon didn't care for threats. He wondered if Carter could have killed his daughter in a fit of temper, perhaps accidentally. Perhaps not. "We'll talk to you again, Mr. Carter. Count on it."

He offered his arm to Mia, and they went on their way.

"I think Hector and I need to take a walk between the dairy and Nether Abbas. If there's something to be found, we'll find it," she said.

"We need to alert authorities in Shaftsbury, too," he replied.

She grinned at him. "Have we created enough gossip for one day?"

"Not quite," he said, and he kissed her right there on the street.

※

CHAPTER TWENTY-SIX

MIA RETURNED FROM her search of the fields with Hector in the guise of a leisurely stroll with nothing to report. The walk had turned up nothing, not so much as the missing milk pail or a hair ribbon. If something had been there, Hector would have found it. She feared for Lizzy but had no idea what else she could do to help. They would have to wait for word from the magistrate in Shaftsbury.

She decided not to distract Gideon from his work on the ledgers. He'd said the sooner done, the sooner they could return to Wales. There was still time to manage it before winter set in in the Welsh mountains, but he needed to focus on the task he had come to do.

A passing footman carried a tray of sandwiches. "Mr. Kendrick and Mr. Marshall requested luncheon in the estate offices. We're laying out for the ladies in the breakfast room now," he said.

Drat. Luncheon with Lady Tavernash, the sour old woman. She sighed. Hunger called, and it would be self-centered to demand servants bring her a tray when they'd already laid out. She dragged herself to the breakfast room. Seeing the old woman scowling from the end of the table while a footman filled her plate, Mia made the shallow obeisance proper to a baronet's widow.

"Good afternoon, Lady Tavernash," she said, going to the sideboard. She smiled at the footman and served herself.

"You spoil them," Lady Tavernash snapped as soon as Mia sat down. "When my son comes into full possession, we'll make short work of that."

Mia found it better not to respond.

"As to you, young lady, what do you mean coming in to luncheon in your dirt!"

I was out looking for a sign of the missing girl…

"I always say blood will out," the Tavernash witch said with a sniff.

"I had a lovely walk this morning. The estate has some exceptional views. How was your morning?" Mia asked sweetly.

"I have no time for walking out. I've been inventorying linens. The ones in the family wing need to be relegated to the lesser guest rooms, and an upgrade purchased. I demanded that Mrs. Morrit see to it, but she confided that Marshall said no—as if my word isn't enough."

"Perhaps you might mention it to Mr. Marshall yourself," Mia said. She hoped the steward would tell the old woman no.

"If I see him, I will. I suspect he avoids me. I shall have to confront him over dinner."

"And Mr. Tavernash? Has he had a productive morning?" Mia asked.

"My son has a fragile constitution. He requires rest. He has been saving his strength to ride out, surveying the land as he should."

Mia finished quickly and departed as soon as she could, drawing another disapproving harrumph from Lady Tavernash. She reached Gideon's—their—quarters with relief. Fresh water and clean towels on the washstand in Mia's bedroom indicated Mercy had come and gone. Mia smiled at the bed. That it hadn't been used since she moved in would have been duly noted in the servants' hall. She couldn't resist a peek into Gideon's bedroom. The bed had been made up, but whether by one of the maids or

Jem, she couldn't tell.

She changed without ringing for Mercy and washed up before taking her place at the table where her work on the family papers had been laid out. When she reached into the box and picked up the first item, a receipt for a tailor's bill, she sat upright sharply, startled to find that the papers in the box had been disturbed. At least, she thought they might have been. She believed a packet of letters had been next, but maybe she didn't remember the exact order of things. Making a predictable order was the point of this exercise, wasn't it? She resolved to keep working.

A few layers down, she came to a packet of three letters she believed to be the ones she'd seen before. Had they always been further down? Upon examination, it became clear they had been opened. This time, she was positive they had been closed more neatly when she'd seen them before. Someone had read them. Gideon? Mercy in her never-ending search for tittle-tattle, more likely.

She read the letters with interest. The first was addressed to Randolph Tavernash, Lieutenant, 7th Regiment of Foot, Charleston, South Carolina, and had been franked by a Duke of Glenmoor. Dated 1782, the duke would have been Gideon's sire's grandfather, if she remembered correctly. Randolph was his father. The sender appeared to be the man's mother, Gideon's grandmother. She begged to make him aware of the death of his cousin Albert, son of his uncle, the duke's heir in a hunting accident. Mia did some quick calculations. Gideon would have been a year or so old, and his father remained in Charleston; he mentioned neither Gideon nor his mother.

The second letter was addressed to Lady Phillip Tavernash, Woodglen, Dorset. He thanked his mother but pointed out that he remained three steps from the title. He wrote that he hoped *the miserly old man will do something for me before he kicks up his heels.* Then he told her, *We've been ordered to begin evacuating loyalist families to Canada lest the gloating rebels do them harm.* He was, he said, dispatched to be part of that evacuation. Again, there was no mention of a wife and son.

The third, from mother to son, stated the situation brutally. Measles had stricken the Elms, his uncle's estate, and both uncle and his remaining son were unlikely to survive. Addressed to his regiment in Nova Scotia, the letter ordered him to resign his commission and return immediately, for *the old man won't live much longer*. As it turned out, Randolph Tavernash waited three more years to succeed his grandfather as Duke of Glenmoor.

She put the letters aside for Gideon to read and set to work on the box, sorting everything she picked up into a pile by year. Letters from distant cousins congratulating him or wheedling for allowances or loans, mixed with bills of sale for property sold and property bought, receipts for livestock, the résumé of a long-gone steward, two speeches given in Lords, and other bric-a-brac. In the end, she stared at the bottom of an empty box. There was no record of a marriage or birth. No letter mentioning an American family. Nothing. For a man who appeared to have a penchant for saving paper, it felt odd. She suspected it was a deliberate omission.

She set the pile for 1790 back in the box, wrote that year in large letters on a blank paper, and laid it on top. Then she added 1789 and did the same, continuing year by year until the top of the pile was a plain paper on which 1780 had been written. She left the letters out, closed the box, and rang for tea.

The sun was dipping low, and the room had darkened. So had her spirits. She had no evidence of Lizzy's disappearance to report and no information about Gideon's birth.

She grew restless waiting, but at last a scratch at the door heralded the arrival of tea. "Come in," she said. A footman entered carrying a heavily laden tray of tea and cakes. Her eyes widened at the sight of Gideon following behind him, and her heart filled with joy and her soul with peace.

He dismissed the servant, laid a set of ledgers on the table, and took her into his arms. A thought flickered to life just before he kissed her. Somehow in the last week, this man had become the source of all her happiness.

⟫⟫⟫✳⟪⟪⟪

GIDEON TRUDGED WEARILY up to his quarters, lugging heavy books but pushing fraud and poor bookkeeping out of his mind, his heart fixated on the woman who awaited him. One of the footmen stood at the door to their suite and scratched on the door.

"I knew you'd be coming," the young man said with a smile. "I had the kitchen lay on plenty for you."

She called, and the footman deftly opened the door while juggling a heavy tray.

"Put it on the table," Mia said. Then she glanced up and rose, and her smile, balm to his soul, made everything right.

"You may go," he said to the footman, his eyes on Mia. He heard the door click shut behind him, laid down the ledgers, and took her into his arms.

She rested her head on his chest and snuggled close. "Difficult day?"

"Long one." He kissed her gently, firmly, possessively, before loosening his hold. "How did you and Hector manage?"

She wrinkled her nose. "Let's have tea before it gets cold, and I'll tell you," she said, running her hand down his arm to take his hand.

He glanced over at the settee. It had become their favorite spot.

"Bring the side table closer, and I'll pour," she said.

He followed her directions. She sat down elegantly and poured while he gave himself over to the sight of her glowing hair, slender neck, and graceful back. Soon she cuddled in, and they sipped tea in silent accord.

She put hers down first, took his cup, and set it on the table. She turned so he could hold her while she laid her head on his shoulder. "There's nothing to report. Hector found nothing," she said, snuggling close. "Did you discover anything useful?"

"Yes and no. I told you the handwriting changed. Six months later, I noticed a discrepancy. At first, it was small amounts, a few shillings at a time widely spaced. Whoever had taken over the books was skimming."

Mia peered directly at Gideon. "We still haven't gotten a sample of Jem's writing," she said before laying her head back down.

"Earlier this year, the amounts became larger and more frequent."

"When exactly did that begin?" she asked.

"About the time Felton Tavernash moved in," he told her.

"Why fraudulent bookkeeping? Why wouldn't he just dispense cash to Tavernash and so note it in the ledgers?"

"Marshall told me he refused Tavernash access to estate funds. I think he meant it. Either he lied or someone else gave Tavernash money and didn't want Marshall or the solicitors to know it."

"We need to confront Marshall about reading. Something isn't right," she murmured. "You told me the solicitors suspected unapproved land sales. Have you found anything like that?"

"Perhaps. There's a page missing from five months ago. The new page picks up where the previous one left off. I asked Marshall about it. He said he made an error and tore it out, but he was flustered. He's hiding something. So I asked him outright about land sales, and he told me that Grimes, the freeholder whose fields border Woodglen just beyond Nether Abbas, tried to claim part of the lower cornfields, and Marshall had to send him packing. He said the man claimed he owned it, then got shifty-eyed when pushed."

Mia groaned. "Another puzzlement. We'll never get to the bottom of what is going on."

"Perhaps not, but it is beginning to appear that several things date to the arrival of our buffoon of a would-be heir."

"But you have no proof of anything."

"Not one iota. I see you packed up the papers. Find anything interesting?"

"No birth records. No marriage records. No family letters rejoicing in or denouncing an American marriage."

"I'm not surprised. I'm sure Phillip would have searched, and he'd have said if he found anything."

She got up and fetched a bundle of letters. "I thought you might find these interesting."

Gideon scanned them quickly. "The snake was in Charleston my first year and more," he murmured.

"It appears so. I'm sorry. More burdens for you to carry. Would your grandfather have let him near your mother if they weren't married?"

He shrugged. "Probably not, but there's nothing here to say whether relations continued."

"More questions. Still no proof," she murmured, snuggling back in.

He busied himself kissing his way down her neck.

"Gideon, does it matter?" she asked in between kissing him back.

Did it? "My birth? To Phillip, perhaps." He moved to exploring the curl of her ear.

"What about Woodglen's finances?" she asked.

He stopped, sighing deeply. "That feels like a matter of honor."

"Then we can't go home until we solve that one."

"Home?"

"To Wales."

A fierce desire to take her there tore through him. He took her mouth, the kiss born of the union that made his home hers. Theirs. She responded with equal passion. He sank his face in her hair. "I want that above all things."

"But..." She sat upright and looked at him directly.

"But I can't abandon what I was sent here to do," he said,

meeting her eyes until she nodded. "Besides, the children will be here next week."

He tried to draw her back, but she resisted. "The children," she gasped.

He stood and took her hand to lead her to his bedroom.

"But Gideon. I'll be a shock to them. Whatever will they make of me?"

"They will love you."

"How can you know that?"

"Because I…know them, little wife." He covered her mouth with his before she could respond and lifted her into his arms. It was a long while before hunger drove them to remember the tray of cakes and sandwiches.

CHAPTER TWENTY-SEVEN

GIDEON, BAREFOOT IN trousers and shirt, shaved while Mia lingered in bed the next morning. When she rolled over, blinked her eyes open, and gave him a languid smile, he saw it for the invitation it was. He was about to join her when a clutter in the sitting room warned him servants had arrived.

He found Mercy building up the fire. She grinned impudently over her shoulder. "Shall I do the fire in your room, Mr. Kendrick?"

Gideon's attention was on Jem, who hovered near the worktable.

"Shall I come back later, sir?" Jem asked.

Was he examining the ledgers? Perhaps the archive box. Either way, it set up a warning flag. "Don't bother. I'm sorry to trouble you—either of you. We meant to say yesterday, Mrs. Kendrick and I are quite able to see to ourselves. We don't require personal servants. We may, in fact, resume meals below stairs."

Two pairs of eyes stared back at him, Mercy's sour with what he suspected was disappointment, Jem's with open hostility. Jem gave a curt bow and stalked to the door. With an avid glance behind Gideon, Mercy followed.

He turned to find Mia, swaddled in his wrapper from toes to chin, standing in the doorway to his bedroom, brows raised in question.

"I caught him hovering by the ledgers and the box. In the light of your suspicions, I think we need to keep our door locked when we aren't here. You can still ring for tea when we are," Gideon said.

Her shoulders drooped. "You're right. I don't require a ladies' maid. If we're going down to breakfast, we best get dressed, though," she said.

"Sorry," he said. "I'll make it up to you."

She gave him a swift kiss on her way to her bedroom. She paused in the middle of the sitting room. "Shall I put the ledgers under my personal linen in my dressing room?"

His bark of laughter echoed around the room. "Excellent choice. I think we'll return this box to the family vault also."

Lady Tavernash had preceded them to the breakfast room. She opened her mouth to spew her usual venom, but she caught sight of the box Gideon placed on a side table and closed it. "What is that?" she croaked a few minutes later.

"Family papers. I'm returning it to the archives," Gideon said while filling a plate for Mia.

"*You* have access to it?" She managed to inject both disdain and outrage into the word *you*.

"Of course. I have the key. Interesting subject, family history," Gideon said.

"It is my Felton's family history as well," she snapped. "That arrogant steward will not give us access." She paused, then added with a haughty lift of her chin, "I know it is hidden in the stillroom; my late husband told me as much."

"I fear the papers from that the distant past are fragile," Gideon said, sipping his coffee.

"I'm sure Mr. Marshall has his orders," Mia added cheerfully. "From His Grace, no doubt."

"You continue to speak as if the duke is alive and hiding somewhere. Dukes do not simply disappear. He's dead. I can feel it in my bones. You of all people ought to know that." Lady Tavernash glared at Gideon.

The old troll might as well accuse me outright. "Your bones notwithstanding, I know my brother is doing precisely what he wants," Gideon said. *Whatever the hell that is.*

"I should think the legitimate descendants would have first claim on the archives," she muttered.

Gideon didn't rise to that bait. To his relief, neither did Mia. In fact, if the twitching in the corner of her mouth was any indication, she struggled not to laugh.

They left the breakfast room with the intention of returning the box and dipping into one or two others. However, Gideon led Mia into his darkened office rather than passing it. He put a finger to his mouth and waited.

Minutes later Lady Tavernash sailed by on her way toward the stillroom. He could hear knocking and banging.

"Kendrick, I know you're in there!" she called, still storming about the stillroom. He pulled Mia deeper into the shadows to the side of the door.

Soon enough she stomped back past his door. They heard her call to a worker piling sacks of grain in the storage room. "Where is Kendrick? Where did he go?"

"I'm sure I don't know, my lady. He ain't here," the man said.

Gideon waited until he was certain the coast was clear and left the office, peering both ways. Mia followed him to the stillroom, where Lady Tavernash had left a candle burning. He closed the door to the hall and handed Mia the box.

She studied every corner of the room, wide-eyed. "I wondered where the herbs were kept," she murmured.

"Watch carefully," Gideon said. He lifted the candle from the wall sconce and twisted the empty sconce. The stone wall popped open. It moved more easily this time, and Mia gaped at the ancient door behind it. Gideon took the key from his coat and opened it.

Using the candle in his hand, he lit ones inside the vault before placing it in a glass jar set up on a table for that purpose. He returned the key to his coat and gazed at Mia, who appeared stupefied by the treasures that surrounded her.

"We could spend weeks in here," she said.

"I think we'd suffocate," he replied.

She poked him with her elbow. "You know what I mean. Where does this box go?"

He showed her, and she replaced it, but she removed the one next to it.

"What are you doing?"

"I just want to take a quick peek," she said. "This one says 1770–1780; it overlaps the time you were born." She put it near the glass-encased candle and lifted the lid.

"Don't remind me how old I am. I already fear I've robbed the cradle," he said.

Her head jerked up. "The age difference bothers you?"

"Doesn't it bother you to be married to an old man?" he asked.

She snorted and sent him a look that said she viewed the question as beneath her and sorted through the papers. The first letter she found was dated 1777. She tossed it back. Another from Manchester in 1772 and a third posted from Windsor in 1773 also merited barely a glance. "Someday it might be fun to read these," she murmured.

"So nothing?" he asked.

"I see one more." She frowned. "Also too early. It is from Sedgewood Hall, however. Isn't that Felton Tavernash's home? Interesting. Perhaps she has cause to be interested in the archives."

"One shudders," he said.

She grinned and opened the letter, which proved to be a florid mess addressed to "my most honorable cousin." Full of flattery, whining, and wheedling, it sought both money and an appointment for a son, Ronald.

"That would be our Felton's father," Gideon told her.

"Well, they didn't get it. Look at this. A different hand on the bottom. A rather arrogant hand, if I do say so." She gave it to him.

Writ large and dark across the bottom, it said, *Returned message telling him never to contact again or show his face, the damned mushroom. Glenmoor.*

Mia's grin was wicked. "That puts our Felton's branch of the family in its place." She packed it back up and returned the box to its spot. "Do we want anything else?"

He searched the box for the current year and, finding it almost empty, put it back. "No bills of sale," he said.

"What now?" she asked.

"I want you to go through the books for the past three years. See if you see what I do. Then we need to meet with Marshall about it. It's time to confront him."

"We never got Jem's handwriting," she reminded him.

"No need if we get Marshall to admit Jem is keeping the books."

"What are you going to do this afternoon?" she asked.

"Ride over to visit this farmer, Grimes. I want his story about the land sale," he said. "And then I want to come back for tea with my wife." To emphasize his point, he took her into his arms and kissed her well and thoroughly, a kiss full of promise.

MIA REACHED THE family wing and found maids going in and out of Lady Tavernash's suite. An idea struck her. She unlocked the door to their suite and wrote a quick note to Jem asking him if he had seen Gideon's gold cravat pin, one she knew to be on the counter in his dressing room. She cornered the maid named Agnes and asked her to kindly give it to Jem.

"Tell him he doesn't need to come up. A written reply will do," she told the maid. The maid frowned, knowing full well she would have to carry the return message.

Mia bit her lower lip, hoping it worked. If he replied, they could compare his handwriting to the ledgers.

Two hours later Mia came to the first discrepancy. She turned a daily entry page to a new date, and it struck her as odd. She went back to the previous day, and sure enough, it ended on a number different from the one the next day started with. The new day was short three shillings. It could have been a mistake, except Jem—or whoever had done this—had been meticulous up to then. Simple trick, odd number, not easily caught unless you were actively searching for trouble.

She stopped adding each column and began searching for other examples of daily end-of-day discrepancies, marking each one she found. They occurred at intermittent intervals throughout that year, always irregular amounts between a few shillings and a pound. Then she found one for seven pounds, a fortune to a footman making eight pounds a year!

Gideon returned midafternoon, and she rang for tea and eagerly shared her findings.

"It's as obvious as I thought, then. It gets worse." He opened the ledger for the current year. "We need to get this one back before Marshall creates a fuss. But look here."

He opened the ledger to the previous February. "I checked with Fillmore. Tavernash came the end of January."

She peered at the page he indicated. It followed the same pattern, only this time, the discrepancy was twenty pounds. "Mercy! Either whoever is doing this got bolder, or Tavernash has his hands in the till and thinks he's untouchable. You said Marshall told you he kept funds away from him."

"There are only a few possibilities. Marshall lied, and he's giving Tavernash estate money. Or Tavernash is blackmailing him. Or Marshall has no idea what goes on with the bookkeeping, and whoever he has doing it has lost all fear of getting caught."

"That's insane. The larger amounts make it all too obvious. He must know we'll catch it," she said.

"Perhaps whoever it is doesn't plan to stay around to get caught," he said. "There's more."

The next example he showed her was from July, ninety-five

pounds.

"That is enough to buy land—except I thought the problem was selling. Odd," she said.

"Yes. Almost. Only, the transaction was never completed. Grimes told me Jem brought him a bill of sale for land Grimes had been coveting, that he had in fact offered one hundred and ten for. He gave over the money and kept the bill of sale. Then Marshall read him the riot act about farming on Woodglen land. They quarreled, Marshall demanded the bill of sale, and Grimes demanded his money back. Marshall refused. Grimes kept the bill of sale. He showed it to me but wouldn't give it over."

"You think someone else gave Grimes ninety-five pounds."

"Yes. He still believes he's getting the rest of the money or the land, 'when the new duke succeeds.' That's all I got out of him."

"Oh dear. Tavernash?"

"He didn't say, but it has to be. When I told him in no uncertain terms that His Grace is alive and well and likely to return soon, his expression was thunderous. I left it at that. Unless I miss my guess, he'll confront either Marshall or Tavernash."

A knock at the door signaled their tea, and Mia was surprised to see Agnes delivering it.

"Ran up before Mercy could, I did," the girl said. "Needed a reason to bring you this back. Jem said you'd grow cold waiting for his answer."

Mia frowned, and the girl rushed on. "I tried to ask him again, but Mrs. Morrit had me running ragged, so I didn't have time to follow him. I went over to Mr. Marshall's office later, but he weren't there, either. No one has seen him since morning." She shrugged. "I brought this back." She reached in her pocket and handed over the crumpled note, the same one Mia had given her in the morning.

There was no handwriting sample, and Mia realized Jem knew they were looking at the books. Mia glanced at Gideon sheepishly. "Oh dear, I may have flushed our bird."

He touched her arm to reassure her. "His flight may have told us what we need to know anyway. Agnes, kindly request a tray of cakes and tell Mr. Marshall we'd like him to join us here for tea."

CHAPTER TWENTY-EIGHT

"I WAS IN the field. You'll have to take me in my dirt. What's so important?" Marshall demanded, glancing between the two of them. Gideon thought he seemed more worried than irritated.

"Mr. Marshall, thank you for coming. Let me put some tea on to steep." Mia indicated the settee with a sweep of her hand, went to the spirit lamp on the chiffonier, and set action to words. She came back with a pot of tea, pausing to whisper in Gideon's ear, "Do you wish me to stay for this?"

Gideon didn't lower his voice. "Yes, please. Your insights may be helpful."

She sat and smiled at Marshall like a perfect hostess, as if he was an honored guest.

"You've never called me up here before. I thought I best come soon," Marshall said. He glanced uneasily at the ledgers.

"We appreciated that, Marshall. It is more private here," Gideon responded.

Marshall waited, warily waving off the plate of cakes when Mia offered it. "You best get to it, Kendrick," he said.

Gideon nodded, meeting Marshall's gaze directly. "First, tell me one thing. Are you able to read?"

Marshall started as if to rise, but he didn't. He opened his mouth and closed it, eyes darting from the wall behind Gideon to the floor. His mouth worked, and he swallowed twice. "How did you know?"

"Does that matter?" Gideon asked.

"Are you going to tell those London solicitors or the duke and get me fired?" Marshall asked, resentment dripping from his words.

Mia shifted uneasily and poured the tea before asking the gentlemen if they wanted something stronger.

Gideon nodded at her before he answered Marshall. "Perhaps I should. Whether or not I do depends on how some other things work out. Who kept records when you first started?"

"My brother, Artie, came here with me. We worked as a team, two halves of one land steward."

"What happened to him?" Mia asked, handing Gideon the brandy and placing a crystal glass in front of each of them.

"He went back home to marry. Came into her father's land. I couldn't hold him back."

Mia's murmur of sympathy seemed to improve the mood of the conversation.

"His work was decent and honest, though his hand was hard to decipher," Gideon said. "Then two years ago, last March, the writing changed. Bolder. Clearer. The calculations absolutely correct. Is that when Jem took over?"

Marshall nodded miserably. He took a deep swig. "What did he do?"

"To begin with, he skimmed from you," Gideon said. "He took small amounts at first—a few shillings here and there—something he could have blamed on error. The thing is, it was obvious. I had Mrs. Kendrick check, and she found it immediately. When he didn't get caught, he did it more often and for increasing amounts."

Marshall cursed under his breath. "The blasted cheat probably laughed behind my back. I trusted him."

"It gets worse, Mr. Marshall," Mia said, sympathy softening her words.

"Starting in February, the amounts increased significantly," Gideon said.

"February?"

Gideon watched him work it out for himself.

"Tavernash!" he cursed again. "Beg your pardon, ma'am. I should have denied that one the house the day he turned up."

"We think Tavernash either bribed or found out, then threatened him," Gideon said.

"Who else may have known?" Marshall exclaimed. "I feel like a benighted fool."

"We don't know. We have one more to add to this, though. In July—"

"Grimes. The man raved and raged but never told me who claimed to sell Woodglen land out from under the estate. Was it Jem or Tavernash?" Marshall shook his head. "I told him whoever did it was a damned liar with no authority and I didn't owe him a farthing."

"Both Jem and Grimes may have been betting on Tavernash inheriting soon. They thought they could wait you out," Gideon said.

"Then you came," Marshall said.

"Yes, complicating their game. There was one more recently. A month or so ago, thirty more pounds went missing. I put that one on the mother."

Marshall sank back, and his head dropped backward. "I've let them steal the estate blind," he moaned.

"Not quite. You've also increased yields and made the entire place twice as profitable than when you took over. That is clear from the ledgers as well," Gideon told him. "From what I can tell, my brother has also invested those profits wisely. Was that your doing?"

"I made a few suggestions, but it was mostly him," Marshall admitted. "I know fields, crops, livestock, a good groom from a slacker." He shook his head. "Didn't keep me from being taken from behind."

"Mr. Marshall, am I correct that the reading problem plagued you as a child?" Mia asked.

"Aye. Teachers tried everything—even beating it into me. Nothing worked."

"And yet you are extremely intelligent. I knew a man like that once. One of my father's friends. His reasoning was superior and his memory prodigious, but he couldn't learn to read. He said the lines on the page looked like squiggles and wiggled away," Mia told him.

"I don't know about wiggle, but they change," Marshall said.

"My papa said it happened sometimes, like a kind of blindness. It doesn't have to keep you from doing your job," she said.

"We'll see about that," Gideon interrupted. "First, we have to deal with Jem and the Tavernash intrusions."

"Aye. First, I'm going to thrash Jem Hawkins within an inch—"

Mr. Marshall!" Mia shouted, horrified.

"It may be a moot point." Gideon explained Mia's experiment and Jem's likely disappearance.

"Bolted like a coward, did he?" Marshall said.

"We'll see. For now, I suggest we play innocent. Tavernash and his lady take me for the idiot my father called me—at least, I think they do. Let's see what they do in his absence."

Marshall sighed deeply. "Wise. Who will keep the books, though?"

The silence that greeted that question stretched while Gideon sorted through ideas. He could do it himself temporarily.

Mia spoke up first. "I could do it," she said.

"Temporarily," Gideon said. He thought for a moment Marshall would scoff at the idea of a woman doing it. He didn't.

"I no longer know who else I can trust. You may as well do it."

"Only if you go over it with me every day. Explain the day's activities and give over the reports and receipts. I'll make the entries and tally the numbers, but I'll read it all to you when I'm finished."

That surprised both men. Marshall blushed.

"My wife is truly wise," Gideon murmured.

"But do you want me sitting boldly in the steward's office or hiding up here?" she asked.

"Our goal is to provoke. Sit in the office," Gideon answered.

Mia frowned. He'd grown used to the expression that meant she was working her way through a problem. "What about Lizzy Carter? Have we heard from the magistrate in Shaftsbury?"

"Not yet. It has only been three days, though."

Marshall agreed to meet daily at three. "That leaves me mornings for other things." He glanced at Gideon. "Harv watches time. He'll make sure."

Mia peered at Gideon. "Where will you be?"

"Nearby, unless I'm with Marshall, learning the work of the estate." The words were out before he thought about them, but it felt right. The business of the ducal estate was more than reports and ledgers. It was time he learned the operation.

BREAKFAST HAD BECOME an ordeal. Tavernash never joined them; he didn't awaken until past noon. Mia wondered how on earth he would ever manage as a country gentleman and sent a prayer of thanks he would never have the opportunity, at least not at Woodglen. His mother was another issue.

They might avoid her if they came down early, but they found new reasons to linger in bed every morning. Lady Tavernash proved to be even more spiteful when her buffoonish son wasn't in attendance. She aimed her complaints at the house, the furnishings, the state of housekeeping, the staff, the horse-flesh, and villagers who failed to give her due respect. Her most pointed darts were reserved for Marshall, who refused to turn over management of the estate to her son, by which Mia assumed she meant turn it over to her. Mia and Gideon rated primarily innuendo and sneering disregard.

Mia stopped any attempt at conversation, and so, she noted, did Gideon. Most mornings, he ate quickly, announced he had to attend "to the business of the estate," and left the woman in a flutter to wallow in her own bile. Mia hastened to follow.

Two days after their meeting with Marshall, a message arrived for Mia while she still sat at breakfast. The address, in Selina's ornate scrawl, surprised her. She wiped her mouth and rose. "I'll just go read this in private," she murmured to Gideon. He ate two bites of egg, grabbed a sweet roll, and followed her to the library.

"Problems?" he asked.

"It's from Selina." She scanned the missive.

He rolled his eyes. "What does she want now?"

"Me. My help. Uncle apparently told her not to bother us after the wedding but allowed that enough time has passed. She wants my opinion on her wardrobe for spring—as if she doesn't have months to plan—and to speak to Eustace about his cruel words to her, since he obviously doesn't listen to Uncle. Oh, and cook has not been preparing the fish course properly lately and I'm to set her straight."

"Send her a note assuring her that she can solve her problems on her own," Gideon said.

She glanced up at him. "I believe I'll ride over and tell her that gently. And tell Uncle that Eustace must stop bullying his sister, since I'm not there to deflect him." At his fierce frown, she went on. "They were kind to take me in, Gideon, and they are family. I agree that Selina must cope without me, but I can at least offer encouragement. Besides—Uncle Ludlow is one more person who needs to see that I'm thriving as your wife."

"Is this part of the Christian forgiveness business?" he grumbled.

"You remember that? Yes, it is, as a matter of fact. My mother taught me that remembering slights does no good and poisons the soul. I don't forgive people who've done me hurt for their sake. I do it for my own because storing resentment creates an ever-growing burden, a crushing weight. As I said, it poisons the soul."

He snorted. "You're a better person than I, in that case. Go if you must, but don't forget your appointment with Marshall."

She didn't. By two, she pried herself free of Selina's clinging, left her with some sensible advice, and promised weekly visits. She had confronted Uncle Ludlow in his study first, laying truth on him about both his children and the management of his servants. "Marriage has made you impertinent, Euphemia," he had grumbled, looking her up and down. "At least I can see it has done you no harm. You may thank me for that."

As she rode back to Woodglen, the Selwyn household's issues receded. Only one part of her conversation with her uncle stayed with her. When asked why he didn't take on the role of magistrate, he had blustered that he couldn't possibly impinge on the duke's rightful role. She raised the issue of Lizzy Carter and pointed out that as highest-ranking man in the shire, the duke being absent, it was his responsibility to see to the problem, not her husband's. She'd left him sunk in thought.

Her time with Marshall went smoothly, and she went up to change for dinner. Gideon didn't follow, deeming himself sufficiently fine for the likes of Felton Tavernash. When she came down to the drawing room to wait the call to dinner, she found Marshall deep in conversation with her husband about what she told them regarding her uncle.

"She's right. Clavering ought to take a hand in the thing. The Carter girl deserves justice—or to be found. I'll send him a message asking him to come round to meet with us." At "send a message," he glanced at Mia and colored a bit.

She'd have someone else write it. Uncle would recognize her writing. "Invite him to dinner, Mr. Marshall. He would like that," she said. "And my cousins, too."

Marshall muttered, "It will improve dinner."

Gideon chuckled. "It can't make it any worse."

Fillmore announced dinner. As they went, Gideon asked Marshall to explain crop rotation again, and Marshall cheerfully obliged.

The Tavernash pair had gone directly to the dining room as always.

Lady Tavernash narrowed her eyes at Gideon and Marshall. "You two have certainly become thick as thieves lately."

You would know about thievery, wouldn't you? Mia thought. "How was your day?" Mia asked the woman politely.

Lady Tavernash sniffed. "Fair. Aside from rude servants. My Felton and I spent a pleasant afternoon discussing our plans for this place." Her son stared glumly at his food. Mia could swear she saw a flash of resentment.

The baronet's widow went on to describe the rooms she deemed in need of total redecoration. At length. Gideon and Marshall continued to discuss the running of the estate without including Tavernash. Mia sat in the middle and nodded at the woman's unrelenting discourse periodically.

Dinner completed, the older woman rose and glared at Mia pointedly. Mia rose as well and followed her out. When Lady Tavernash sailed on down the hall to her favorite parlor, Mia lingered behind. A thought had occurred to her over dinner.

She waited until Fillmore came out after delivering port to the gentlemen and approached him. "Do you need something Mrs. Kendrick?" he asked.

"How often do you inventory the silver?"

Fillmore bristled. "Annually, ma'am. In early December, as the duke prescribed."

They were deep into November. "You might want to do it early this year," she suggested.

The crusty old man glanced in the direction the lady had taken and back at Mia. *No fool, this one,* she thought. Stealing the silver would be crude and blatant, but given the woman's greed, her belief that the estate owed her, and the absence of any single authority over the massive household in the duke's absence, it felt entirely too likely.

He studied her intently. "Perhaps I will if I find a moment," the old man said.

Chapter Twenty-Nine

G IDEON ESCORTED VISCOUNT Clavering to the library, where Marshall joined them. Mia in the meanwhile had set off to escort her cousins on a tour of Woodglen. Eustace Selwyn, the puppy, attempted to insert himself into what he called with a sly wink, "gentlemen's activity." Gideon put him off, declaring their discussion a legal matter requiring discretion. That and a frown from his father sent him on his way.

Marshall, as prearranged, spoke first as soon as Gideon had served drinks all around. "Mrs. Kendrick tells me you are reluctant to tread on the duke's privileges here in the shire."

"Yes, yes, precisely. The position of magistrate in this county has long resided with the Dukes of Glenmoor as appointed by the Crown. But we seem to have a vacuum, and Euphemia reminded me of the duties and privileges due to my rank. What is it you need, gentlemen?" Clavering tented his fingers together.

"I knew we could count on you, Clavering," Marshall said. "This business with the Carter girl had our female servants on edge, and I'm hearing the village as well. Kendrick here has the power to act on the duke's behalf, but he isn't a local man, and well, you can see where certain unfounded rumors hamper his ability to deal with problems."

"Carter is fearful about the girl's fate; he approached me at the wedding breakfast," Gideon said.

"Foul-tempered man," Clavering murmured.

"Indeed," Gideon said. "One wonders if she may have simply run off. There being no one with obvious authority investigating, I decided to search."

"Bad business either way. Young girl like that? Can come to no end of harm." The viscount squared his shoulders with all the dignity he attached to the role of magistrate, albeit a temporary one, and studied Gideon. "Your reputation here—which I'm beginning to perceive may have been undeserved—isn't helpful. What is this about power to act?"

Gideon and Marshall exchanged glances. He left Marshall to explain it.

"As if 'duke in all but name'?" Clavering exclaimed. "I never heard of such a thing."

"On behalf of the Glenmoor estate, I'm delegating you to take leadership in matters of law and public order until such time as my brother sees fit to return. If it appears this will be a long-term arrangement, we can petition the regent for a permanent appointment," Gideon said. "Is that clear enough?"

"I understand a search was carried out. What else has been done so far?"

Gideon quickly outlined what they had learned from Mrs. Millbrook and the villagers. "My wife retraced the route from the village to the dairy with that great hound of hers. He turned up nothing. I've written to the magistrate in Shaftsbury. I got this back today." He handed Clavering the pompous note informing them that no loose girls had been found on the streets and that he saw no purpose in a door-to-door inquiry. "My next step was to send the question to Standish, the physician who cared for your daughter. He has not yet replied."

"What is it you want me to do?" Clavering asked.

Marshall spoke next. "We'd like you to make a public show of interest. Call Carter in and question him. Ask around the village. Put your authority behind it. Can you do that?"

"Easily enough," Clavering said. "If Kendrick is at my side."

Gideon felt like he had been hit with a cricket bat.

Clavering went on. "He has the real authority. I can see that. And the will to do it. I'll lend my position, Kendrick, but you have to carry the thing."

Gideon shook his head. "The village needs to see you acting alone, my lord. It will be seen as objective. They don't trust me."

A knock at the door heralded Fillmore's arrival. "My lord, gentlemen, Mrs. Kendrick has ordered tea for the green drawing room if you would care to join them." He drew in breath. "Lady Tavernash has already done so."

Mrs. Kendrick has ordered… Gideon couldn't suppress his smile.

THE KITCHEN DID Woodglen proud; Mia suspected a visit from the viscount was cause for pride.

"Shall we wait for the gentlemen to pour?" she suggested.

Eustace wandered the room, picking up figurines and putting them back down, examining paintings, and making a nuisance of himself as he had all afternoon. "Is Kendrick coming? I'd like to get a good look at him. Rowley will be jealous."

"Did you invite the heir?" Selina whispered.

"Mr. Kendrick is meeting with your father and will be here soon. As for Mr. Tavernash—"

A commotion outside the room made her groan. Lady Tavernash's strident tones echoed in the grand corridor. Mia ought to have formally invited the woman but had secretly hoped she wouldn't notice they had guests. She had begun to wonder if Lady Tavernash had spies in every corner of Woodglen.

The baronet's widow swept into the room, chin high.

Mia rose, curtseyed, and spoke before the woman could. "Lady Tavernash, you are just in time. Fillmore brought this lovely tea just minutes ago, and my uncle, the viscount, will be here momentarily."

It seemed to take the wind out of the woman's sails.

"Lady Tavernash, may I make known to you my cousin, the Honorable Eustace Selwyn? You have met the Honorable Selina Selwyn once before, I believe."

Eustace strolled over and managed a decent bow that almost offset the rude way he studied the lady.

Selina dipped a curtsey and asked hopefully, "Will Mr. Tavernash be joining us?"

Lady Tavernash examined both as if they were some species of bug. "My son has more important things to do than—"

The arrival of the gentlemen put period to her pronouncement, and Mia managed to see everyone seated with little difficulty. "Shall I pour?" She didn't wait for a reply.

Eustace grudgingly agreed to carry a cup to each person. "You've become quite the lady of the manor, Fee, for all you're married to the village troll," he whispered in her ear.

Lady Tavernash pounced quickly. "Are we to know what this mysterious meeting was about?" she asked, eyeing Gideon over her teacup.

Uncle Ludlow straightened and clutched one lapel. "Mr. Kendrick has delegated me to act as magistrate until such time as the duke returns."

Lady Tavernash turned a shade of putrid purple. "Mr. Kendrick has delegated? Who is he to delegate? My Felton is the highest-ranking man here. He is the heir presumptive. He should decide such matters. If the Crown were to get word of this…"

"Your Felton can't even get his substantial bulk out of bed this early," Mia muttered under her breath, drawing a frown from Selina, the only one close enough to hear.

"I remind you, madam, that Mr. Kendrick has power to act on the duke's behalf. He has authority to act as magistrate himself, I would warrant, but he has requested Viscount Clavering's assistance in a delicate matter regarding the…the shire," Marshall said.

Eustace, who had been studying Gideon intensely, bobbed up at that. "Power to act?" When Gideon ignored him and his father did as well, he went on. "Is it about Lizzy Carter? I heard Kendrick had been snooping around," he said.

Gideon glared at Eustace, and her cousin shrank back to Mia's delight.

"The girl that was abducted? You are investigating," Lady Tavernash said, glaring at Gideon. "That is sending the fox to inspect the chickens!"

"My dear madam," Uncle Ludlow intoned, "Mr. Kendrick had wisely distanced himself from the matter and requested my help. We will see justice done."

The old bat subsided in a flurry of ruffled feathers. Mia, for her part, wanted to smack the woman. Instead, she picked up one of the elegant platters in front of her. "Lemon cakes, anyone?"

CHAPTER THIRTY

MIA CLIMBED THE stairs, exhausted and out of sorts after the excruciating visit. When Gideon followed her up, she wished he hadn't. His grim visage and irritable manner added to her own despondent feelings. The cramping in her belly that had begun right after the Tavernash dragon invaded them didn't help, either.

Gideon swung on her as soon as they reached their quarters. "Why in God's name did you invite that prancing fool Eustace Selwyn? It was bad enough that I had to put up with the Tavernash harridan."

"Eustace may be rude, but he is as much my cousin as Selina. I could hardly leave him off the invitation," Mia replied, stunned by his uncharacteristic display of temper.

"He kept staring at me as if hoping to find scales or a tail—or information for the White's betting book," Gideon spat. "I don't want him in this house again."

"It isn't your house, though you've been given leave to act as if it is," she retorted.

"It isn't yours, either," he snapped. "When did you become lady of the manor?"

Mia choked on Gideon's cruel remark, echoing as it did the mocking words Eustace had whispered in her ears. She swallowed her tears and glowered at him. "You invited my uncle for tea. I assumed you wished him treated properly. I won't do it again," she said.

"Mia—" He reached out a hand to her, but she moved away.

"As it happens, I am feeling indisposed. I am going to rest. In my own bed. I would appreciate it if I were not disturbed." She glared at him. "And I will not be available for a few days—or nights."

She turned her back and walked to her room with as much dignity as she could lest she succumb to tears. He may have tried to follow, but she couldn't tell. She slammed the door with a satisfying whack, and he didn't try to open it. She fell on her bed and allowed the tears to come until she sobbed, and her pillow became wet.

Her cousins were horrid, Lady Tavernash was worse, and Gideon had hurt her. One other thing came into focus, pushing the other hurts aside. There would be no baby this month. She wept for disappointment over a hope she wasn't even aware she had cherished.

It was long after dawn after a sleepless night when Gideon, shaved and in shirtsleeves, paced the sitting room. He stalked to Mia's door for the third time, raised his hand to knock, but dropped it back. He'd been married for six years and certainly knew the signs of a woman's monthly discomfort. He had sent Mercy up with hot bricks the night before but had not approached his wife. There was more to Mia's distress, however; he had hurt her with his bitter words about her cousin.

Perhaps you should wait, Kendrick. Give her time and apologize when she feels more the thing. They had been married in haste less than a full month ago, and Mia had had no time to adjust to her new role.

He rang for breakfast to be brought up. Two footmen arrived with trays and a message.

"Mr. Fillmore respectfully requests a word with Mrs. Kendrick, when she has time, sir," John told him.

Respectfully? That's a first. He glanced at Mia's door after they left and sat to eat in glum solitude, hoping the delicious odors would bring her out of her room. They didn't. He pushed eggs around on his plate and nibbled toast, coming to a decision. He would go find out what his old nemesis wanted.

He gulped down his coffee, donned his coat and waistcoat, and started for the door. The door to Mia's room opened, and she stood there, pale and wan in a plain wrapper, her hair a mess around her face. Her eyes held a world of hurt.

"Mia, I—"

"I can see you're leaving. Don't stay on my account," she said, refusing to meet his eyes.

Perhaps now was not the time for reconciliation. "I'll return soon, and we can talk," he said.

She nodded, still staring at the breakfast table. "Is there tea?"

"Shall I make you a cup?" he asked.

"No. Go on."

He did, feeling like a brute. He found Fillmore in the butler's pantry. "You wished to speak with my wife? She is indisposed this morning," Gideon said.

Fillmore, sour faced as ever, sighed. "You'll do. This won't keep. At your lady's suggestion, I counted the silver yesterday. I got through the tableware. I've not yet inventoried the big pieces. Her suspicions appear to be correct. Three spoons and two butter knives are missing."

If the county suffered under a vacuum in the enforcement of law and the public peace, the household of Woodglen had an even bigger one. It appeared his wife was stepping into the breach. *Lady of the manor indeed.* She didn't have to seek the role; she was being thrust into it. That needed apology lodged itself in his heart.

"What do you suspect, Fillmore?"

"The viscount and his family have always been honorable."

True enough. "But?"

"We have many unwanted visitors this autumn," the old man said.

"You have a lock on the silver pantry?" Gideon asked before rushing on so as not to offend the butler's dignity. "Of course you do."

Fillmore's nod was a choppy dip of the head. "There is a problem, however. Mrs. Morrit's keys have gone missing. Or so she said."

Interesting. Gideon suggested methods for securing the door even from someone with a key, including a few the butler seemed amused by.

"Perhaps we should put Mrs. Kendrick's massive beast in the room," Fillmore suggested.

Was that an attempt at humor? "That would cause more problems," Gideon said.

In the end, they agreed to station footmen at the door around the clock. There was no need to make explanations public. The presence of a guard would be enough of a message to the perpetrator. Gideon wondered if Mrs. Tavernash would make a scene when she found the room guarded, though neither of them had said her name.

John, coming at a dead run, interrupted them. "Beg pardon, Mr. Fillmore, but a fancy traveling carriage has arrived—and it is full of children, sir," he said, clearly shocked.

Gideon left with as much speed as he could. Fillmore passed him on the way. Gideon rushed on. *My children are here!* A bright light had just shown on his dismal day.

CHAPTER THIRTY-ONE

MIA HEATED HER brick over the spirit lamp and wrapped it in a towel. She made willow bark tea and returned to bed with both. She struggled not to think about the previous night's quarrel. There would be time for that when she felt better. For now, she couldn't shake several kinds of misery, from Gideon's treatment at the hands of her cousins and the neighbors, to Lizzy Carter's fate, to poor Hector confined to the Woodglen stables. She closed her eyes and tried to sleep.

Hours—or perhaps moments—later a knock at the door woke her up. She stuffed the pillow around her ears.

"Mia, may I come in?"

Gideon!

"Something has happened. I need to speak to you," he said, his voice muffled by the door.

"Wait." Blessedly he did while Mia straightened herself up and sat up against the pillows. "You may come in."

He approached the bed and searched her face so intently she had to drop her gaze to her hands. "What has happened?" she asked.

"My children have arrived," he said.

"Oh! I am so sorry. I have to dress." She tossed the covers aside and began to rise. Gentle hands urged her back down.

"Easy, love. They are getting settled in the nursery. I thought perhaps they could come down here for tea if you are feeling up to it."

She nodded. "I will be. I'm not usually such a layabout."

"Do you need anything?" he asked.

"No. Mercy has been quite proficient at seeing to what I need. Of course, now the entire shire will know I'm not with child."

His startled expression amused her. "I hadn't even thought of that. I—Were you disappointed?" His distress touched her heart.

She managed to smile at him. "A bit, but there's time for it. Perhaps the gossip is a good thing."

"Have you eaten?" he asked. "I brought toast."

"Thank you," she murmured. "Kiss me now and go see those children of yours. I have no doubt they've missed you as much as you've missed them."

His kiss, tender and compassionate, soothed her. Before he left, though, he had one more thing to report.

"Clever of you to guess the silver might be disappearing."

"Someone has interfered with your family papers, diddled with your saddle, extorted money, and God knows what else. It seemed likely," she replied. "Again. No proof. Certain people have been poking around in all the public rooms and most of the ones in the family wing. Fillmore ought to check those, too."

"Feel better. We'll focus on the ledgers for now."

Her eyes flew wide open. "I am supposed to meet with Marshall at three."

"He'll manage for a day without you. I'll warn him you are under the weather."

"And I want to scan the journals I spied on the upper shelves in the family archives," she replied, feeling more energized by the moment.

"Good idea, but for today, take care of yourself and get ready to meet the children."

MARSHALL'S LACK OF surprise over Mia feeling poorly reminded Gideon forcefully that they had no privacy. As long as they stayed at Woodglen, their most intimate business would be public knowledge. He needed to get his family home, but for now he would make the best of it.

He spent the afternoon with his children in the sunlit but dismally bare nursery. There had been no children at Woodglen since Phillip and no other for two generations before. Their wise governess had brought a good supply of books, Daniel's tin soldiers, paints, kites, and stuffed bears. The girls, of course, each brought a doll.

Helen, at nine, had too much dignity to jostle for his attention. He took Jessica, who was seven, in his lap and let her tell him all the news from home, mentioning each of the servants and neighbors who came to call while Daniel hopped from foot to foot, waiting his turn. He crawled into Gideon's lap as soon as Jessica stepped down, eager to tell his father news about his pony; their dog, Hero; and the den of foxes in the near woods.

When Daniel wound down and ran off to unpack his soldiers, Gideon beckoned Helen. She came to his side and accepted a side hug but didn't climb into his lap. *My oldest is growing up!*

"What news do you have for me, Helen?"

"The biggest news is that my father has gotten married. When will we meet her?" Helen asked.

"She would be here now, but she isn't feeling well," he said.

"Is she one of those fragile ladies who takes to her bed all the time, like Esther Caddell's mother?" she asked.

He remembered Mrs. Caddell, a miserably unhappy woman who succumbed to a bout of nerves at the slightest provocation. "Not even close," he replied. "She's strong, healthy, and bright as a new penny. You'll like her."

His daughter appeared skeptical. "But when will we meet her?"

"Perhaps for tea. We'll see."

"'We'll see' is what adults say when they don't want to say no or give unpleasant news."

"Are you unhappy with me?" he asked.

Helen furrowed her brow. "You've been gone a long time. And now you married without us even being there." For a moment, he feared tears, but Helen was made of sterner stuff. "I can see why you like living in all this luxury, but you can't expect us to enjoy being pushed aside for it."

His heart sank. "Is that what you believe I did?"

She met his gaze steadily.

"I'm sorry, Helen. Nothing is or ever will be more important to me than you are," he said.

"Not even this new wife?"

He'd walked into a trap. *What do I say now?* He swallowed and made an attempt. "We are not so paltry a family that we cannot welcome Mia in."

"Mia? What am I to call her? She isn't my mother," Helen said.

"I'll let you discuss that with her," he said, feeling like a coward.

He didn't feel much better in late afternoon when he escorted them downstairs for tea. The younger two were wide-eyed at the opulence of Woodglen. Helen, by contrast, was withdrawn.

Mia stood at the window, smiling in greeting, with roses in her cheeks that hadn't been there in the morning. He hoped they hadn't been artificially assisted, but he was grateful for whatever effort they'd taken.

"Is this the dining room?" Daniel asked, drawing laughs.

"This is the suite I share with Mia. This is our sitting room," Gideon said.

He introduced the children to his wife, proud of the girls' curtsies and even Daniel's bow.

"I'm so pleased to meet you all. I've been waiting and waiting for you," Mia said. "Come sit at the table."

Helen glared skeptically at Mia's words but sat nonetheless.

"Lemon cakes!" Daniel exclaimed, reaching for one.

"Sandwiches first!" Gideon told him.

Jessica stared at Mia. "What are we to call you? Helen says we mustn't call you 'Mother' because we already had a mother even though Daniel and I don't remember and she does."

"My name is Euphemia Forbearance Kendrick. Your father calls me Mia. You can call me any of those or—" Mia leaned forward with a mischievous wink. "—make up one of your own."

That satisfied Jessica, who sat back considering the possibilities.

"Forbearance?" Helen wrinkled her nose.

"Euphie," Daniel said. "That's a funny name."

"If we call you Euphie and Papa calls you Mia, it is Euphemia all together," Jessica pointed out.

"Why don't you wait and see what you think when you know me better?" Mia said, passing a platter of sandwiches. She poured nursery tea—primarily milk with a splash of tea.

"Daniel, would you like a tour of Woodglen?" Mia asked.

"Yes! This is Uncle Phillip's grand house. I want to see it all."

"He might like the stables best," Gideon said. "So would Jessica."

"Hector would love to meet them!"

Is Hector your son?" Daniel asked.

Mia laughed, and Jessica said, "Or your horse?"

"He's almost as big as a horse, but Hector is my dog."

Soon Mia and his younger children were in an animated conversation about the relative merits of horses, dogs, bunnies, foxes, hedgehogs, and other wildlife. When Jessica brought up zebras, Mia treated the idea with perfect seriousness. He breathed a sigh of relief. She had charmed the two of them.

Helen, however, sat in stony silence, systematically demolishing her sandwich.

CHAPTER THIRTY-TWO

Jessica pronounced the ballroom larger than their entire house in Wales. Helen deemed that an exaggeration. Mia wondered. Daniel gaped in awe before discovering he could slide on the highly polished floor. Mia was relieved when Gideon grabbed the boy by the shoulder.

"You'll give Fillmore heart palpitations," Gideon said.

"Who is Fillmore?" the boy asked.

"He's the butler. He's a sort of general of the army it takes to keep this place all shiny, including that floor," Mia explained.

"Why does it need to be so shiny if no one is in here?" Helen asked.

"I've often wondered that myself," Mia said.

Having explored the wonders of the colonnaded entry hall, multiple ornately decorated drawing rooms with brilliantly colored wallpaper covered with fabulous paintings, and the stairway hall, into which multiple marble staircases descended, Jessica asked Mia how she found her way around.

"Better than at first. The middle part of the building is a square. That is where we are now. The west wing has the ballroom, where we just were, on the lowest level and the family suites and rooms above. The nursery is on the highest level of that wing. The other wing has billiard and music rooms on first with guest rooms above," Mia explained.

Distracted by the conversation, Jessica stepped on Helen's foot, and Helen let out a yelp. Helen turned a rosy hue with embarrassment and mumbled an apology. Unfortunately, her yelp echoed through the massive stairway hall, quite enchanting Daniel, who couldn't resist testing the sound.

A few squeaks and a hoot later, Jessica joined him, and Mia saw Fillmore approaching from the far end of the central corridor. Before the butler could get there—or Gideon could quiet the children—the great purple vision that was Lady Tavernash emerged from the chinois drawing room and descended on them.

"What is the meaning of this? How dare these ill-bred urchins upset the peace of my house!" she shouted. "Fillmore! These children are intruders. See that they are removed."

Gideon opened his mouth to object, but Daniel got there first. "This is my Uncle Phillip's house," he insisted.

Oh dear. Mia felt rather than saw servants lurking in alcoves, taking it all in.

"I beg your pardon?" The woman huffed, shaking purple ruffles in all directions. "Who, pray tell, is your uncle?"

"The Duke of Glenmoor," Helen answered. "And this *is* his house. He said we were to visit anytime."

The Tavernash woman waved that away with a haughty gesture. "The duke is missing. He is unlikely to return. This house will be my son's and therefore my home. I will thank you to respect it."

Helen turned to her father, stricken. "Won't return?"

"Your son can't have it," Daniel announced loud enough for all to hear. "Uncle Phillip told me it would be mine one day, but I don't know if I want it. What will I do with all those drawing rooms?"

Lady Tavernash's mouth gaped in a most unladylike manner.

Daniel turned to Mia. "Will you show us the dining room now?"

"And the library," Jessica added.

Mia feared Lady Tavernash would have apoplexy. "Stop right

there!" Lady Tavernash shouted. "The duke is gone, and you have no rights here. You"—he aimed a bony finger at Gideon—"are a bastard and an upstart attempting to steal my son's heritage by any means possible. Where is this brother of yours if indeed he is alive? Rumors of his death are rampant, some believe at your hand. While you and this, this strumpet swan through the halls and—"

"Uncle Phillip is dead?" Jessica howled. She sobbed into her father's leg.

"I think that is quite enough. You will not terrorize my children with unfounded rumors about a beloved uncle and lies about their father. Insult my wife again and I will have you and your precious son removed from this house. You are well aware I have authority to do so." Gideon glared at the woman with an unblinking gaze.

"You—She. Fillmore…" The woman glanced around frantically.

Fillmore peered implacably back, a study in calm.

She swallowed. "Fillmore, that little brat claims he can supplant my son. Explain to him that this is impossible."

Fillmore bowed. "I regret, my lady, that isn't my place to say."

Mia turned to the children. "Shall we continue the tour of your uncle's house with the dining room? Wait until you see the chandeliers."

"But when can we see the stable, M…that is, Euphie? I want to see the horses," Jessica said.

"Dining room, library, then stables," Mia said. "This corridor is very long. Shall we skip?"

And so they did. Lady Tavernash, Fillmore, and Gideon all stared after her.

WHEN GIDEON ELECTED to take the children on a tour of the estate and piled them all into a landau with Bert driving, Mia reluctantly stayed behind to meet Marshall in the steward's office. He handed her a packet of receipts, notes, and messages. She picked up pen and paper and made notes while he listed expenses and payments from his prodigious memory. The man had proven to be as talented and effective as she'd anticipated.

Mrs. Demming, the cook, joined them. Marshall shrugged and ran a hand over the back of his head. "I thought she might as well give you the kitchen finances directly. Mrs. Millbrook will bring the weekly dairy numbers tomorrow." With a dip of his head, he bid them goodbye.

The cook turned to Mia, wide-eyed. She handed over some scribbled notes that Mia managed to figure out with a bit of diplomacy. "Do you have everything you need, Mrs. Demming?" Mia asked.

"Need?" the cook asked.

"Supplies, help, tools…"

Mrs. Demming sat back with a sigh. "I've been trying to explain to Marshall and that dried-up old raisin Mrs. Morrit why I need an undercook. All they allow me is Peg, the one kitchen maid and a lazy one at that."

"You manage those dinners with just Peg for help—and that excellent tea you served when my uncle visited as well? My dear Mrs. Demming, you are a wonder-worker!"

Mrs. Demming glowed under the praise. "It dint matter so much last year with His Grace gone and no visitors—and no Tavernash to keep us running. Then the mother came with her snooping and demanding. I'm run off my feet."

"Now Mr. Kendrick and I have added children to your burdens," Mia murmured.

"Young ones aren't burdens. They are a joy. It's the housemaids complaining about fetching meals up to the nursery," the cook replied.

"It is too much for one person. I can tell you that from my

own experience! I'll speak with Mr. Marshall about hiring an undercook and second kitchen maid, at least as long as we're here," Mia told her. She wondered how Marshall had been so shortsighted, but then, men had no idea what it took to work miracles in the kitchen.

"And the Tavernashes?"

"Especially as long as they are here," Mia answered. "Now tell me how you've been managing all this."

Mrs. Demming started describing her methods and struggles, but the conversation quickly devolved into a cozy chat about recipes, favorite dishes, men who liked their food, and shared anecdotes about kitchen disasters. The cook asked Mia if she wouldn't like to begin approving menus.

"I'd be honored to. Two heads are always better than one," Mia replied.

"Millbrook will be glad to see you sitting behind that desk, madam, I can tell you. I know I am." Mrs. Demming rose to leave looking happier than when she'd dragged in but paused as she reached the door. She clutched her skirts and frowned as if groping for words.

"Is there a problem, Mrs. Demming?"

"No, ma'am. I just—I want to say that husband of yours is nothing like what they say. He's a good man." With that, she scurried away.

"He is that, Mrs. Demming. He is that," Mia whispered at the woman's retreating form.

HELEN REARED BACK when Hector came loping through the stables to greet Gideon. "He's a monster!"

"Hector, sit." The dog obeyed Gideon instantly and earned an ear scratch. "Hector is Mia's dog. He's a sweetheart, actually. And more obedient than some children I know."

Daniel had no fear whatsoever, even though the beast topped him by over an inch. "May I pet him?"

"Of course!" Gideon showed him some of Hector's favorite spots for scratching. "He'll love you forever for that. Why don't you three take him for a walk out behind the stable while I have a chat with Bert?" He taught them a few simple commands. Helen remained skeptical, but Jessica was delighted to command such a magnificent canine.

Left in private, he approached the groom. "What is eating you, Bert? Something aggravated you mightily back there."

"It was Vincent," Bert said.

"One of the field workers?" Gideon tried to picture the young man. The son of Alger Collins, Woodglen tenant, he thought. They had stopped by to watch the workers putting in winter wheat and turnips. He'd kept his distance while Gideon chatted with the others.

"He was keen to call me vermin for..." Bert stuttered to a stop.

"Spit it out, Bert. I've probably heard worse," Gideon sighed.

"Yer none of the things they said when you came, sir. I know that. Yer no cripple and smart as they come. The maids have no complaints. So I figure the rest of it is all lies, too."

"What is the rest of it?" Gideon prodded.

"That you're after Woodglen for yourself. That you did something to the duke to get him out of the way, and then came with papers saying you could run the place."

"Get him out of the way?" Gideon asked.

"Vincent said maybe you didn't kill him, but you probably have him locked up in your mine in Wales," Bert said.

It was so uncannily like what his father had actually attempted to do to him that Gideon was momentarily taken aback. "And you, Bert, what do you think?"

"You've been nothing but fair with any of us here," Bert said.

So if I'm stealing Woodglen, you don't care... "But do you believe the stories?"

"It don't seem likely to me, and the rest of it was lies, so no. I don't," Bert said as if making up his mind, his face still troubled. "Still, I heard your boy told Lady Tavernash that he is to have Woodglen. How can that be? Begging your pardon, Mr. Kendrick, but bastards can't inherit."

"No offense taken, Bert." Daniel's words had flown through the staff faster than Gideon had expected. He could only wonder how much more trouble they would cause.

CHAPTER THIRTY-THREE

WHEN MIA SUGGESTED that they take the children to Nether Abbas two days later, Gideon expressed reluctance. She wouldn't take no for an answer.

"You were right that people needed to see me after our marriage. We haven't shown ourselves enough. As long as we're hidden here, rumors continue to fly. People need to see you with your children," she insisted.

He frowned down at his morning coffee, looking for excuses to avoid facing down the gossips, she suspected.

"Your work is caught up," she went on, and she was right. There was nothing more to be gained staring at the same ledgers. Gideon had been riding out with Marshall, reviewing and learning about estate management, but he was frustrated at the lack of progress in other areas that kept him here. Unless they caught Jem or found proof Lady Tavernash embezzled, there was little they could do. Nor, had they heard anything from Dr. Standish in Shaftsbury about Lizzy Carter. Mia had taken some of the old journals from the stillroom archives but had not yet read them.

"A day with the children would be good for both of us," she said. "We can let the girls buy some hair bows or fripperies at the drapers, and maybe stop for tea."

He gave in.

They took the open landau with Bert at the ribbons once again. Gideon, however, rode Hannibal alongside.

They left Bert with the horse and carriage at the livery at the edge of town and walked. Curtains twitched as they passed, and the back of Mia's neck tingled with the sense of watching eyes.

Helen lingered at the window to the apothecary. "You promised me lavender soap, Euphemia," she said.

Mia, delighted that she'd unbent enough to address her by name, agreed that was so. Mrs. Duger, who Mia suspected had hurried from her post at the window, glared at them from behind the counter.

"We're interested in more of that lovely lavender soap," Mia said, her smile forced and her jaw stiff.

"Is this the boy who claimed Woodglen will be his one day?" Evelyn Duger demanded, staring at Daniel.

Helen raised her chin and gazed directly at the woman with all the hauteur of a potential duchess. "My uncle, His Grace of Glenmoor, has assured my brother that is so, though why it should be of your concern, I cannot say."

Mrs. Duger glanced away, muttering about disrespectful children.

"I think I don't want that soap after all," Helen announced, turning on her heels and leaving the shop.

Mia glanced up at Gideon, who reined in his temper with obvious effort. "Then we may as well be on our way." He tipped his hat, and they left.

"What a horrid woman! She shouldn't have our patronage," Helen pronounced.

Mia couldn't argue. She smiled, certain that this newfound stepdaughter would grow into a formidable woman someday.

"I agree, Helen. And she won't. However, kindly refrain from repeating or announcing what your uncle said. Remember what I told you about expectations and legalities?" Gideon cautioned.

"And greed," Helen said solemnly. She turned to Mia. "Papa's American uncle tried to use Daniel to take money from Uncle

Phillip last year."

Mia wondered how long before they had to explain the entire truth to the children. Gideon's vague "expectations" may have merely confused them, but Helen's story had to terrify them. No wonder Gideon tried to keep their family mess quiet.

Mr. Pettifer the draper filled their order for ribbons in silence, but his furtive glances at Gideon and Daniel made his curiosity obvious.

They left quickly and made their way to Mrs. Hinson's little tearoom, confident Martha Hinson, at least, would be polite.

As they walked, Mia's sense of unease increased. It wasn't helped when she caught sight of Bill Carter watching them from the front of the smithy with Vincent Collins and some bullyboys from the Cockcrow at his side.

They sat at a table in the tearoom, one large enough to accommodate all of them. None of Martha's former pleasantness was in evidence. She appeared tense and subdued.

"Good morning, Martha," Mia chirped. "I hope you have those delightful ginger biscuits today."

Martha nodded. "Will you want tea?" Her eyes darted to Daniel as she spoke.

"Yes, please," Gideon replied, "and nursery tea for my children."

"Children, Mrs. Hinson's biscuits are the best in the area," Mia said, attempting to break the tension in the room. "And if I recall correctly, so are her honey buns."

Martha blinked at Mia. "I can bring those, too."

"That would be lovely," Mia said. She glanced at Gideon warily, wishing she hadn't proposed the outing.

They were served in good time, but Martha didn't linger to speak with them. Even the children seemed subdued as if picking up on the tension. They ate quietly.

Two women Mia knew to be shop employees came in and took a table. The pair of them studied the children avidly. More nasty Nether Abbas gossips. Now she was certain the outing had been a bad idea.

Martha came in to take the women's order. She turned to ask the Kendricks if they needed anything else. Mia thanked her politely but said they were finished.

"Mrs. Hinson," Gideon asked before Martha could leave, "has there been any word about Lizzy Carter?"

The woman's brows shot up. "You'd know before I would," she said, turning to go. They went back through the grocery and were almost to the door when Martha approached Mia. "Might I have a private word, Mrs. Kendrick?" she asked.

Mia glanced at Gideon. He nodded and led the children out. "What is it, Martha?" Mia asked.

"Be careful. My Alvin says talk at the Cockcrow is growing ominous with Carter ranting about Lizzy not turning up and now this business about the boy," she whispered.

"What about Daniel?" Mia asked, keeping her voice down.

"They say Mr. Kendrick done something bad to the duke to take Woodglen for the boy somehow, that his papers are a pack of lies."

Mia's heart sank. In spite of their efforts, the gossip simply worsened. It was as if someone was actively feeding it. *But who at Woodglen frequents the Cockcrow? A few of the grooms, perhaps. Yet Bert seems loyal. The footmen?* "Tell me one thing, Martha. Has Jem Hawkins been seen hereabouts? He left Woodglen without warning, and we've not seen hide nor hair of him."

Martha bit her lower lip, glanced around, and nodded. "Aye. Turns up at the Cockcrow and then disappears every day or so." She put a hand on Mia's arm. "You be careful. I always liked you," she said.

Gideon gazed at her expectantly.

"I'll talk to you after we get back," she said, anxious to be away.

They drove along the main road around Woodglen's lower fields. Helen, to Mia's left on the rear-facing seat, sat deep in thought. Jessica, sitting across from Helen, pointed out flowers and animals to Daniel. Gideon rode a bit faster, the distance between him and the rest of them lengthening by the time they turned up the road that led to the manor and to Selwyn Court. Hedges lined the narrow road on both sides as they drove on toward the break in the hedgerows where Mia had encountered Gideon that first day.

Noise and some scuffling behind the shrubs to Helen's left drew Mia's attention. Jessica went up on her knees to watch the spot as they passed. "Do you suppose it is deer or a fox?" she asked.

Daniel's scream, quickly muffled, sent ice through Mia's veins. She turned back as he was pulled over the side of the moving landau. She grabbed his foot with one hand and flung open the door, shouting to Bert. At the same moment, a shot rang out, and the horses bolted with Mia only halfway out of the landau. She landed on the dirt with a shoe in one hand as a figure in black carrying Daniel disappeared through the break in the hedge.

Mia scrambled to her feet, cursing her lack of weapon, and charged through the hedgerow only to stumble again. This time, she almost hit a good-sized rock. She grabbed it in one hand as she rose, picked up her skirts with the other, and ran.

"Drop that child now!" she shouted. Daniel, bless him, kicked and fought while the man who snatched him tried to control flailing arms. It slowed the man some, but her skirts and the field stubble slowed her as well. She finally drew within ten feet—her breath heaving—dropped her skirt, and let the rock fly. It bounced off the top of the man's head and brought him to a halt. He turned, groping in his belt for his knife.

Mia froze at the sight.

"Follow me and I'll cut him," the brute said through the scarf that covered his face. Daniel, now held one-handed, squirmed, and the hand with the knife pointed outward rose to secure him across his chest. The boy latched on to the hand, biting down hard.

The miscreant shouted and dropped the knife but not the boy. Before he could turn and run, Mia had the rock back in her hand. This time, from close quarters, she didn't miss. She hammered the man's face, and when he screamed, she brought it down with both hands and all her strength against the side of his head.

"Run!" she yelled to Daniel, who had broken free. She hit the abductor repeatedly. The man, blood streaming down his head, grabbed her arm, and the rock fell. His hands came to her throat, but he let go abruptly when Daniel bit his thigh through cotton trousers.

The man grabbed Daniel by the hair, letting Mia escape his grasp, then stopped abruptly, eyes wide with fear. A great black horse sailed over the hedge with a figure of fury on its back, hit the ground at a gallop, and closed on them. The abductor turned to run, fell over Mia's outstretched foot, and landed hard, while Daniel hid behind Mia's skirts.

Gideon leaped off Hannibal, fell astride the man, and raised back his fist. He put it down. "It appears a woman has already beaten you," he said, yanking down the scarf. One eye had swollen almost shut, and the gash on his brow bled profusely. He smelled of spirits—bottled courage.

Mia gasped, hugging Daniel close.

"Yer supposed to be a cripple," the man whined. Gideon ignored him.

"Do you know him?" Gideon asked his wife.

She nodded. "It's Sam Duger, the apothecary. This is hardly his usual thing."

"I would hope not. Abducting a child may just get him transported if not hung."

"No!" Duger shouted. "I—"

"You what?" Gideon growled.

"Carter said as how you deserved it, since you took his Lizzy," Duger whined.

Gideon did hit him then, and Mia took bloodthirsty satisfaction.

Daniel threw himself at Gideon when he rose. "I fought him, Papa, like you taught me, even better than last time."

"Last time?" Mia gasped in horror, remembering that Gideon's maternal uncle had attempted to use Daniel as a pawn just a year before.

DEEP IN HIS soul, Gideon cursed the power of the duchy and the envy, machinations, and evil it inevitably attracted, particularly the ones visited on children. It took him the better part of an hour to calm his children while Helen, Jessica, Daniel, Bert, and Mia all told their versions of what had happened. They had trussed Duger up with Gideon's cravat and a ruffle torn from the bottom of Mia's gown and handed him over to Marshall, who'd tossed him in a storage bin and locked it.

In the cacophony of stories, only a few things were clear. Duger was an incompetent amateur, not a professional kidnapper, and he had not acted alone. None of them had seen who made the commotion behind the other hedge to distract them, and none had any idea who'd shot one of the carriage horses.

Gideon was fairly certain the shot had come from the same side as the commotion no doubt designed to distract attention from the grab, but whether there were one, two, or even more involved, he couldn't say. No one had come after the carriage or the girls. No one had come to Duger's aid, either.

They wound down, exhausted at last. Helen wept. "He almost took our Daniel." Gideon reached for her, but she threw herself at Mia. "You saved him. I was so frightened when you jumped down and ran after him, but you didn't hesitate. I'm so sorry I've been mean to you. I—"

Mia wrapped her arms around Helen's shoulders. "Hush now. Of course I was a shock to you, and of course that vile man frightened you. It's over now. Let's see if we can have tea sent up to the nursery." She glanced plaintively at Gideon.

He kissed her cheek. "I'll tell you everything I learn," he whispered. He kissed his children, too, and urged them off.

Marshall had been hanging back, but he approached now.

"Well, Bert, what else do you know?" Marshall demanded.

"Nothing, I swear, but I think maybe you ought to ask Peter and Frank. They've been back at the Cockcrow lately," Bert shrugged. "That Duger's a regular there. So is Bill Carter."

Marshall rounded up the two grooms, Frank from the hay he was baling and Peter hiding in a stall. It wasn't clear if he was hiding from work or Gideon. Marshall shoved them both down on a bench. "Tell us what you know about this attempt on Mr. Kendrick's son and don't bother lying!"

"His *son?*" Peter gasped. He appeared genuinely shocked, but Gideon didn't miss the emphasis on the word *son.*

"I take it Daniel wasn't the intended victim. Or perhaps the originally planned victim. What did they plan to do to me?" Gideon asked.

Peter studied his feet for a moment before glancing sideways at Frank.

"Frank?" Marshall growled.

"We don't know much. Only gossip at the tavern," Frank said.

"Repeat this gossip," Gideon demanded.

"Mostly fast talk. Some said you needed a lesson about coming here and throwing your weight around. Some said you needed what they did the night the old duke threw you out, that you had no business coming back," Frank said.

Peter nodded, braver with a friend talking.

"Who?" Marshall asked.

"What do you mean?" Peter asked.

"Who are the big talkers?"

The groom shrugged. "Duger always had a bad mouth in his cups. Bill Carter kept telling folk they should beat the truth out of you about Lizzy. Selwyn—" Peter glanced up sharply. "He'd be yer cousin now. No wonder he's quieted lately. May've gone off to London anyway."

"Who else?" Marshall demanded.

"Mostly Jem," Peter said, drawing a ferocious frown from Frank.

"You mean Jem has been hanging around since he disappeared from here?" Gideon asked.

Frank nodded morosely.

"Jem Hawkins has been at the Cockcrow? Why didn't you tell me?" Marshall shouted.

"He asked us not to. Jem's a mate. Didn't want to cause him trouble, did we?" Peter said.

Marshall cursed under his breath and bemoaned beetle-brained grooms.

"What exactly has Jem been saying about me?" Gideon asked coldly.

The two men shifted in their seats.

Frank glared at Peter. "Just the usual. What folks say."

Gideon suspected folks would have nothing to say if Jem didn't feed them rumors. "Specifically, please," he said.

"Yer a bastard. Thinking you can take Woodglen's a pipe dream," Peter mumbled.

"True that, ain't it?" Frank put in.

"Go on," Gideon drawled, unabashed.

"Jem said you diddled with Woodglen money, taking what you want. Said you stole from the duke. Said the maids all have to hide from you even now that you're married. Other folk ask if you dint take Lizzie, who did? Things like that," Peter said.

Marshall cursed colorfully, out loud this time. "Damned Jem Hawkins put his own thieving ways on you, Kendrick. The snake."

"Where might we find Jem Hawkins?" Gideon asked smoothly.

"Aside from the Cockcrow? Don't know. He may be sleeping

rough," Frank said.

"Or at the smithy," Peter suggested. "We done?"

"For now," Gideon said. "I suggest you avoid the Cockcrow for a while."

"Altogether if you hope to keep your jobs," Marshall added.

Peter looked up at Marshall. "Jem's the one stealing?" he asked.

"Damned right. Now get on with you," Marshall growled.

Gideon stood lost in thought after the two grooms left. Marshall studied him closely. "Not alone, you're not," Marshall said at last, guessing his intentions. "That little wife of yours would have a fit."

Gideon grinned ruefully. "I wasn't going alone. I thought I'd take Hector."

CHAPTER THIRTY-FOUR

G IDEON RODE BACK to Nether Abbas in the gloaming with Hector loping along at his side. He found Carter's smithy dark, cold, and empty. Cursing fate, he tied Hannibal in front of the one place he had been determined to avoid at all costs, the Cockcrow tavern, determined to confront Bill Carter in spite of the ache in his back caused by leaping off Hannibal earlier.

Lights shone from the window, and the jovial sounds of the evening regulars filled the air. He inhaled a deep breath and took a step over the threshold he'd been tossed over when he was sixteen. Hector followed him in, dropping to his side when the voices stopped, and all eyes turned to Gideon and his great beast.

He planted both feet apart, stood tall, and let the silence linger for several moments. "I am, as you see, the troll of Woodglen. Mute and stammering." He scanned the silent crowd. "That is how you describe me when you're in your cups, is it not?"

No one responded. The men continued to stare. He recognized some—Hinson the grocer, Gratis, his old nemesis Adcock, and Rogers, the same man that had thrown him out twenty years before, a bit grayer but every bit as nasty-looking. There was no sign of either Bill Carter or Jem Hawkins.

"Where can I find Jem Hawkins, the lying snake?" he demanded.

No answer.

"Hawkins has been stealing from Woodglen for years. It wasn't even difficult to detect. He ran when we uncovered it, but I hear he hung around blaming others. Where is he?" Gideon said, using a voice that had cut through brawling miners more than once.

No answer.

He tried again. "The assizes may take up the matter of those who aided his crimes by hiding him."

His words had no effect. He turned to leave.

"Where's Lizzy Carter, then, if yer looking for folk?" Gideon recognized the speaker as Vincent Collins, the tenant Bert had warned him about.

"Where is the father that drove her off?" Gideon retorted. The more he saw of Bill Carter, the surer he was of that.

That remark drew a few sympathetic nods. Only a few. The Cockcrow was a sewer of small-minded speculation and poison. He turned to leave and called Hector to follow. A pewter mug hit the back of Gideon's head, Hector growled, and Gideon braced for further attack. It didn't come.

He turned and peered at them, face-to-face, one after another. The coward who hid in the crowd and took his courage from drink could have been any of them. "Tell Jem Hawkins to quit hiding like a frightened rabbit and come confront me at Woodglen."

He mounted and rode out of the village under a darkening sky. It occurred to him that the two he sought may not have gone far from the point of attack. Instead of following the road, he turned Hannibal onto the fields that lay in stubble after harvest, moving in the direction of Woodglen's dairy. Mrs. Millbrook seemed the type to lock the place up good and tight, but he recalled a storage shed behind the place, one with shrubs for cover. It wasn't far across the field from the hedges and convenient to the village as well.

Before he could approach closely, a shadow—a huge, lumbering figure—emerged from the sheltering bushes. Clearly Gideon on his massive horse had been outlined against the sky, his approach obvious and perhaps expected.

"What are you looking for out here in the dark, Kendrick?" Bill Carter boomed.

"Hiding from your crimes, Carter?" Gideon asked, reining in his horse. Hector inched forward, a growl deep in his throat. "Stay!" Gideon ordered.

"I ain't done nothing," Carter said. "Searching for my Lizzy." He walked toward Gideon, ignoring Hector, who inched forward on his haunches.

"You set Duger on my family," Gideon said, his words as cold as his heart facing the man who'd tried to harm Daniel. "We're calling in Clavering tomorrow to sit as magistrate and question Duger. I have no doubt he'll hand your minion over to the assizes for trial and you with him. If you have a defense, I suggest you be there."

Gideon had come out with no assistance, not even rope to tie the man. He didn't mean to drag him in, merely to confront him. He'd been too angry to consider it might force Carter to run. Belatedly he realized how badly he'd miscalculated.

"I have a defense all right," Carter snarled. He grabbed Gideon by the arm and yanked him from the horse. Hannibal sidled. Hector came round and attacked. Gideon's arm snapped, blinding him with pain.

Hector barked and snapped, launching himself at Carter. Carter held on to Gideon's broken arm. Gideon, half fainting from pain, shook it off and clamped his free hand on Carter's throat. Still Carter hung on.

"Help me, damn it!" Carter shouted. A shot rang out, and Hector fell to the ground.

"Hold him," said a second voice. Jem Hawkins emerged from the shrubbery, tossing his gun aside and taking out a vicious-looking knife. "We'll cut him and dump his body in the ash heap behind your smithy until we can deal with it," he said, waving the weapon.

Gideon struggled for consciousness as Carter yanked him by the arm.

"I dunno, Jem. Selling the boy to a press gang is different from murder. Can't we do the same with Kendrick?"

"Don't be a—" At the new voice, Jem swung to the right.

Marshall! Thank God, Gideon thought.

"Put it down, Jem. My pistol is faster than you can move." The sound of a hammer pulled back accompanied the threat.

Jem hesitated. "You owe me, Marshall," he said.

"Put it down," Marshall said, emerging from the gloom. "You back off, too, Carter. Move over by Hawkins."

"I kin snap his neck with one hand," Carter growled.

Before Carter could move, Gideon summoned all his strength and jammed his knuckles into Carter's throat, followed quickly by a finger poke to his eyes. The big man went down choking.

"Put the knife down, or I'll shoot you where you stand, Jem," Marshall said.

Jem dropped the knife. "Let me go, or I'll tell the world your secret, Marshall. What good is a land steward who can't read?" he spat, taking a step sideways.

"Move again and you're a dead man," Marshall said.

"Too late with that threat, Hawkins. We know about Marshall. It doesn't stop him from doing his job well. He just needs to choose his assistants more carefully," Gideon said, breath heaving.

"Now help this buffoon to his feet and into that shed behind you," Marshall said. "Now! It would give me great pleasure to shoot you for what you've done."

Marshall herded them into the shed and barred the door with a piece of wood. "This won't hold too long. We need to set a guard until morning when we can move them up to the house."

Gideon had dropped to his knees next to Hector, his left arm hanging uselessly at his side. "He's still breathing. Leave me that pistol. I'll keep watch over them and this good-hearted animal. Take Hannibal and come back with Harv and Bert and a wagon to carry Hector."

"That arm needs looked at. They'll keep for a few hours."

Gideon shook his head. "I'm not leaving this dog. It may break Mia's heart if he doesn't make it." He glanced up and took the weapon from Marshall. "Thank you for following me. That was close."

"I told you you weren't going alone, you daft man," Marshall said. He left with both horses and a whistle.

WEEPING OVER BELOVED fur-bearing friends and foolish husbands served no one well. Mia managed to avoid it. Just. How could she lash out at Gideon when he'd lain, racked with pain, at Hector's side for over an hour until help arrived? Nor could she succumb to the tears that threatened at his agony when Dr. Gratis, who turned out to be a better bonesetter than physician, stabilized the arm. She almost lapsed into weeping when she tore herself from his bedside to check on Hector and found Helen lying at the great beast's side, whispering encouragement in his ears.

"What are you doing up in the middle of the night?" Mia asked.

"I couldn't sleep thinking about what happened to Daniel. Then I heard noise and came down. I peeked and, and… How is Papa?" The girl choked back tears.

"In pain but well. His arm is broken, but it has been set and should heal with no trouble," Mia assured her with a hug. "How is our Hector?"

At his name, the massive head rose, and Mia bent to pet it. He settled back down.

"Mr. Marshall removed the bullet and saw to the wound. He said Hector should recover if we can keep him from running around. That's a job I can do," Helen said.

"Thank you," Mia whispered. "You were doing very well

when I came in."

"See to Papa, Mia. I can care for Hector," Helen said.

The use of her diminutive name touched Mia deeply. She kissed the girl's cheek, glanced at Marshall hovering nearby, and left her to it.

A sleepless night didn't prepare any of them for the day to come, but Mia's uncle arrived midmorning, summoned by Marshall, and there was no avoiding it. Uncle Ludlow and Marshall came up to the Kendrick sitting room, and the men discussed how they might proceed.

Gideon insisted on being present, regardless of his pain. Helen had been summoned from the stables, and the children's governess made sure all three were groomed and waiting in the breakfast room in case the viscount had questions for them. Mia prayed they wouldn't be summoned.

The green room, largest of the drawing rooms, had been rearranged and filled with more people than Mia expected when she entered to find her uncle, dignified and serene, at one end of the room, in a large chair. She helped Gideon to a comfortable chair near the front and propped pillows around his splinted arm before approaching her uncle. The viscount took her hand and kissed it. "Bad doings, niece," he said.

"Thank you, Uncle," she whispered.

She turned and scanned the folk crowded into the room. Alvin Hinson surprised her, as did Dr. Gratis. Evelyn Duger wept openly. There were other villagers, and Mia worried they were there to spread lies about Gideon. Mrs. Millbrook sat next to Mrs. Demming. Mrs. Morrit stood, pinch lipped, in the back.

Mia returned to Gideon's side, just as Lady Tavernash sailed in on her son's arm. They ignored most of the room and approached Uncle Ludlow directly. "What is happening here, my lord? Why are all these people milling about my drawing room?" the lady demanded.

"There were difficulties in the village yesterday," the viscount replied. "Perhaps you might like to observe the proceedings."

Lady Tavernash glanced at her son, raised a haughty chin, and took a seat with Felton beside her.

Fillmore slipped in to stand next to Mrs. Morrit just before Marshall arrived with all four grooms following. They surrounded three prisoners with hands tied in front of them and led them to three wooden chairs placed near the viscount for that purpose. Lady Tavernash blanched at the sight of Jem. The grooms and Marshall stood along the side.

"We'll begin with the issue of the attempt to abduct Daniel Kendrick yesterday. I call on the groom Frank to testify."

Jem appeared contemptuous and Carter surprised. Duger's hands shook, and he kept his eyes on the floor. Lady Tavernash kept her expression blank.

Uncle Ludlow smiled at the groom. "I understand you are a regular attendee at Mr. Rogers's establishment in Nether Abbas." That brought general laughter. "Is that so?"

"Aye. Loyal, I am," Frank said. More laughter.

"Can you please repeat for me some of the talk you've heard?"

Frank described various vicious lies about Gideon, all of them familiar.

"And did this talk take the form of threats to the Kendricks?" the viscount asked.

"Yes, my lord. There was some as wished to drive Mr. Kendrick away," Frank said. "They said as how he ought to have a good thrashing. At least."

"I see. Was kidnapping mentioned? Or murder?"

"Not in my hearing," Frank said.

"Are any of those who made threats present?" Uncle Ludlow asked.

Frank laughed. "Oh, aye. Sitting right in front of you. Carter, Jem, and Sam Duger. Others, too," he said, glancing at Rogers.

Mia's uncle let him step away and called Sam Duger.

"Softest target," Gideon whispered.

Sure enough. It took little prodding to get Duger to describe how threats to beat Gideon morphed into a plot to kidnap Daniel and sell him to press-gangs in Weymouth. "Why would you do that?" Uncle Ludlow demanded.

"Kendrick is strutting around Woodglen like he owns it, claiming it ought to go to his son," Sam Duger said.

Mia wondered if she was the only one who watched Lady Tavernash's lips tighten at that.

Sam wasn't finished. "Besides, Carter here said Kendrick deserves to lose one of his, him taking Lizzy and all."

A murmur met that announcement, and Carter glared pure hatred at Gideon. One voice, small but sharp and clear, cut through the noise. "Da? What is going on?"

Mia spun around to see Lizzy Carter standing in the doorway, next to Dr. Standish. She approached the front.

"I heard you were looking for me. Why would you think Mr. Kendrick did something? It was her that arranged it." All eyes followed the girl's finger. It pointed at Lady Tavernash.

⇶⫷

"Sorry for the delay, Kendrick. Took me days to find her working for a merchant's widow in Shaftsbury as a tweeny," Standish said, drawing up a chair next to Gideon while Viscount Clavering called for order. They'd been right. Lizzy had run to the bigger town for work.

"The Tavernash witch arranged it and set rumors loose blaming you," Mia said out loud, fire in her eyes.

Gideon felt simply grateful that looks could not kill because if they could, Lady Tavernash's certainly would. The woman, of course, called Lizzy a liar and denied everything.

Lizzy laughed in her face. "Your nose should fall off for that bouncer. You paid me ten quid and had him take me to Shaftsbury by wagon," she said, pointing at Jem.

Carter was on his feet, shouting. "You got ten quid and dint hand it over? You run from me? You can't do that. You're my daughter. You belong to me."

Lizzy shrank from him, obviously fearful. She peered around and went to hover near Standish. Gideon's determination to see Carter transported hardened.

The viscount called for order. In the end, he had Carter removed by two grooms and a footman. He warned Lady Tavernash he would do the same to her if she didn't quiet down. He called for Jem to testify.

"Mr. Hawkins, I suggest you take this opportunity to tell the truth. We have witnesses to attempted kidnapping and threats of murder already. Are Miss Carter's words true?"

Jem glanced at Lady Tavernash. "Yes, and that isn't all." It all tumbled out then, so much perfidy that not one person even reacted to the revelation that Marshall couldn't read, so buried was it under extortions, threats, and thievery by the Tavernash pair and Jem. He even admitted vandalizing Gideon's saddle as part of a campaign to drive him away.

"You have no proof!" Lady Tavernash shouted.

"My lord," Gideon interjected, "may I suggest that Mr. Marshall and I search the lady's suite while she remains here?"

She was halfway out of her chair but subsided when Harv and Frank stepped in front of her.

Standish helped Gideon up. "I'll check that arm before I leave," he murmured.

Gideon leaned on Mia, and they followed Marshall up to the family wing. What they found exceeded even their suspicions.

CHAPTER THIRTY-FIVE

MIA STARED AT the growing pile on the sitting room table. Silver spoons. A teapot. Mrs. Morrit's missing master keys. Large amounts of cash.

"Count it, Kendrick. Does it match what was taken?" Marshall asked. He set down a pearl-handled revolver and a long-bladed knife. "I found these in Tavernash's drawers."

Mia glanced up. "We haven't gone through the lady's drawers yet."

Marshall pinked up. "I thought maybe you might do that."

Mia opened a drawer full of shawls and found nothing. In a drawer of delicate and very expensive lady's unmentionables, she found two packets of letters. There was nothing else.

"You were right, Gideon. Someone did rifle through the family papers." She spread them out to read. "Oh my!"

"What is it?" Gideon asked.

"Your great-grandfather obtained the services of an inquiry agent in 1783, not long before he died. There being no living sons, the man sorted through his three grandsons, all from different fathers. The son of the oldest had died the winter before. One was deemed ineligible, being from a younger son. The last was found in South Carolina in the army."

"That would be my father," Gideon said. "I think that younger cousin died without issue."

"Yes. Your father was deemed the proper heir and called home. The letter goes on to discuss Tavernash's grandfather," she said.

"Not his father?"

"No. His grandfather, apparently a younger cousin of *your* grandfather. Confusing. This is the interesting part. 'We are pleased to locate an heir in your direct line. Your brother Roland Tavernash's line is riddled with questionable marriages.' It goes on to tell the old duke (your great-grandfather, I think), 'Your nephew's marriage is undoubtedly illegal under the marriage act and his son of doubtful parentage.'" Mia wrinkled her nose. "The nephew would be Felton's grandfather, and the son of doubtful parentage would be Felton's father." She grinned at Gideon. "We can see why she stole them from the archives."

She opened the second one, from the same agent, and laughed out loud. "Your father had his doubts about our Felton also. Apparently, there is—or was—a midwife prepared to swear that Felton was born to one Eunice Battersea two weeks before she married your grandfather's second cousin and should be in no way considered eligible to inherit."

Gideon appeared to struggle to take it in. "That may be why the Committee for Privileges is so slow to approve him inheriting his father's title. Aside from the fact they can't prove the duke is dead."

"Perhaps we should share this letter with them," Mia said, grinning impishly.

"I'll let you two handle this whole inheritance business. If you don't mind, we have a viscount waiting to deal with theft, kidnapping, and attempted murder—yours, I might add. I'd like to get to it," Marshall said.

Mia picked up the letters and kept them to herself. She couldn't resist letting Lady Tavernash see that she had them while Gideon and Marshall presented the hard evidence from her room before huddling in a whispered conference with Uncle Ludlow.

The viscount ordered the three prisoners bound over to the assizes for trial. The likelihood was that none of them would ever see Nether Abbas again. Marshall and the grooms would transport them to jail in Dorchester to await the judge.

Lady Tavernash sat as if made out of marble, moving only to hush her very confused son a few times while Viscount Clavering stared at her, pondering, or so he said.

When he spoke at last, Mia was certain he would let the woman off, convinced he would believe that a gentleman did not put a titled lady on trial. She was wrong.

"Lady Tavernash, you are a disgrace to your husband's title. I'm ordering you held under house arrest at my home, Selwyn Court, until trial can be arranged."

"This is an outrage!" Lady Tavernash shouted.

"Poor Selina," Mia murmured.

"Quiet!" Uncle Selwyn said. "I further declare that there being no evidence tying Felton Tavernash to any of these crimes, he is free to go. I do, however, order him to leave Woodglen immediately and not come back."

"But I'm the heir," Felton Tavernash whined, turning this way and that as the prisoners were led away.

"If, God forbid, evidence should come to light that the duke is dead, you may press your case in Lords. Until then, stay away."

CHAPTER THIRTY-SIX

SATED AND AT peace, Mia curled around her husband's warm body, careful to avoid the side with the splinted injury. "You continue to astonish me, Gideon. I had no idea what a miraculous lover you could be one-handed."

He smiled contentedly without opening his drowsy eyes and kissed the top of her head, twirling bits of her hair with his free hand.

"As wonderful as this was, however, I will disown you if you do something that boneheaded again," she said.

His eyes snapped open. "You will what?"

"Dis—"

Lightning fast, he had her under him, his injured arm carefully to the side, his mouth devouring hers. "Never," he whispered against her mouth.

"I was terrified," she said when she was able. "They might have killed you."

He kissed across her cheek to her ear before raising his head to reply. "You've no desire to be a wealthy widow?"

She pushed against him then. "Don't say that. Don't ever say that. It isn't funny. I love you. I couldn't bear it."

A feral smile formed on his lips. "You do?" He kissed her neck. "I'm glad." He kissed his way lower. "Because I love you, too."

She opened her mouth to demand his promise he would never put himself in that sort of danger again, but his words and his busy mouth pushed all coherent thought from her mind.

Sometime later, she snuggled close again and sighed. "Is it really over? Can we go home now?"

"Home?"

"To Wales. Helen wishes it. Jessica says she needs more time in the stables."

"What about Daniel?" Gideon asked.

"He wants another chance to slide across the ballroom floor when Fillmore isn't looking."

She could feel his laughter rumble through his chest. "I long to go home, but we have some loose ends to tie up." He kissed her again.

"What loose ends?" she asked.

"Ask me in the morning," he said, kissing her in earnest.

⁕

MARSHALL RETURNED FROM Dorchester two days later and reported to Gideon. The two men sat with their feet on the steward's desk, sipping brandy.

Gideon lifted his glass. "It has been a pleasure working with you, Curtis Marshall."

"Does that mean I'm not fired?" Marshall asked.

"Goodness, no. I'd have to stay here and do the damned job myself. My family and I will be leaving now that new staff are on their way," Gideon said.

"What new staff? From where?"

"London. I wrote to a friend and asked him to hire you a reliable secretary. While he's at it, I requested an undercook for Demming and a new head housekeeper."

"I was only gone two days! What happened to Mrs. Morrit?" Marshall asked.

Gideon laughed so hard he had to put all four legs of his chair down flat on the floor. "She left with Felton Tavernash. I don't think it was an accident they had a master set of keys. She wasn't waiting for us to find out."

"Who's this friend of yours you trust to hire staff?" Marshall asked.

"The Earl of Clarion, my stepmother's brother. He or his brilliant steward will find you just the person. In the meantime, Mrs. Millbrook has agreed to help. Mia discovered she's an excellent bookkeeper," Gideon said. "Does that suit?"

Marshall nodded. "I expect she'll do. She and the new secretary may just keep each other honest."

"Wise."

Marshall sobered. "I'll miss you. Will you come back?"

"Count on it. My wife will want to visit her uncle. The children will want to visit Bert and the horses. At least once a year. More often if you need me, but I doubt you will," Gideon said. He glanced down at his feet. "More often if my blasted brother comes back where he belongs," he said more softly.

He shook off thoughts of his missing brother. "Have that secretary of yours send monthly reports. Not the numbers. Tell me how everyone is getting on. I'll send you some birds from my pigeon flock. In an emergency, send one of those."

There seemed little else to say.

"When are you leaving?" Marshall asked.

"You and Clavering can handle the trials, so soon. Tomorrow if Helen has her way. It will take more than that to pack and arrange carriages."

"Promise me you're taking that great mass of a dog with you."

Gideon grinned. "He's one of the things to arrange. He'll need his own carriage!"

The two men walked back down the central corridor in amiable silence. Footmen touched their forelocks as they passed, and the tiniest maid dipped a curtsey. The house had always seemed too silent before, an ominous sort of silence. This felt different, more of a sense of expectation. He almost thought contentment.

Before he could dismiss that as a foolish thought, they reached the central stairway hall, and three children, laughing and skipping, hopped down the stairs, shouting greetings to the two men. Their governess followed at a more sedate pace.

"Mother says we're leaving in three days, Papa. We're on our way out to hike up to the folly and enjoy it while we can," Jessica said. Helen had determined that since their mother was always "Mam," "Mother" would be perfectly acceptable for Mia. The younger two, who barely remembered their mother, had readily agreed.

A disturbance at the front entrance occurred just as Gideon sent the children on their way. He and Marshall turned their attention to the door, where the porter had admitted a travel-stained stranger in a military uniform. Mia came out of the guest wing, where she had been taking stock of the music room to see if changes were needed, and joined them.

"No need to call for Fillmore, John. We can handle this," Gideon said.

"May we help you?" Mia asked the stranger.

"Is there a Gideon Kendrick here?" the man asked.

"I'm Gideon Kendrick."

The stranger relaxed a bit as if relieved of a burden. "I'm under orders to put this in your hands and no other. I hoped you would be here because the solicitors in London told me I would have to go to Wales next if not." He handed Gideon an oilcloth pouch bound with leather thongs.

"You appear to have come a long way. May we offer you refreshments, Lieutenant?" Mia asked.

"Captain, ma'am. Captain James Hargrove. And yes, a bit of a rest would be welcome."

Gideon broke out of the absorption that had come over him at the sight of the stained pouch. "Perhaps you can explain how you came to be here. Where are my manners? I am Gideon

Kendrick, and this is my wife. This other gentleman is Curtis Marshall, the steward here." He gazed at the man expectantly.

"It does all seem a bit mysterious. I met Mr. Phillip Tavernash in Philadelphia," the soldier said.

"Mister? Are you sure?" Mia asked.

"Yes, ma'am. That's how he introduced himself. There were rumors among the British community that he had a title, but he never claimed one."

"Rascal," Gideon sighed. "But Philadelphia. I should have known. He went to Charleston."

"Yes. He spoke of the port there. He said he preferred Philadelphia. In any case, I was being posted home, and he asked me to deliver this to you. He was quite emphatic about putting it in your hands." The young man colored. "I have to admit he paid me for my travel."

"I fear we need to peruse this in private, Captain. John, please escort this gentleman to the breakfast room and ask Mrs. Demming to feed him well. Notify Fillmore to prepare a room for the night." Gideon spun toward the courier. "You will stay over, won't you? Perhaps we'll see you at dinner and you can tell me more about how my brother gets on."

"I'll leave you to it," Marshall said when the footman led the captain away.

"No. Stay. If this is what I think it is, you may as well know. You've already had a glance at our family secrets. If we're to keep working together, you should know it all."

They sat in the little waiting room, the one where Gideon had waited for Marshall that first day, and unwrapped it. A thick packet came first. Gideon unfolded it to reveal church records, carefully copied, and a formal statement with a seal. He met his wife's wide eyes and nodded. "He found it. They were married. He sent a copy of the parish record and a vicar's testimony signed and sealed." Gideon also lifted a scrap of paper on which was written in Phillip's hand, *This will make it easier for Daniel—or you, if I die first.* He handed it to Mia.

"Who were married?" Marshall asked.

"Gideon's mother and father," Mia replied, absorbed in reading the papers.

Marshall considered it for a minute. "But that means you're—"

"Not a bastard," Gideon said.

"You never were," Mia added with a grin. It was their private joke about the long list of myths about Gideon that were never true.

Marshall whistled low and slow. "And the duke—or whatever he is—knows."

"My brother, Phillip, had his title confirmed by the Crown. They won't rescind it, and neither we nor they would want the scandal."

"But the boy was right."

"About the house being his? I fear so," Gideon replied. "My brother is determined to right what he sees as a wrong, drat him. I don't want any of this and never did."

"I'm glad one of you is taking an interest; I can tell you that," Marshall said.

Gideon fingered the other thing in the pouch. "What is it?" Mia asked.

"A letter from my brother."

"That I know is private. I'll leave you to it." Marshall paused at the door. "I can now attest to the gossips that the duke is indeed alive with an honest face. I know you love him, but I'm happy for you—Your Grace." He left before Gideon could retort.

Mia snuggled over and put her head on Gideon's shoulder. For a long moment, he just held her, one-armed. Then he opened it and read.

Dear brother,

As you can see, I found records to confirm what we believe. When it comes time for the title to pass, this should make it easier. Guard it with care in the family archives. You should have found them by now. Or send it to Sadler for his vault. In the meantime, care for Woodglen, the Glenmoor estate, and its people. I have every confidence that you can manage the thing as well, or likely better, than I could. Have more sons! We need a spare or two.

I dispensed with the title somewhere in the middle of the Atlantic, and I find I quite like being plain Mr. Tavernash. I would like access to funds, however. There are wondrous opportunities to be had here, any one of which might with luck make me rich. Do retain all the entailed assets and divide the rest. My solicitors, Sadler and January, will see to providing credit on a Philadelphia bank. Does half seem fair to you? You decide.

There is no rush. I'm about to embark on a marvelous adventure, overland to Pittsburgh. It has become, I hear, a manufacturing hub. I want to see, but I won't linger. I will take a ship downriver, visiting Cincinnati, Madison, and other towns in the newly formed states. The fever of growth is exhilarating here. At Saint Louis, which I understand is still rather French, I'll have a decision to make, whether to continue on to New Orleans or hire a wilderness guide and set out into the unknown. You may not hear from me for a few years, but I expect to return to Philadelphia eventually. Know that you'll be in my thoughts and have my trust. Good luck to us both.

Your brother,
Phillip, the duke in name only

"Drat that man!" Gideon swore.

"He seems determined to prove he can do as well as you did with your mines," Mia said.

Gideon hadn't considered that. Could Phillip have envied him all this time?

"We'll have to go to London," Gideon told her. "There's a packet in here for Sadler and January that I best deliver in person. We won't stay long."

"Will I meet that stepmother you've spoken of?" Mia asked.

"Her primary residence is there, so yes. Madelyn would like that," he answered. "The two of you will get along famously, and she adores the children. Besides, she can help you shop for a new wardrobe."

Mia blinked, as if momentarily stunned by the idea of shopping in the capital. "The children will enjoy the sights in London, don't you think?" she asked.

"Briefly. Then home to Wales. I long for the hills. I long for home." He kissed the side of her head.

"Yes. We need to go home. I rather like what your brother said about more sons. I don't give a fig about that spare business, but—"

He silenced her with a fierce kiss.

MIA WOKE IN the night alone. She put on her nightgown. When Gideon wasn't in the sitting room, she donned a wrapper and slippers and left their suite to search. She tried the library but found it dark. She wandered through the kitchen and on to his office. Light from a lantern at the end of the hall caught her eye. "Gideon? Where are you going?"

He smiled in greeting and reached out a hand. "I'll show you."

He led her to a path that stretched away from the stables, one she hadn't explored. It was a bit overgrown, and her slippers and the hem of her nightclothes got damp. They walked, he with his swaying gait, she matching her steps to his, for fifteen minutes before they came to a low stone wall surrounding scattered gravestones.

"No great vault for the Dukes of Glenmoor," he murmured. Some stones were small, some crumbled. A few were ornate. The newest, a granite obelisk, stood at the far end. He raised his lantern and read, "Randolph Tavernash, Duke of Glenmoor, 1754–1808."

She said nothing. She merely held his hand.

"Few enough words to cover a life," he murmured.

"You came out looking for information?" she asked.

"No. I have one more thing to do before we leave."

For a terrible moment, she feared he planned to spit on his father's grave.

"A wise person told me recently it is important to forgive lest hurts and resentment take root and grow and corrode our soul. I have made my peace with Woodglen and even with Nether Abbas." He leaned over the grave and whispered, "Thank you for Phillip. He is a better man than you ever were. As to the rest, I forgive you."

He enfolded Mia in his arms for a fierce hug. He took her hand, and they walked away together, into their new life.

The End

Author's Note

One of the joys of writing historical romance is learning new things, in this case the rules of inheritance. We all know, for example, that if Prince Charles had predeceased Queen Elizabeth, Prince William would have inherited. The royal family's line of succession is well known. What about other titles in the peerage?

This story (as will others in this series) hinges on legitimacy and inheritance of a title in a ducal family. Inheriting a title can be tricky, but the rules are simple. The oldest legitimate son of a duke always inherits the title or, in the case of his death, the son's oldest legitimate son. But what is the legal process?

1. The new duke petitions the Lord Chancellor for a writ of summons to the House of Lords for the current or the next session of parliament.
2. The claimant submits proof that his parents were legally married and he is the son of that marriage.
3. He has to prove that he is indeed that son, over twenty-one, and a member of the Church of England.
4. The Committee for Privileges reviews the proof. Once the proof is accepted, the new duke is sent a writ of summons to parliament and confirmed in his title.
5. Once confirmed, a title is unlikely to be overturned. A challenge would be an embarrassment to the Crown.

The situation involving the Dukes of Glenmore hinges on

item two. Phillip's parents were not legally married, and Gideon's were. Phillip was confirmed in the title that should have gone to Gideon.

Phillip had grown up believing he was heir apparent. What about the cousin? Felton Tavernash claimed to be heir presumptive, assuming Phillip to be the legitimate duke, lacking a legitimate heir apparent and likely dead. Proof becomes trickier and more time-consuming. An heir presumptive had to prove not only his own legitimacy but the legitimacy of his entire line of descent.

As for Gideon's deformed back, he was cursed with severe scoliosis. It can cause chronic back pain as it does in Gideon's case. According to the Mayo Clinic, the disorder can worsen over time, causing more pronounced changes in the individual's appearance: tilted waist, uneven shoulders/hips, protruding ribs on one side, and so forth. Scoliosis was known by Hippocrates. Treatments over the centuries varied. In Gideon's era, an iron back brace was known. It is likely the doctor in Wales may have suggested it to him. It is also likely Dr. Gratis tried more sadistic quackery at the old duke's request. Gideon's own determination is to not let it hinder him.

Early in the writing, I puzzled over whether he could/would be an excellent horseman. The answer came in a surprising form. One of my favorite shows, *Secrets of the Dead*, did a program that answered that very question, in that case regarding Richard III, who had severe scoliosis (*Secrets of the Dead*, season 13, episode 6, "Resurrecting Richard III"). My ideas about Gideon's custom saddle came entirely from that episode.

About the Author

Award winning author of family centered romance set in the Regency and Victorian eras, Caroline Warfield has been many things (even a nun), but above all she is a romantic. Someone who begins life as an army brat develops a wide view of life, and a love for travel. Now settled in the urban wilds of eastern Pennsylvania, she reckons she is on at least her third act. When she isn't off seeking adventures with her Beloved or her grandson down the block, she works happily in an office surrounded by windows where she lets her characters lead her to even more adventures in England and the far-flung corners of the British Empire. She nudges them to explore the riskiest territory of all, the human heart, because love is worth the risk.

Website: www.carolinewarfield.com
Amazon Author: amazon.com/Caroline-Warfield/e/B00N9PZZZS
Good Reads: bit.ly/1C5blTm
Facebook: facebook.com/groups/WarfieldFellowTravelers
Twitter: twitter.com/CaroWarfield
Email: warfieldcaro@gmail.com
Newsletter: carolinewarfield.com/newsletter
BookBub: bookbub.com/authors/caroline-warfield
You Tube: youtube.com/channel/UCycyfKdNnZlueqo8MlgWyWQ

www.ingramcontent.com/pod-product-compliance
Lightning Source LLC
Chambersburg PA
CBHW071224210726
48293CB00002B/564